PRAISE FOR
THE WEAVING MYSTERIES

Weave of Absence

"Della and her friends . . . [are] fabulously entertaining. The weaving 'biz' is full of intrigue, and the books make for incredibly fun mysteries that hold on to the revelation of the culprit until the very last pages."

—*Suspense Magazine*

"From start to finish, it's one of those books that you have a really hard time putting down. . . . If you're looking for a fun and exciting series, you'll want to pick up the Weaving Mystery series. It's definitely worth a read!"

—*Marie's Cozy Corner*

"Carol Ann Martin has . . . created a tantalizing mystery in *Weave of Absence.* Readers don't have to be a weaving expert to relish this charming story."

—*Thoughts in Progress*

Tapestry of Lies

"This second book in the Weaving Mystery series knocks it out of the park. There are plenty of twists and turns to keep you guessing whodunit. I enjoy the cast of quirky characters that are Della's friends and neighbors. The plotting is stellar. . . . If you like your mystery with a crafty touch, then you should be reading *Tapestry of Lies.*"

—*MyShelf.com*

"The characters get better and better."

—*Kings River Life Magazine*

continued . . .

"With her direct approach and fearless sleuthing, the second Weaving Mystery finds Della throwing herself into an investigation and uncovering several surprise twists. The charming small-town setting and Della's likability add dimension and warmth to this intriguing mystery that keeps readers guessing until the very end. Weaving tips are included." —*RT Book Reviews*

"Martin's second mystery is as interesting as her first. . . . The mystery is sufficiently devious." —Fresh Fiction

Looming Murder

"I loved *Looming Murder*."
—Amanda Lee, author of *Wicked Stitch*

"The small-town setting and community vibe of the weaving studio enhance the mystery by providing a central location to introduce key players. Della is a smart and likable sleuth who has a penchant for high heels and nasty spills. Her sleuthing skills and her relationship with Matthew provide plenty of drama to keep readers hooked."
—*RT Book Reviews*

"Martin scores a real hit with this one. . . . The book was very well written and I loved all the information about weaving . . . a great book." —Debbie's Book Bag

"I really love it when I find a new series and can't put down the book until I finish it. There are quirky characters and red herrings that will keep you turning the pages."
—MyShelf.com

"Martin has started an interesting new series with some quirky and fun characters. . . . The mystery was especially complex and ended with a big surprise." —Fresh Fiction

Also by Carol Ann Martin

Looming Murder
Tapestry of Lies
Weave of Absence

Loom and Doom

A WEAVING MYSTERY

CAROL ANN MARTIN

AN OBSIDIAN MYSTERY

OBSIDIAN
Published by New American Library,
an imprint of Penguin Random House LLC
375 Hudson Street, New York, New York 10014

This book is an original publication of New American Library.

First Printing, August 2015

For more information about Penguin Random House, visit penguinrandomhouse.com.

ISBN 978-0-451-47488-9

Printed in the United States of America
10 9 8 7 6 5 4 3 2 1

Penguin
Random
House

This one is for the girls, Coco, Alish, and Becca.
You three are the best.

Chapter 1

Today was the day. After two months of remodeling, Dream Weaver, my craft shop, would finally be getting a fresh coat of paint — the finishing touch in a long series of steps before reopening. The work had taken twice as long and almost three times as much money as I'd been promised. I'd have to sell a lot of place mats and dish towels to recover my costs.

I flew through my morning routine and ran down the stairs, two at a time, from my apartment to my store. I knocked on the door of Coffee, Tea and Destiny — the shop right next to mine — and signaled to my good friend Jenny that I'd be right back, and hurried on to the newspaper dispenser two blocks away. Minutes later, I tapped on her window again and waved her over. Then I walked into my shop.

Soon, the door swung open, throwing the bell above the door into a tizzy. Jenny walked in. "Rather late coming in to work this morning, aren't we? I take it you decided to laze around in bed for a while?" Jenny said with a twinkle in her eyes. "Were you alone? Or, perchance, did you have company?"

I felt the heat rise to my face. I tried to hide my embarrassment by glancing at my watch. "If what you're asking is whether Matthew spent the night, the answer is no. He was in New York yesterday for a meeting with his publisher."

Matthew and I were still a relatively new item, and thrilled as I was that he seemed to be as smitten with me as I was with him, I didn't feel comfortable discussing the romantic details of our relationship, not even with my closest friend.

"He should be landing in Charlotte right about now, but he won't be home for at least another hour and a half." Eager to change the subject, I looked around.

I was standing in the middle of what used to be my weaving shop. At the moment it looked more like a war zone than a high-end craft boutique. My lovely pendant school lights had been taken down and were now hidden behind the counter for safekeeping. The gorgeous old wide-plank wood floors were covered with brown construction paper. My beautiful lead glass windows were lined with newsprint, and every one of my handwoven pieces was gone—stored upstairs in my apartment. The only things still in the store were a few of my larger display cases, empty and wrapped in plastic. But what really made the place look like hell was the layer of plaster dust that covered everything. It was so thick it looked almost like snow, except that this powder had a life of its own. Every step I took sent another cloud in the air. But none of that mattered anymore, because, today was the day.

"Isn't this exciting?" I said. "The painters should be here any minute. Why don't we start cleaning up for them? We can save some time."

"I think maybe we should wait."

There was something in her voice that made me suspicious. "Uh-oh. I don't like that tone. What's up?"

"I don't know any more than you, but Syd called a few minutes ago, saying he had something to talk to us about."

This did not sound good. Syd, our contractor, had originally told us the work would take no more than a month—at the most. But, like clockwork, every week he'd come up with another story as to why the work would take even longer.

I groaned. "I don't know about you, but I could use a cup of coffee."

"I just made a fresh pot. Come on over," she said, heading back to her shop. She paused in the doorway. "I still can't believe I have my very own shop."

"You've already had your own shop for a year."

"Yes, but it feels different now."

A couple of months ago Jenny and I had the bright idea of remodeling our shops, so that our businesses would be side by side rather than both sharing the same space. Until then, we had shared, with hers in the back of mine. We discussed it at length and decided that logistically, the project should not be too complicated. All we wanted was to divide the floor space by building a wall running from the front to the back, and then creating a separate entrance for Jenny's side. That way we would each have our own display window. But more important, our clients would be able to enter directly into each shop, and would no longer have to cut through my boutique to get to her café.

The only disadvantage was that I'd lose the occasional extra sale I'd make when one of her clients bought an item while on their way into the coffee shop. This had seemed like a small price in return for all the advantages we'd both gain. Besides, there was one more benefit. With Jenny having her own entrance, I would no longer have to open at the same time she did. (Eight o'clock. Whoever heard of starting work at such an uncivilized hour?) I'd open at ten, like the other shops in town, and enjoy two extra hours of sleep every morning. Heaven.

So, after analyzing the pros and cons, we had done what any wise businesswomen would. We'd gone for it.

We interviewed contractors, requested a slew of quotes and hired Shuttleworth Construction, which had given us the cheapest price. I should have known that selecting a contractor based on the amount he charged was not the smartest way to do it. But what else could a struggling entrepreneur do?

Now, I just knew that Syd was about to drop another bomb on us. *Good grief.* My good mood of a moment ago was slipping fast.

I locked my shop and followed my friend to hers, stepped in and looked around.

"I hate to say this, but your place doesn't look much better than mine."

"What do you expect? We're renovating," she said, handing me a fresh cup of java. "You can't have the improvements without dealing with a mess first."

"It still doesn't make it any more pleasant."

"Just think how beautiful everything will be once it's all finished."

I was just taking my first swallow of coffee when the door opened and Syd ambled in, wearing his work overalls over a light blue T-shirt and looking ill at ease.

"What fresh hell are you visiting on us this morning, Syd? Every time I think you're done, you come up with, 'just one more thing,'" I said, making air quotes.

"I don't blame you for being upset," he said, avoiding my eyes. "But don't worry. It's just a small setback—no biggie." Maybe not for him. "Once everything is all completed, you'll see it was worth it. Right now, the mess makes it look way worse than it is. Once all the dust and debris is gone, this place will look great."

"It's not the mess," I said. "It's the business we're losing." I crossed my arms. "So I'm right? You're telling us there's something else that needs doing?" He looked down. "What is it this time?" I asked, trying hard not to lose my cool.

"There was a problem with the occupancy permit," he

said, and raised his hands in a pacifying gesture. "I know this comes as a disappointment to you, but I'll have the problem fixed in no time."

"You can't be serious," Jenny said. "No occupancy permit?"

He shuffled from one foot to the other. If he'd been holding a cap in his hands he would have been twisting it. "It's not all that bad."

I swallowed hard. I just knew we were about to get another convoluted excuse. "Give it to me straight."

"The good news is that your side is ready to go, Della. All I have to do is stop by city hall and get the permit signed," he said, looking at me. "The inspector stopped by at seven o'clock this morning and approved it, but couldn't find the paperwork. I can get you his John Hancock by the end of the day. But that shouldn't be a problem 'cause you still have to get the place painted. So, no rush, right?"

My scowl melted. And then, suspecting what the bad news might be, I frowned. "What about Jenny's store?"

He dropped his gaze to the floor. "Well, that's where the problem lies. But, honestly, it's not my fault. I did everything according to code—or, rather, according to the old code."

"What does that mean?"

"Well, I just found out that there's been a change in the code. I'll have to move the electrical panel to somewhere in full view. Turns out they don't allow them inside closets anymore."

"You have to relocate the electrical panel?" Jenny said. "Isn't that a huge job?" I knew that tone. Any second now, she would be having a meltdown. "But Mr. Swanson approved our plans two months ago, and everything was done accordingly. He can't do that, just change the code and enforce it on a project that he already okayed, can he?" Her eyes swung from Sydney to me, as though looking for my support.

Howard Swanson was the building inspector. I had glimpsed the man only once—thin face, darting beady eyes and a tight mouth. He reminded me of a rodent. I wasn't in the habit of taking an instant dislike to people, but for him I'd made an exception.

Sydney shrugged, looking miserable. "I'm afraid he can. He's got the power to do pretty much whatever he wants."

"Why is he doing this? Is he trying to make me go bankrupt?" Jenny's voice cracked. I moved closer and patted her back.

"Don't worry. I'm sure I can get it done real fast," Sydney continued. He looked nearly—but not quite—as miserable as Jenny. I wasn't at all certain it was sincere.

"If I don't reopen soon, I'll never get my clients back from Good Morning Sunshine," she said, her voice tight with controlled emotions. "For all I know, it might already be too late."

"Your clients love you," I said. "They're just waiting for you to reopen. As soon as you do, you'll see, they'll be flocking in again."

"I sure hope you're right," she said, sounding no less worried. I hoped I was right too.

But Jenny had every right to be concerned. The previous owner of the shop up the street, called The Coffee Break at the time, had closed her business and moved to Charlotte after her husband's death about a year ago. That had left Jenny's shop the only game in town. Then, one week after Sydney had started demolishing our space, the other shop had suddenly reopened, renamed Good Morning Sunshine. The timing couldn't have been worse for Jenny, or better for them.

Over the next few weeks, while Jenny put up a brave front, her old customers kept dropping by to share more disheartening news. The new owners, Jim and Lori Stanton, were newlyweds. They just moved to town to be closer to family. They were lovely and everybody liked them.

I had caught a glimpse of the Stantons a few times over the last few weeks. She was an attractive brunette, still dressing more city than small town, as I had when I'd first moved here. It had taken me nearly two years to adopt a more casual style. Now, slacks and sweaters were the norm rather than the exception. But I'd never been able to give up my four-inch heels, but that was because of my height—five feet nothing. I liked seeing the world from a little higher.

Jim Stanton was a pretty boy. He looked like he spent a lot of time in suntanning booths and gyms—he was golden brown and sported lots of muscle. The story was that they had come to Briar Hollow to visit family, and happened to drive by the shop. They'd taken one look at it and fallen in love with its possibilities.

Within weeks they had moved into the house in back. Then after putting up a new sign, showing a bright yellow sun with rays beaming down on the name, they'd thrown an opening party and announced that Good Morning Sunshine would be offering coffee, tea and light meals, putting itself in direct competition with Coffee, Tea and Destiny. Except for Jenny and her closest friends—namely Marnie and me—it seemed the whole town had gone.

Marnie and I tried to cheer her up. "A lot of restaurants open, but few of them make it. I bet they won't last six months," I said.

"They're city folk," Marnie had added. "They won't be able to stand the small-town life. You'll see. They'll be gone before you know it."

Then, as if the universe had conspired to keep Jenny's hopes down, an old customer had dropped by and announced that the couple had just been to a lawyer and signed the papers. They were no longer renting; they had just purchased the place. The Stantons were here to stay.

I thought Jenny would have a heart attack. But all she did was smile and nod. I wasn't sure how long she could keep up the good front. And, truth be told, I was worried about my own situation too.

I faced Syd, with my hands on my hips. "How much is this going to cost me?" I couldn't see how I could come up with more money. "I've already spent way more than you originally quoted."

Because the building belonged to me, and Jenny was my tenant, I was responsible for all carpentry, electrical and plumbing costs. She was responsible only for the cosmetic work of her space—namely, her share of the painting.

Sydney dug his hands in his pockets, bobbing his head from side to side. I could almost hear the gears clicking in his mind.

"I feel bad for you guys," he said. "I know this turned into way bigger a job than we first anticipated. But that's what happens when we open up old walls. We never know what we'll find in there. I had no idea when I made my calculations, that all the electrical wires were knob and tube and would have to be replaced." He paused. "How about this? I'll charge you only the cost of the materials, and I'll pay the electrician out of my own pocket."

"You will?" I said, only slightly mollified. Technically, this latest delay might not be his fault, but as the contractor, he should have been better informed about the city's construction code. Still, I could live with the arrangement he proposed. But I couldn't help wondering why he would make such a generous offer.

"That's very kind of you," Jenny said. She always saw the good in everyone. "You shouldn't have to pay."

"No. I insist. And I don't want you to feel guilty about taking me up on it," he added.

I didn't, but I kept that thought to myself.

"I give my electrician a lot of work," he told her. "So he'll give me a good deal."

"How long will it take?" she asked.

"I swear it'll get done in record time. I'll make sure I have a team of electricians here first thing in the morning."

There was no sense in belaboring the point. So, "I'll hold you to that," was all I said.

"Well, I'd best be going if I want to start getting things organized," he said, picking up his electric saw. "And remember. This is not my fault. It's Swanson's, the city inspector."

"Hold on a second," I said. "Where are you going? You said you were going to start painting today. You might not be able to do Jenny's shop, but you can start on mine."

He gave me an apologetic smile. "Gee. I'd like to, but there's no point in starting one side before the other. I'd only have to come back again in about a week. I'd rather wait and do both at the same time." And without waiting for a reply he was gone.

I closed my mouth, which had been left hanging open after his answer. "Can you believe this guy?"

It occurred to me that Jenny had been uncommonly quiet these last few minutes.

"What are you thinking about?" I said, studying her. "If you're worried about your business, don't. You know—"

She cut me off. "No, that's not it. There's something that man isn't telling us. Normally his aura is blue, but it changed to muddy gray just now when he mentioned the city inspector again. I have the feeling he's hiding something."

Chapter 2

I-have-a-feeling comments were typical of Jenny. Two years ago, when I'd left my career as a business analyst in Charlotte and moved to Briar Hollow, Jenny was one of the first people I'd met. We had formed an instant friendship, even though she and I couldn't be any more different. She was one of those naturally beautiful women—tall, blond and slender. Standing next to her at my full height and in my highest heels invariably made me feel like a midget.

And our differences were not only physical. Jenny believed in things like tarots, crystals, tea leaves and auras, and regularly made predictions about the future.

With my background as a business analyst, I was a pragmatist. I looked at all that woo woo stuff as a whole lot of nonsense. But I also knew better than to make light of Jenny's convictions. She did not take well to anyone making fun of her.

So all I said was, "Really?" keeping a straight face. She stared at me, trying to read my mind no doubt. I gave her my most sincere look.

"Can you believe it? All this time and money and we're still not ready to open. All he had to do was build a darn wall and put in a new door." One quick glance at her told me she was as unamused as I was.

Jenny's shoulders drooped. "I guess things could be worse," she said, nodding toward the *New York Times* next to her coffee cup on the counter. "Whenever I feel as if the weight of the world is on my shoulders, all I have to do is read the paper. There's nothing like a good dose of world news to remind me just how good I've really got it."

"Amen to that. But I'd rather not even read depressing news first thing in the morning. At least in the local paper, the worst news one is likely to read about is a house fire." I was referring to a recent tragedy. A house fire had erupted during the night, killing a mother and severely injuring her two children.

"Did you hear anything new about that story?" she asked.

"I haven't even opened my paper yet." I was in the habit of picking up a paper every morning, but I'd been so excited about the prospect of seeing the end to the renovations, that I hadn't so much as glanced at it yet. It lay unopened next to the telephone. "How's Ed?" I asked. Ed, Jenny's boyfriend, was a doctor. He worked at Belmont General, the closest hospital in the area.

Before she could answer, the door swung open and Marnie Potter came bursting in carrying a package that she set on the dusty counter. Marnie was a flamboyant redhead who had recently lost about forty pounds on what she called "the heartbreak diet." She swore if she'd known a breakup would cause her to shed so many pounds, she would have gladly gotten dumped ages ago. But she must have been getting over her broken heart because the pounds she'd lost had already started coming back.

As to Marnie's exact age, that was a mystery; however, judging from her frequent hot flashes, I gauged her to be in her early- to mid-fifties. Today she wore cherry red pants with a fuchsia tunic and purple earrings. On anybody else it would have looked ridiculous. Somehow, on her it looked only cheerful.

"Morning, sunshine," she called out, and then she glanced around, wide-eyed, at the construction mess.

Jenny instantly said, "Please don't use that name in here." Marnie looked confused for a second.

"Sounds too much like a certain coffee shop up the street," I said.

A flash of understanding lit her eyes. "Oh, sorry. It never occurred to me. I guess I'll have to find new endearments for you." And then, looking around, she planted her hands on her hips. "What happened? I thought the place would be finished today. I came over to help you bring all the stock back down from your place."

"It *is* finished," Jenny said. "At least Della's side is — except for being painted. But it seems the inspector won't give me a permit until the electrical panel gets completely redone."

"I thought the electrical was all done?"

"It seems they changed the code. They don't allow electrical panels to be installed inside closets anymore. Can you believe it?"

"What? That's just plain ridiculous." She must have remembered that I'd had mine installed in plain sight, because she said, "Did you know about this?"

"I didn't. The only reason mine is in full view is because I don't have a closet. I was going to place an armoire in front to camouflage it. I wonder if that will be okay."

Marnie waved my concern away. "Once you have your permit you can go ahead and do whatever you want." She crossed her arms over her ample chest, looking thoughtful. "You know, there's a reason these inspectors are so disliked. I was just talking to Norma at her house — "

"Norma?" I said. "Do I know her?"

"Oh, that's right. You never met her. She's a neighbor of mine who lives a few doors down. She was in a snit a few weeks ago because she wanted to have a new window installed in her basement suite. She felt that, in case of fire, a window would give her tenant an extra exit. But the building inspector turned her down. He says — listen to this for weird reasoning—it's too risky because, if her tenant happened to crawl out the window when somebody was coming up the walk, they might collide."

Jenny frowned. "He thinks the possibility of two pedestrians colliding is worse than the danger of burning alive? That doesn't sound very logical."

"I swear that's what he said to her. Anyhow. I didn't come here to complain about the inspector. I want to help you get things organized. We won't be able to get your place ready, Jenny, but we can start on Della's at least."

"I'd love to," I said. "But I still have to get the place cleaned and painted. And Sydney won't do it until Jenny's place is ready too."

"Bah. We don't need him. We can do it ourselves." She waved her arms around. "Look. The floors and windows are already covered. All we have to do is clean up the dust, tape the edges and get going. Have you picked out your paint colors?"

"I've got them." They followed me to my shop where I marched over to my armoire, lifted the plastic sheet and got the color chips from a drawer. "I'm not changing anything. I'm staying with the same buttery yellow I already had on the existing walls. That way I won't have to repaint the whole store. And here is the soft blue I've been using for the ceiling, and the white I used on baseboards, window trims, and doors. What do you think? Is that okay or should I go for a complete change?"

"It worked for you up till now, so why change it? Your merchandise always looked amazing against those colors," Marnie said.

I had originally chosen yellow for that very reason. Everything looks happy in a yellow space.

She picked up the swatches. "Here's what I can do. I'll go pick up the paint, rollers and brushes, and meanwhile you two can start with the masking tape. The sooner the place is finished, the sooner I can come back to work."

"Ah, so *that's* the reason you're so eager to help," I said. "You're bored at home by yourself."

"You've got that right. I've been going crazy these last few weeks with nowhere to go. You wouldn't believe the amount of weaving and baking I've been doing."

Marnie was my right hand in the shop. As a talented weaver herself, she was one of my suppliers from the day I'd opened, regularly bringing in beautiful pieces of her work. And then a bit over a year ago, she'd finagled herself a job as my assistant. As she'd pointed out, it made sense. I may not have had the budget for full-time help, but I did need someone part-time. The arrangement was good for her too, she insisted. She was lonely by herself all day. And she could just as easily weave here, on one of my looms, as she could at home. That way, she could do weaving demonstrations in the shop, showing customers the amount of work that went into each piece. And to make sure I couldn't turn her down, she'd insisted on charging me only for the time she helped with sales.

Marnie was also an incredible baker. And being an insomniac she thought nothing of whipping up a couple of batches of cookies and muffins during the night. A year ago, when she'd heard about Jenny's plan to open a coffee shop, she'd hightailed it over with an assortment of tasty treats for Jenny to sample. The two women had made a deal on the spot. Now Marnie was one of Coffee, Tea and Destiny's best suppliers of baked goods. The only problem with all of this was that Jenny and I could have used another Marnie—or two.

"The one good thing from all the time off I've had," Marnie told Jenny, "is that I did so much baking, I have enough goodies in my freezer to keep you supplied for the next few months." Turning to me, she added, "And don't you worry. I've got some pieces ready for you too. I must have a dozen sets of place mats." Place mats were the one item I could never keep in stock.

"Great. I won't have to bug you for a while. But before we get started, I really should wait for Syd to come back with my permit."

"I thought you already had it," Marnie said.

"I do. I mean, he approved it, but he didn't sign it while he was here."

"Where does Syd have to go to pick it up?"

"City hall, he said."

"So, why wait for him? Go get it yourself. In the meantime, Jenny and I will have plenty to do."

"I think I should change first," I said, noticing my jeans were covered in splotches of red paint, stains I'd gotten repainting my front door a few days earlier.

"Who are you planning to impress?" Marnie asked.

I shrugged. "I suppose you're right. It shouldn't take long. Be back in half an hour or so."

Marnie crossed her arms and gave me a suspicious look. "Come on. Out with the truth. You're just trying to weasel out of doing the cleanup, aren't you? You're hoping that by the time you get back it'll all be done."

I laughed. "Now that you mention it, that's not a bad idea. Don't worry if I'm late." I grabbed my raincoat and took off.

Chapter 3

Like many small towns, Briar Hollow could not afford its own infrastructure. Instead, it shared the city hall, police, fire department and hospital with the nearby town of Belmont. That was where I was heading when I hopped into my Jeep and took off. The drive there would be no more than fifteen minutes on a normal day, but the way I drove, it would take only ten. Along the way, I pictured how wonderful my remodeled shop would look with my new merchandise.

Being closed for two months had been frustrating; however, it had allowed me one luxury—the luxury of time, which I'd used to prepare an entire new collection of pieces. During all my years of weaving, I'd mostly worked classic weaves and traditional pieces. This collection was different from anything I'd ever done. It didn't even resemble any merchandise I'd carried in my shop before. And because I wasn't sure how it would be received, I'd kept it secret.

The inspiration had come a few months ago when I'd visited a museum collection of Native American art. Among the many spectacular pieces were Navajo blankets, some almost two centuries old, each more stunning than the last. The colors were bright, the patterns sharp geometrical designs that dazzled the eye. I had been entranced.

It was after that visit, when I couldn't get it out of my

mind, that I first contemplated preparing an entire collection based on Native American weaving. Over the following weeks I thought about it, going online to learn more about the specialty. Had I not been able to keep my attempt private, I would never have dared to try. But, by the time the shop renovations began, I was ready to take the plunge. And now, in just a few days, I would be unveiling my new work for the whole town to see.

To say that I was happy with the results was to put it mildly. They went far beyond my expectations. Now I was planning an entire window display around it. I only hoped everybody else liked it as well as I did. Something told me that with the new direction my shop was taking, I might have a few rough months, but everything would turn out all right in the end.

As for Jenny, I was certain her store would do well, too. Maybe she could do some kind of opening-day promotion, something that would attract all her old customers back. But what?

Of course, she had a core group of clients that I had no doubt would return. But after being closed for so long, there was a good chance the majority of her old regulars had made Good Morning Sunshine their new haunt. We'd simply have to come up with something.

The City of Belmont WELCOME sign flashed by. I slowed to thirty and drove along Main Street all the way to the other side of town until I spotted the old city hall building. I was just pulling into its parking lot, when a car came careening out of the driveway, straight toward me. I swerved, narrowly avoiding a collision, then swiveled in my seat, watching the car and its driver speed away.

Idiot! I mouthed, my heart still racing at the near miss. *Somebody should arrest that guy.* The whole thing had happened so fast, all I was left with was the vague impression of a driver wearing large sunglasses and a light blue baseball cap, in a silver hatchback with a bumper sticker proclaiming something about judgment day. Well, if that was the way that person always drove, no wonder he was worried about the hereafter.

Probably some teenager with too much testosterone and not enough brains.

I gathered my scattered wits and continued on into one of the parking spots. Although I had already been here a few times, I still marveled at the lovely old building. It had been built almost a century earlier—a one-story redbrick structure with a pitched roof, blue doors and white trim. From the front it looked deceptively small, but from the parking lot in the back one could see the building jutting out in two long wings.

I made my way to one of the back entrances, where I rattled the door a couple of times before accepting that it was locked. I then retraced my steps and rounded the building to the front. I walked in and found myself in a lobby that opened into a large room. It reminded me of a bank, with a gray marble counter, behind which were only a few employees. By the far wall a long lineup of customers waited for the next available teller. I was debating if I should join the queue, when I noticed that there was an information panel across the room.

I followed the directions to the building inspector's office down a dimly lit corridor with flickering lights. Not in a million years would these pass the current building codes, I thought. And had I not needed Howard Swanson to give me a permit for my own building, I might have been tempted to point this out to him.

The corridor made a sharp turn, and another twenty feet farther I found myself before an office marked BUILD-ING SERVICES. I looked at the exit door nearby. Unless I was mistaken, that was the same door I had just tried from the parking lot. I could see now that it had one of those automatic locks that allowed it to open only from the inside. I turned back to Swanson's office and knocked.

Silence.

Somewhere in the back of my mind I noticed how quiet this part of the building was. There were no telephones ringing, no sounds of voices from the lobby, not even the hum of office machines. I looked back down the hall I'd just come from. There were half a dozen other offices— every one of them was closed. I shrugged off the spooky feeling, and waited a few more seconds before I knocked again. Then I pressed my ear against the door.

Still nothing.

Then, it hit me. Swanson, being an inspector, was probably out inspecting, and I should have made an appointment with him before coming. But seeing as I'd come this far, I could at least write him a message before leaving. To my surprise, when I tried it, the door swung open, and I found myself looking into a large dimly lit room.

"Hello?" Again, I was met with silence.

I glanced out into the hall, and seeing nobody, I made up my mind. I felt along the wall and flipped on the lights. The place was a mess. Along one side, the room was lined with industrial-beige file cabinets, above which were stacks and stacks of rolled-up plans. It was a wonder the man could find anything in there. In the center of the space was a heavy metal desk that looked not much younger than the building itself. On it were masses of envelopes, some opened, some still sealed. *Good God.* Hadn't the man ever heard of filing?

I stood in the doorway frozen with uncertainty for a few moments, and then I gathered my courage and marched over to the desk, looking for a piece of paper on which I could write him a note. I was tearing off a page from a message pad when something caught my eye. I glanced at the floor, and yelped.

There was Swanson, not three feet away. He was lying on his back in a pool of blood, his eyes staring blankly at the ceiling, his mouth half open, as if in surprise. I had no doubt that he was dead. Even his complexion was gray. I was swept in a wave of guilt as I remembered all the unkind thoughts I'd had toward him earlier this morning.

All at once I became aware of my stomach, roiling dangerously. If I didn't get out of there fast there'd be more than just a bloody mess for the biohazard team to clean up. I dashed blindly down the hall with my hand over my mouth. As I ran through the main room an older gentleman had the misfortune of stepping in front of me. I bumped right smack into him and we both went crashing to the floor.

He was back on his feet as quickly as I was, and was starting to apologize, but I was already racing for the entrance. I made it outside in the nick of time and was still bent over, gagging and gasping, when a trio of city employees wandered out to check on me.

"Are you all right?" the same gentleman I'd mowed down asked. He took a few steps closer.

I waved him away. It was embarrassing enough to be caught bent over and throwing up, without having anyone come too close.

"Poor thing—she's sick," the woman said. Rummaging through her pocket, she came out with a tissue, which she handed to me. "Would you like to come in and sit down?"

I wiped my mouth, and shook my head. I was taking long deep breaths, and my stomach was slowly settling.

She turned to the others. "Somebody get this lady a glass of water."

I suddenly noticed the spittle of vomit on my jeans. Embarrassed, I wiped at it and excused myself. I hurried to my jeep and slipped into my raincoat. When I returned to the group, the younger man was back with a paper cup.

"Here, drink this."

After a few sips of water I began feeling more like

myself. "Thank you." The three of them stared at me with worried eyes.

"She's looking a little less peaked," the old man said. He was tall and slender and had gray hair.

"We have to call the police," I blurted. "Mr. Swanson is dead. There was so much blood. I think he might have been murdered." There was a collective gasp.

"How can you be sure he's dead?" the woman asked. "What if he's just passed out? Maybe we should call an ambulance."

Should we? I wondered. But I had seen death before and knew what it looked like. There was no question in my mind that Swanson was dead. But it wouldn't hurt to agree. "Yes. That's a good idea. I could be wrong."

"He can't be dead," the younger man said. He looked like he was in his early- to mid-thirties, and was dressed like a professional in a suit and tie. "I just saw him yesterday." He no sooner had said this than he marched toward the building, as if intent on proving me wrong. He had just entered the building when the gentleman said, "I think I'll go with him." He hurried after him. I was wondering if I should join them too, when the woman placed a hand on my arm.

"I'll wait here with you," she said. "You're just starting to recover from the shock. There's no point in getting yourself all worked up again." She was right. The nausea had passed, but I still felt weak. "Oh, it's just too terrible," she continued. "Poor Mr. Swanson. Surely you're wrong about him being murdered. It had to have been an accident. Who would want to hurt him? I simply can't believe it."

She had blond hair, blue eyes and the quirkiest eyebrows I'd ever seen. They were penciled in an odd shape. Her dress was too short. She wore a heavy layer of foundation on her face and her oddly bouffant hair was bleached blond. I had the impression of a middle-aged woman trying to look half her age. She gave me a friendly smile.

"There, there. You'll be fine."

Over the last few minutes more people had come out of the building. Some must have overheard our conversation because there were now half a dozen observers standing around looking shocked and whispering among themselves.

"Do you think anybody called an ambulance yet?" I asked the woman.

"Oh, dear. I have no idea. I'll go do that right now."

"Never mind," I said, rummaging through my bag. "I have my cell right here." In my rush to dial, I dropped my phone not once but twice before I got through.

"Nine one one. Do you need the police, an ambulance, or the fire department?" the operator asked.

"Police, please — and ambulance," I added.

"What's your emergency, ma'am?"

"I'm calling to report a . . . er . . . I think he's dead but I could be wrong," I said, trying to keep the tremor out of my voice. "It's Mr. Swanson, the building inspector at city hall. There's a lot of blood, and I'm pretty sure he was attacked."

"I've got an ambulance on its way," she said, and proceeded to ask me all the pertinent information.

"Are you with the victim now?"

"No. He's in his office, where I found him. There was so much blood, I had to get out."

"Has anybody taken his pulse?" At that moment the two men stepped out of the building, wearing grim expressions. They made their way over.

"Not me, but the men who just went to check on him are coming back. You can ask them." I handed the phone to the older man. He took it, a question mark in his eyes. "It's the emergency dispatcher."

"There's no point in standing here. Come on inside and sit down," the woman said. "You look a little wobbly on your feet. We have a staff room. We might as well wait in there for the police."

I followed her into the building to a small room with a coffeemaker and two worn sofas. She offered me a cup of coffee, which I gratefully accepted.

"You're getting a bit of color back in your cheeks," she said after I'd had a few sips. "Are you starting to feel better?"

"I am. Thank you. I'm Della Wright, by the way."

"I'm Johanna Renay. I'm a clerk for the department of revenue." She shook her head, her eyes tearing. "I can't believe it. Why, just yesterday Howard was talking about the new house he was planning on buying. It was his dream house. Oh, his poor wife will be devastated." Hearing the sorrow in the woman's voice as she spoke of him, and knowing the man had a loving wife made his death all the more tragic somehow.

The two men walked in and the older one handed me my phone. I introduced myself again.

"Nice to meet you. I'm Tom Goodall," the gentleman said. He shook my hand and turned to Mrs. Renay. "How are you doing, Johanna. I know you and Howard were close."

"I'm all right," she said, not very convincingly.

The younger man introduced himself. "Ronald Dempsey," he said, adjusting his tie and raising his chin self-importantly. He wasn't a city employee as I'd first thought. I recognized his name as that of a local builder. And if I remembered right, this was the same man who was financing a project right here in Belmont—a new development of luxury houses. I hadn't seen the prices, but judging by the advertisements all around town, they were in the stratosphere.

"I'm the owner of Prestige Homes," he added, as if reading my mind. "Mr. Swanson was buying one of my houses—the Mountain View model."

This surprised me. I'd always thought city employees earned modest salaries. How much did a house in the Prestige Homes project cost? I wondered.

"Aren't you going to take your coat off?" he asked me. "You must be getting hot."

"I'm fine. Thanks." I was just beginning to get over the shivers. The shock, I supposed.

"And by the way," Dempsey said. "You were right. Swanson is as dead as a doornail."

I nodded.

Mrs. Renay was taking the news terribly. She wiped the moisture from her red-rimmed eyes, and when she spoke, it was with a tight throat. "Poor man. I can't believe somebody killed him."

"I can," Dempsey said. All eyes turned on him.

"What would make you say such a horrible thing?" Mrs. Renay said.

"The man was impossible to work with. He nearly drove a lot of contractors out of business, having them demolish and rebuild things that were perfectly fine, and making them wait and wait for their permits," he said, looking as if he was dying to name names.

"Like who?" I asked.

"Smithy, Clarkson, Shuttleworth."

"Shuttleworth?" I said, shocked. "You mean Syd?"

"I don't mean him in particular," Dempsey said, now backtracking. "You have to understand, in real estate, time is money. Builders have to pay interest on their loans. An extra year on a project is enough to eat up all a man's profits." I only half listened to what he was saying, my mind preoccupied with Syd Shuttleworth. Dempsey's words supported what Syd had told us, that the inspector had caused all the delays in the project.

"Weren't you worried he'd find flaw after flaw to complain about in any house he bought?" asked Mrs. Renay.

"I was lucky he liked my work. Besides, if I'd refused to sell to him, he'd probably have given me a hard time, just like he did to everybody else. Besides, a sale is a sale."

At that moment, I heard the sound of sirens getting closer. Dempsey, who had taken a seat on one of the sofas, looked at his watch. "Is it already eleven o'clock?" He jumped to his feet and dashed to the door.

"Hey," Tom Goodall said, "you can't leave now. The police will want to talk to all of us."

"Mr. Goodall is right," I said. "You can't leave until the police allow it. You may think you have nothing to add, but sometimes a person will see things he doesn't even realize is important."

Dempsey's face turned red. "I don't have to stay here. I didn't hear or see anything. You did. Besides, I have more important things to do than to sit around talking to cops." He pulled a card from his breast pocket and threw it on the table. "There. If they want to talk to me, they know where to reach me." He turned and walked out.

"Looks to me like he really didn't want to talk to the police," Tom Goodall said. "Or maybe he thinks he's more important than the rest of us."

Mrs. Renay pulled herself to her feet and sighed. "I guess we'd better go outside. They'll be here in a minute."

From past experience I knew just how grueling a police questioning could be. And since I was the one who'd found the body, I was likely going to be the principle player.

Let the torture begin.

Chapter 4

We traipsed out through the main hall. To my surprise there wasn't a customer in sight. The few employees who were still inside were huddled behind the counter, looking worried.

"I told everyone to keep the office closed for now," Goodall explained. "There's no point in having people walking around all over the place until the police are finished here. Besides, everyone is upset. I doubt they could focus on doing their jobs right now."

We waited at the front of the building.

"Mr. Goodall mentioned you and the victim were close. How long did you know him?" I asked Mrs. Renay, more for the sake of conversation than curiosity. The prospect of being questioned was making me nervous.

"All my life. He and I were in college together." The faint smile she gave, remembering, made me suspect the two might have dated back then. "Then," she continued, "a few years after I started working here, he was hired as the city inspector. He's been here nearly as long as I have. And I knew his ex-wife. Though, I haven't seen her in about a year—since she and Howard got divorced. He just got remarried to a younger woman only six months ago. Men are so stupid—marrying a woman half his age. Can you imagine?" I was surprised at the anger in her tone. She seemed to read my mind. "I'm just thinking about Sondra."

"Sondra . . . you mean the ex-Mrs. Swanson?"

She nodded, then frowned. "Oh, dear. I suppose I'd better call his new wife and give her the tragic news after the police are done with us. How long do you think these things take?"

"It shouldn't take terribly long. No more than half an hour I'd say. They'll only want the important details. They'll contact us later with all further questions."

At that moment a black-and-white cruiser came to a screeching halt at the curb. The officers stepped out and hurried over. A second later, an ambulance showed up and the emergency team hopped out.

"This way," Tom Goodall said, waving at them toward the building entrance. "Follow me."

One of the cops yelled out to the ambulance attendants. "Hey. If the victim's dead, don't disturb the crime scene."

The younger officer turned to our small group. "Which one of you called to report this?" he asked through his mustache.

"I did," I said, stepping forward. "I found him. Do you want me to go with you?"

"No," the older officer replied.

"Hey, Jack. You think one of us should go in? Make sure those guys don't touch anything?"

"Good thinking," he replied. He was a heavyset man with a ruddy complexion. "I'll talk to the witnesses."

Mrs. Renay stepped forward and introduced herself with the bearing of someone taking charge. "After Miss Wright discovered the body, Ronald Dempsey and Mr. Goodall went to see if he needed an ambulance. Miss Wright and I waited out here."

The cop looked around. "Where's this Ronald? Is he inside?"

"He had an appointment. Seems like it couldn't wait." She sniffed, making it clear she did not approve of his leaving. "But he left his business card so you can reach him if you need to." She handed it to him.

The officer scowled. "He shouldn't have left. He should have known we'd want to talk to him."

She nodded. "That's what we all told him."

His eyes wandered over to me. "So you discovered the body. Can you recall what time it might have been?"

"I think around ten thirty." I looked at Mrs. Renay for confirmation.

"That sounds about right," she said. "It was only a few minutes past ten thirty when you ran through the main office."

A second police car drove into the lot and, cringing, I recognized Officer Lombard as she stepped out. She came forward, her thumbs hooked on her belt.

"Why is it that every time there's a murder around here, you're sure to be involved?" she asked. I felt my blood simmering. So it was going to be like that, was it? Let's just say that Officer Lombard and I had a bit of history.

"I think 'involved' is a strong word to use, considering all I did was find the body and call the police."

"But, you have to admit, you sure have a knack for finding dead bodies." Her tone was only slightly less contentious.

I cracked a tiny smile. "You're beginning to sound like my mother. But I'd say it's more a case of really bad luck rather than a skill. Believe me—I would rather somebody else had found him." I shuddered, remembering the bloody scene.

"Hope you guys don't mind," she said to the other officers. "But I'm taking Della with me." We walked in the direction the ambulance men had just taken. The city employees who had gathered by the entrance now moved out of the way to let us by.

"It's this way." I headed down the hall toward Swanson's office and stopped outside the door. Inside, the two ambulance attendants and the mustached officer were bending over the body. I began shivering afresh. I wasn't the only one having some difficulty with the situation. Tom Goodall stood a few feet away, looking slightly jaundiced.

I dared a quick look at the victim, this time noticing the hole in the side of his head. My stomach lurched at the sweet metallic smell of blood. Suddenly the room tilted and I dropped into a crouch.

"Put your head down and take a deep breath," Lombard said. She opened the side door, the same one I'd noticed earlier and a welcome breeze of fresh air wafted in.

"He's dead all right," one of the attendants said. "Looks like he was hit over the head with that bookend." I had seen the bookend, shaped like a horse's head. It looked like marble or granite, probably weighed a ton. I didn't turn to look.

"I called the coroner," the cop said.

The two attendants stood. "No point in us sticking around. The coroner will want to see the body before it's picked up."

"We need to get the forensic team over here," the cop said, pulling out his cell phone.

"Did you see anyone coming out when you arrived?" Lombard asked.

"Not a soul. In fact, I remember noticing how quiet this area of the building is."

She nodded. "The killer could just as easily have come in and out through that window." I glanced in the direction she was looking. The window was on the back wall. It was slightly open.

She walked over. "See how easily it opens and closes?" She demonstrated. Then she leaned out, looking at the ground below. "There are footprints here. Steve?" she said to the other cop. "I want you to make sure the technicians get plaster casts of those imprints."

He gave her a who-died-and-made-you-boss look, but he got his cell phone out, nonetheless, and made a second call.

"Della?" Lombard was looking at me strangely. "Are you all right? You're awfully pale." I was surprised at how considerate she was being.

"It's the smell."

"You still have to walk us through what happened when you came in this morning, before you discovered the body."

Ah, that explained her attentive behavior. Her concern was not for me but for her investigation. I swallowed hard, and stood, grasping the doorframe for support. "I knocked a couple of times, and got no answer, so I tried the handle—"

"Why?" Lombard asked.

I shrugged. "I wanted to leave him a message. I was surprised when the door opened. I went over to the desk." I gestured toward it. "I was looking for a piece of paper, something to write him a note. That's when I saw him on the floor."

"What did you do then?"

"I turned around and got the hell out."

The mustached officer had finished his call and was leaning out the open window, examining the ground. "It looks like somebody trampled the flower bed all along the side of the building. What do you want to bet those footsteps are the gardener's?"

Lombard threw him a nasty look and sniffed, as if insulted. "We can't jump to conclusions. When we get the casts, we'll get forensics to compare them to the gardener's shoes."

"Forensics?" I said. "The police department has a forensics team?"

She reddened. "The department might bring in experts." I seriously doubted that. Considering how little experience the local police had with murder, bringing in experts would be a good thing, but the town did not have that kind of a budget.

"There's another entrance right outside this office," I said. And then seeing the suspicion in her eyes, I explained. "I happened to try it from outside, but it was locked."

Officer Lombard stepped out and examined the door, pulling the edge of her sleeve over her fingertips, she gave the handle a try—opened it and closed it. "It latches automatically when you close it," she noted.

"Somebody could have exited the building that way, but unless it had been left propped open, they would have had to come in by the main entrance," I said. Lombard nodded slowly, still eyeing me with mistrust.

The young officer came over, opened the door and looked out. "Even if someone had left this way, there wouldn't necessarily be fingerprints on the door. They could have used gloves."

Lombard regarded him with a scowl. "And now, whatever fingerprints might have been on the handle are covered with yours."

He looked down at his hand. "Oh, shoot." And then brightening up, he added, "But I didn't touch the outside handle."

"But *I* did," I said. This was followed by groans all around.

Officer Lombard turned to me. "You're sure you didn't notice anyone when you came in?"

"Not a soul. And I didn't hear anything either." My eyes had automatically paused on the body as I said this. "Do you mind if I go back outside? I'm not feeling very well."

At that moment Officer Harrison, Lombard's partner, stepped in, followed by Dr. Cook, the county coroner. I had met Dr. Cook before. He was a nice old man and too kind a person to be a coroner. The problem was that after a lifetime of caring for the town folk, the good doctor could never believe that any of his neighbors—as he called everyone who lived in the area—could be killers. As a result, he had in the past signed off on some deaths as natural, only for them to be identified as murders at a later date. He nodded to me and went straight to the victim.

"Did you touch anything?" Lombard asked me, narrowing her eyes.

"Not a thing. All I did was knock. When there was no answer, I tried the door and walked in. I got out of there as soon as I saw him."

"So you touched the doorknob of his office, not just the outside knob?" she said.

"Er, yes, but that was all."

She shook her head, sighing. "Okay. Let's get out of here. The tech guys should be here any minute."

I headed down the hall, happy to get away from the sour smell of death.

"By the way. You never did tell me why you wanted to see the victim."

"I had my shop remodeled and he'd just approved the occupancy permit. I came by to pick it up."

One of the officers inside said, "There's a whole stack of permits right here." He pointed to a pile of yellow forms on the desk.

"Can you see if mine is in there?" I asked, stepping forward. "I need it to open my shop."

Officer Lombard planted herself in front of the door. "You can't have anything from in here. You should know that by now."

"But my permit has nothing to do with his murder."

The cop inside said, "I just went through and none of them are signed."

Lombard stared at me through narrowed eyes. "Are you sure your permit was supposed to be ready when you came here?" Her expression said what her words didn't. She considered me a suspect.

My mouth dropped open. "You think I killed him because he refused me a permit? That's just nuts." Lombard knew me well enough to know I was no killer. But looking at her now, I couldn't decide whether she was seriously considering me as a suspect or if she was just playing with my mind.

"Don't worry. You're not on my radar," she said almost grudgingly. "But you know as well as I do that I have to ask you all these questions." She paused, getting her notebook and pen from her pocket. "One more thing. Did you have any reason to be angry at Mr. Swanson?" she asked. I felt the blood rise to my face.

"No, of course not. I never had any dealings with him."

Her eyes lasered into mine. "But you did have dealings with him. He had the power to allow you or refuse you your permit. Are you sure he'd approved it?" It sounded to me as if she was intent on pinning this murder on me. Her tone was sounding more and more accusing by the second.

I met her gaze straight on. "This is crazy, and I don't have to listen to this. Unless I'm under arrest, you can't force me to stay here."

"Hold on a second. I still have a couple of questions. Are you sure you didn't see anyone leave the building?" she asked, her tone less accusatory.

"I already told you twice that I didn't."

"What about in the parking lot?"

All at once I remembered the car that had almost smashed into my Jeep. "You're right. I *did* see someone, or rather, a car. It was a small silver hatchback."

"Silver? That's not much of a description. Half the cars in Belmont are that color. What about the make and model?"

"Sorry. I couldn't tell the difference between one manufacturer and another."

"What about the driver then?" She didn't sound as if she believed me one bit.

"I couldn't describe him. It all happened too fast. One second he was about to crash into me, and then I swerved and he flashed by. All I saw was someone wearing sunglasses and a light blue baseball cap."

"So what you're telling me is that you saw some mystery person speed by in a car you can't describe. I suppose you want me to believe the reason he was in such a hurry is because he was running from the scene of the crime? Am I right?" Now she was mocking me. Still, I answered her seriously.

"At the time I thought it was probably some crazy teenager."

"How sure are you that the driver was a male?"

"Er . . . actually no. I just figured—because of the baseball cap."

She seemed to think all of this over for a moment and then she mumbled something indistinct and scribbled a few words in her notebook. I wondered if she believed me after all.

"Well, with all the information you gave us, we'll probably have this case solved by the end of the day." She gave me a smile that was more like a sneer.

"Can I go now?"

"I know where to find you if I need you. I'll probably have more questions for you so don't leave town."

I made my way to my Jeep on shaky legs and automatically headed over to Matthew's house. I was in dire need of a good ear, a soft shoulder, some reassurance and a hug. Mostly a hug.

Chapter 5

Matthew Baker and I went back a long way. His mother and mine, having been college friends, had kept in touch ever since. His family and mine got together for holidays and special occasions for as long as I remembered. And then, a couple of years ago, the friendship I felt for him caught fire. Unfortunately, Matthew's feelings took longer to ignite. But it all turned out well in the end. We had recently become an item, a turnaround that threw both our mothers into a state of rapture.

I parked in front of his house and called his name as I walked in.

"In here," he answered from the kitchen.

I dashed over and caught him standing in front of the coffee machine, wearing nothing but a towel around his midsection. He turned to face me, giving me a view of his wide shoulders and tight abs. I quashed an impulse to run my hands over him.

"Guess I caught you at a bad time," I said instead.

"Or a good time," he said, coming close and giving me a kiss. "Uh-oh. What's wrong?" And then, before I could answer, he continued. "Give me a minute. I'll go jump into some clothes and be right back."

I watched him hurry away with butterflies in my stomach. Matthew was everything I had ever wanted in a man. He was warm and loving, smart, and most important, he and I shared the same values. The rest was just gravy. But what nice gravy it was. He was gorgeous, tall— I barely reached his shoulders—with dark hair and beautiful light brown eyes that had a way of turning golden when he smiled, or dark brown when he was angry.

A minute went by and then he came back down, wearing jeans and a sweater. "I was just making coffee. Want a cup?"

"Thank God you're here," I said, coming over for a hug. "You won't believe what happened." He was patting my back, making reassuring noises.

"Whatever it is, I'm sure it's fixable."

For some reason, all the emotions I'd been holding in came surging forth at his display of sympathy. I was able to handle Lombard's lack of compassion and sarcasm, but in moments like this, I couldn't take kindness without falling apart. The next second I was weeping inconsolably.

From the mat in front of the stove, Winston, Matthew's French bulldog, came bouncing over, wiggling his butt—a great big ball of slobbering love.

Winston had a fierce flat face on a squat, muscular body. For all his brutish appearance, he was twenty-five pounds of pure teddy bear. Matthew and I often joked that an assailant might be in mortal danger of being licked to death.

He jumped up and rubbed his wet nose against my hands—an attempt, no doubt, to console me. Even the dog was being sweet.

I pulled out of Matthew's arms and scratched Winnie behind the ear. "Hi, boy." He barked his pleasure. "Yes, I'm happy to see you too."

"Here. Have a seat," Matthew said, pulling out a chair. "Looks to me like you could use a cup of coffee."

I nodded and pulled myself together. "I'm so glad you're here. How was your meeting with your publisher?"

He grabbed a mug from the cupboard and gave it to me. "Never mind that now. Tell me why you're so upset."

"I had to go by city hall this morning, to get my occupancy permit." I explained that it had been approved earlier, but somehow the inspector had neglected to leave one with Syd. "But when I got there, he was dead," I said, fighting a fresh surge of tears. "I found his body." I grabbed a paper napkin from the basket on the table and wiped my eyes. "You should have seen all the blood."

"No wonder you're so upset."

"I'm feeling better now, but I doubt I'll have much appetite for a while."

"You called the police, of course." I nodded. "And more important, you didn't tamper with the crime scene did you?"

Much as that comment stung, I couldn't blame him. I had once borrowed something from a murder scene. Okay, so maybe I'd done that twice—but only to help the police with their investigation of course. And the important thing was that I put it back. But no matter how much explaining and apologizing I did, Matthew had been livid. The thing is, before becoming an author, Matthew taught criminology at UNC. And before that, he was an FBI agent. Lately the local police had taken to calling him in on some of their cases as a consultant. From this, I had learned one important lesson. One might be able to get the man out of the FBI. But one could never take the FBI out of the man.

"I did not touch a thing, except for the doorknob when I opened the door." I said nothing about the light switch and the message pad. "And I got out of there the minute I saw him."

"Thank God for small favors." He came over and wrapped his arms around me again, gathering me into a warm embrace that soothed all remaining stress right out of me. I melted into his arms. He smelled divine, an intoxicating mixture of citrus and musk. I breathed him in.

"Well, I'm flattered you come to me when you're upset." He released me and refilled both our cups. "So tell me everything."

I did. I told him about how I'd found him, how I'd been sick in the parking lot and how the police had come and questioned everyone. "And of course, which officer would show up, but Lombard."

He looked at me puzzled. "What difference would that make?"

"I may be wrong, but I have a bad feeling she's going to try to pin this on me."

"You have a *feeling*?" He gave me an amused smile. "You're starting to sound like Jenny."

"I'm being serious, Matthew."

He squeezed my hand. "I think maybe you're worrying for nothing."

"If you're suggesting that I'm being paranoid, you're wrong. She all but said that she thought I'd killed him. She seems to think that Swanson wouldn't grant me a permit and that I killed him over that."

"That sounds like a pretty thin reason for murder if you ask me."

"Maybe, but she warned me not to go anywhere, that she'd have more questions for me."

"She was just teasing you," he said. "And if you hadn't had such a shock you would see that too."

"I hope you're right."

"Even supposing I wasn't. You know how the police work. After a murder, everyone is a suspect." He stroked my cheek with his finger. "You have nothing to be concerned about. Trust me."

"You really think so?"

He nodded. "Now, I'd like you to do something for me."

"What?"

"Repeat after me, 'I will not get involved.'"

I was just taking a sip. I put down my cup, perhaps a

bit hard because coffee spilled over the rim. "That is not fair. All I did was find a body. You can't blame me for that. Unless you think I should have walked away without calling the cops."

He raised an eyebrow. "Repeat after me," he said again, his voice tighter this time. "I will not — "

"Wait a minute. I just want to understand this. Are you giving me an order?"

"I'm telling you that I don't want you to get involved, because I care. Is that so difficult to grasp?" Suddenly, the atmosphere had changed. A moment ago it had been warm and loving. Now it bordered on explosive.

I took a deep breath and in a calm voice, said, "I don't tell *you* what to do or not do. I don't have that right. And neither do you."

"Della, if you start snooping around, you could get yourself into some real trouble. And I don't want to have to worry about my girlfriend all the time. If you get yourself into another jam, I swear I'll . . . I'll . . ." He paused.

"You'll what?" I asked, my voice now rising. "You'll break off with me?" He stood there glaring at me, his mouth an angry line. "Fine," I said. "If that's the way you want it." I grabbed my bag and stormed out of the house.

Chapter 6

I drove away in a screech of tires. Much as I loved the man, sometimes he could make me spitting mad. If he thought I was going to become a biddable girlfriend, he had another think coming.

I parked behind the shop and took a moment to calm myself down. After a few deep breaths I decided to keep this argument to myself. No point in rehashing all the details with Jenny and Marnie. I already knew what they'd say—that I'd overreacted, that I should call him and apologize. In other words, all the things I was already telling myself. *I'll wait a day and then I'll decide.*

Satisfied with my decision, I dashed upstairs to my apartment and changed into a pair of clean jeans and a T-shirt. These were hardly better, but at least they didn't have paint splotches and spittle. I looked at the ones I'd taken off, decided they weren't worth keeping and chucked them into the garbage. And then I hoofed it downstairs to my shop.

"Wow. How in the world did you manage to accomplish so much so quickly?" I said, walking in. "I hardly recognize the place."

The entire space had been cleaned from top to bottom. Gone were all the newspapers that had littered the floors and been taped to the windows. And better yet, gone was the dust. I took a few steps, and could have kissed my friends when the white powdery clouds failed to appear. If not for the virgin wall and the painter's tape masking the baseboards, the shop would have looked ready to stock.

Marnie and Jenny were covering the armoire and furniture with fresh plastic drop cloths.

"We had to rewrap everything. The old sheets were covered in dust," Marnie said.

A few feet away I noticed a gallon of paint, a roller and tray and some brushes.

"You like?" Jenny said, wiping her hands on her jeans.

"I can't believe how much work you did in so short a time."

"Well, it wasn't such a short time. You didn't exactly come right back, as you promised," Marnie said, her tone implying a wagging finger. "Where were you for so long? You've been gone for nearly three hours."

The image of Swanson's dead body came flooding back. Jenny must have sensed my mood because she shook her head, a silent signal to ignore Marnie's attitude.

"We decided to speed things up," she explained. "Syd takes so long for everything. But if we keep going, we could paint both sides by the end of the day tomorrow. Then we could set up and open day after tomorrow. What do you think?"

"That sounds a bit optimistic, but if you're game, so am I."

"Don't look so depressed. We'll get it finished. I promise," Marnie said.

Jenny looked at me strangely. "What's wrong? Did he give you your permit?"

"Uh, not exactly. There was a problem."

Marnie froze. "Don't tell me he turned you down. He did the same thing to my friend I told you about. She was just at the end of her rope. Damn that man for being so ornery. I could just strangle him."

"Somebody beat you to it."

"What is that supposed to mean?" Her face fell. "Don't tell me he's—"

"Dead," I said, nodding. "Somebody killed him."

"Oh, no," Jenny said, covering her mouth.

Marnie planted her hands on her hips. "That's just great. How are you supposed to get your permit now?"

Jenny gave her a light slap on the arm. "Marnie! How can you even say such a thing? The poor man is dead."

"You always were nicer than me," Marnie replied, not looking the least bit repentant. "I'm the more practical one." She turned to me again. "What are you going to do?"

"I don't know. I suppose I should call city hall and ask. Maybe they can give me a temporary permit until they get a new inspector."

"Something else is upsetting you. I can feel it," Jenny said. "What is it?"

I scowled. "It's nothing."

"Did you and Matthew have a fight?" she asked.

Was I that transparent? "I don't want to talk about it."

"Whatever it was about," Marnie said, "I wouldn't worry about it. A young lover's quarrel, that's all it is. You'll be kissing and making up in no time." She held out her hand. "Give me your apartment keys. I'll run upstairs and call the city. We might as well find out what we should do about this permit situation."

"I doubt there's anybody there. All the employees had been sent home when I left."

"I'll find out soon enough. Now give me those keys."

I handed them over. Seconds later her footsteps clattered up the stairs.

"Poor man," Jenny said. "I know he was difficult, but no one deserves that. Surely he wasn't killed for that reason?"

"At this point, God only knows the reason."

"Are you absolutely sure he was murdered?"

"There's no question about it."

"He was just here—no more than a few hours ago. He had to have been killed between the time he left and the time you found him. He couldn't have seen very many people in that time. They'll probably catch the killer in no time." I nodded. "How did you learn about his death?"

"I'm the one who found him."

"Oh, poor you. No wonder you look so distraught. Are you all right?"

"I am now, but I was pretty upset for a while. There was a lot of blood. Somebody knocked him over the head with a marble bookend."

She grimaced. "Ouch."

"And then, who shows up but Officer Lombard. Let's just say she wasn't thrilled to see me. She did everything but come right out and tell me that she thinks I did it."

"Surely she was just toying with you?"

"She sounded serious to me."

"I suspect she's still sore at you for solving her case last fall."

I hadn't thought of that. "You think? She should be grateful, not resentful."

"You showed her up in front of her coworkers."

"I didn't try to show up anyone. Why is she taking it so personally?"

Jenny shrugged. "Some people are like that."

"I told Matthew she would try to pin this on me. He said I was worrying about nothing."

"He's right," Jenny said. "There's a big difference between being irritated with you and trying to pin a murder on you. Is that what your argument with Matthew was about?"

Talking about that was just about the last thing in the world I felt like doing. Luckily, the door flew open and Marnie came in, wearing a self-satisfied grin. "I don't know if all the employees were back, but I spoke with a very nice young man—the clerk in the permit department and listen to this. It turns out that the occupancy permit for the *building* was approved."

"We already know that. What I need is to get my hands on it."

"You're not listening. The permit was approved for the entire building. That means your side too, Jenny."

"What?!" Jenny and I exclaimed at the same time.

"How can that be?" Jenny continued. "Syd said I wouldn't get it until I changed my electric panel."

Marnie shrugged. "Don't ask me why, but according to the clerk I spoke to, both places are ready to go. In fact, they're registered as a single municipal address, so the one permit is all you *ever* needed."

"Hm. Swanson told Sydney the complete opposite," I said. "But I, for one, am not going to complain."

"Neither am I," Jenny said. "But what I can't figure out is why would Swanson have lied to Sydney? I'd better call him before he books that electrician. He'll be happy he won't have to spring for all that work."

I was thinking about what Jenny had just said. "Why *would* Swanson have lied?" I said. "I might have been inclined to think Syd made it up in order to stretch out the work, except that one of the people at city hall this morning said that Swanson was in the habit of giving contractors a hard time with permits—that they all hated him for it."

"Now I feel bad that Syd was willing to pay for the labor out of his own pocket. He would have been losing a bundle on this job."

Marnie gave me a puzzled expression. "That hardly makes sense. No contractor offers to pay for work out of the goodness of their hearts. If he offered, it can only be because there was something in it for him."

Now that she put it that way, I had to agree with her argument. "Like what?"

Marnie frowned. "I don't know yet, but trust me, nobody works for nothing."

"You do," I pointed out. "You don't charge me anywhere near what you should."

"That's because I get something other than money out of the arrangement. I get companionship. You know how lonely I am when I work at home."

"I wonder," Jenny said. "Do you think Syd could have misunderstood? I can't imagine the inspector giving him a hard time for no reason."

I doubted that. They're both in the building business and both spoke the same language—constructionese.

"Where are our building permits?" Jenny said, marching over and tearing mine off the wall where it had always been prominently displayed. She handed it to me. Glancing at it, I saw that each step of the construction had been initialed as proof that they had all been completed. "If Swanson approved my side," she said, "he would have initialed the electrical work." She marched out of the shop and into hers. Marnie and I followed her. As we walked in, Jenny was already looking around, searching under tarps and cardboards.

"According to the rules, we were supposed to make sure the building permits were in plain sight," she said. "Well, wherever it is, I don't see it."

"Hold on," Marnie said. "If both places were considered a single unit all along, it would make sense that you only ever had the one building permit. And Sydney being a contractor, he would have known if there was only one permit for the entire building."

I planted my hands on my hips. "In that case, he would have also had to know that if my side was approved, Jenny's was too. It's beginning to sound like Swanson was up to something, and Sydney was in on it."

"In on what?" Jenny said, looking confused.

I was just as perplexed as she was.

Marnie and I returned to my shop, while Jenny prepared a fresh pot of coffee. A few minutes later she appeared in the doorway with a tray of steaming coffee mugs. "I called Syd to tell him he didn't have to move the electrical box. He sounded surprised, not at all like someone who'd been caught in a lie."

"Ha! Maybe he sounded surprised because he didn't expect you to find out," Marnie said.

Jenny disregarded the comment. "He's just a few minutes away, so he'll drop by and pick up the rest of his tools."

"Did you tell him about Swanson?"

"I didn't have the heart. I hate being the bearer of bad news."

"It might not have been bad news," I said. "According to Dempsey, one of the contractors who hated Swanson the most was Syd."

"I don't believe that for a minute," she said. She always believed the best of everyone.

When I glanced at her, Marnie was watching me with a peculiar smile. "Why are you looking at me in that way?" I asked.

"No reason."

"You've obviously got something on your mind. Tell me."

"I was just noticing the gleam in your eyes as you were trying to solve the puzzle. You are playing detective again. Aren't you?"

Chapter 7

Jenny and I started in my shop since mine was already prepped. Meanwhile, Marnie armed herself with brooms and mops and countless rolls of masking tape, and began cleaning Jenny's store.

"This paint job might not be as perfect as what Sydney's crew could do," I said, dipping the roller into the pan. "But it'll be finished faster."

"Which is a good thing," Jenny said.

"And we'll be saving ourselves some money."

"Which is an even better thing," she added, laughing. "But I think you're not giving us enough credit. I bet we can do it just as well." She was on the ladder already cutting the edges of the ceiling with an angled brush. "As long as we stay inside the masking tape." She chuckled. "But staying inside the lines was always a problem with me."

"Not me. I used to be a business analyst—almost as anal as accountants. All inside the lines all the time."

Fifteen minutes later, we had just started with the coat of primer, when Marnie came bursting in.

"Sydney's here. He's looking for his tool belt. Any idea where it might be?"

"Oops. That's my fault," I said. "I borrowed it to put up a few pictures on my living room wall and forgot to bring it back down." I'd put up lovely pictures of Native weaving all over my bedroom wall as inspiration for my new collection. It had worked. So far, I'd completed two blankets, a dozen place mats, a few runners and some squares I planned to make into decorator cushions.

I wiped my hands with a rag. "I'll be right back." I raced up the stairs to my apartment, returning a few seconds later. "Here it is," I said, walking into Jenny's shop.

"Ah, that's a relief," Syd said. "There's not much I can do without my measuring tape and hammer." He grabbed the tool belt.

"By the way, did you hear about Swanson?"

"You mean about the electrical panel?" he asked, dropping his measuring tape. "Jenny told me I wouldn't have to move it, and Marnie just told me the city had already passed it. I can't figure it out, unless I misunderstood. Lucky for everyone she checked." He made a production out of rearranging all the tools in his belt, the whole time, avoiding my eyes. I glanced at Marnie again, wondering if she was also noticing how fidgety he was.

"I was talking about his murder," I said, watching for his reaction.

"Murder? What are you talking about? Are you telling me that Swanson is dead?" I wasn't sure what was behind the expression in his eyes, except that it didn't look like surprise. There had been an instant of something like elation, quickly replaced by fear. Already my mind was jumping to conclusions.

"I'm afraid he is."

"Swanson is dead?" he repeated, this time, as if he was trying to sound sad. It was a poor attempt.

"He was murdered. Somebody hit him over the head hard enough to split it open."

He leaned against the wall as if his legs could no longer support him. "I knew a lot of people hated him, but I never imagined—"

I waited, hoping he would expand on this.

He blew out a breath. "He was a city inspector. He had

a way of making enemies." That was pretty close to what Ronald Dempsey had said just a few hours ago. He shook his head, as if in disbelief. This reaction also seemed off. "Poor guy. That's a real shame." I wondered if Marnie and Jenny heard the insincerity in his comments as I did. "That'll be especially hard on his family. He just got married again a few months ago. At least his wife won't be entirely by herself. Her sister and brother-in-law moved here." He paused. "Do the cops have any idea who did it?" This time, the nervousness in his voice sounded real.

"Not that I'm aware," I said. "How well did you know Swanson?"

"Considering I've been a contractor for the better part of my life, not all that well. A lot of my jobs didn't involve permits — you know, flooring, kitchen cabinets, painting. That sort of stuff. I know he was buddies with some of the local contractors, but except for the occasional job, he and I never had much in common. He was a lot older than me."

"Who was he friends with?"

He shrugged, glancing at the door as if he couldn't wait to get out of there. "I don't really know." I waited, and after a few seconds of silence he expanded on that. "I saw him a couple of times at The Bottoms Up, with Ronald Dempsey." I hid my surprise.

"You said Swanson was friends with other contractors. But Dempsey is a developer."

"Developer, contractor, same difference." He was now inching his way backward toward the exit. "He needed building permits just as badly I do. And he must have liked Dempsey's work because I heard he was buying a house from him." He reached the door. "Marnie tells me you'll be doing the painting yourself?"

"Yes. I hope you don't mind," I added, "but the renovations ended up costing way more than I expected. I figured I could save myself some money."

"I understand," he said. "So I guess that's it then. Here's my last bill." He pulled an envelope from his shirt pocket and handed it to me, almost dropping it in his rush to leave. "I'll pick up the check the next time I'm in the area." He slung the tool belt over his shoulder, picked up the red toolbox at his feet, and stooping under the weight, he scurried out.

Marnie, who had been standing a few feet away, stared at the closed door. "Well! He sure was in a rush to get out of here. Don't you think?"

"I got the same impression. In fact, I think it was really weird that he didn't ask to be paid right away. I could have run upstairs to get my checkbook."

"But then he would have had to stick around for another five minutes. Why do you suppose he was in such a rush?"

"He looked as nervous as a thief who'd just triggered a burglar alarm. What really surprised me is that he hadn't heard of Swanson's murder," she continued.

"I'm surprised you didn't tell him the second he walked in," I said.

She winked. "Because I could have bet my best brownie recipe that you wanted to tell him yourself. I knew you'd want to see his reaction." She tilted her head sideways. "I know you. You're just dying to start snooping, aren't you? In fact, I bet you already have a suspect. Judging by the way you were looking at him while you asked him all those questions, I could tell, you think Syd was the killer."

I wouldn't have put it that strongly, but after watching him squirm and then rush out the door, I was convinced that he was guilty of something. I just wasn't sure what. Jenny mentioned something strange earlier," I said. "According to her, Syd's aura had been gray this morning instead of its usual blue—not that I believe any of that stuff. Her interpretation of that was he was lying." I shrugged. "In this case, I think she might have been right—about the lying, I mean."

Marnie nodded. "She told me the same thing."

I remembered the fleeting expression of delight in the contractor's eyes. It had been an odd reaction upon learning about someone's death.

"I think Syd knows something," I said.

"You mean about Swanson's murder?"

Before I could answer, the door flew open and Jenny came storming in. "You won't believe this. I was curious about what Syd was up to. So I followed him and—"

"Now *you're* playing detective?" Marnie said, giving her the eyebrow.

"Yes, I am, and for a darn good reason too. The more I've been thinking about it, the more I feel that Syd was trying to slow the work progress for as long as he could. But since it wasn't for the money, there had to be another reason. And I suspected it had something to do with Good Morning Sunshine."

"What in the world are you talking about?" Marnie asked.

"I think they're all conspiring against me," she said.

Good grief. Jenny was starting to lose it. What she was thinking was just plain nuts, but I kept my mouth shut. Marnie was not so polite. "Sugar pie, I think you need a good night's sleep. You're starting to imagine things."

"Before you start thinking I'm crazy, listen to me. I waited in my car until he left, and then I followed him. And guess where he went." She looked from Marnie to me and continued. "He made a beeline straight to Good Morning Sunshine."

"That doesn't necessarily mean anything," I said gently.

She harrumphed. "Do either of you remember that he was the one who told us we needed the electrical box moved? How long do you think he would have stretched that out for?"

"We don't know whether that was him or Swanson," Marnie pointed out.

Jenny rolled her eyes. "Fine. Go ahead and believe whatever you want. But you know how I get feelings about things. By the way, do either of you know the new owners' names?"

"Jim and Lori Stanton," I said.

"Actually, he calls himself Jack," Marnie said. She looked from me to Jenny. "I met them at the grocery store. I was in line behind them at the cash register. They were chatting up everyone and handing out coupons for free coffees."

Jenny gasped. "You never told me that."

"I didn't want to upset you. Did you go?"

"Good grief, of course not. You would never forgive me if I had."

Jenny gave her a rueful smile. "That was smart of you." She sighed, and then said, "I bet you anything that Syd has a connection to them."

Marnie froze. "I just remembered something," she said. "Syd was there that day, at the grocery store with them. I didn't think anything of it then, but now . . . I wonder if they might be related."

Jenny crossed her arms. "So, still think I'm being paranoid?"

Chapter 8

I still thought her theory was a stretch. However, of the two of us, Jenny had always been the calmer, more levelheaded one. When I got frantic, she would talk me down. When I got angry, she calmed me. That is why it was so strange to see her so agitated. Could she be right about any of this? Was I dismissing her suspicions too swiftly?

I had questioned, more than once, why the renovations were taking so long. I had even wondered if Syd was moving so slowly on purpose. But thinking that he was plotting with the owners of the coffee shop up the street sounded paranoid—at least upon first examination. But what if she was right?

I chose my words carefully. "I can understand why his behavior might seem suspicious, but how do we know he wasn't just stopping for coffee?"

"If he'd wanted coffee, he could have asked. I had some ready here," she said.

"Considering we had just told him he was wrong about you needing the electrical panel moved, I think it was completely natural for him to want to leave ASAP."

She thought this over and shook her head. "I'm telling you—there's something going on. I just know it." An idea lit up her eyes. "Didn't somebody say they moved here to be close to family? I think Marnie is right. Syd is probably family. Or maybe they're paying him to keep me closed."

Now she was beginning to scare me.

"I don't think there was any conspiracy," Marnie said, looking worried. "He probably wasn't purposely stretching out the work. He was only doing what all contractors do. He took on too many contracts and juggled his time, giving everybody a few hours here and there, hoping to keep everyone happy."

"I'm sure Marnie's right," I said.

"When I had my professional kitchen built," Marnie continued, "the contractor told me it would all be done in three months. Well. It was more like five months by the time it was finished. And it cost me twice as much as I'd expected. That's just how it is with renovations."

A while back Marnie had decided that with the amount of baking she was doing for Jenny's shop, she needed to be equipped like a professional. She ordered an industrial kitchen complete with a walk-in freezer. She had spent an inordinate amount of money on it, but in the end she had a setup to make any baker proud. In spite of its cost, she was happy and had since doubled her output.

"Everything you're saying sounds logical. And any other time I would say you're right," she replied. "But if you'd seen the way the new owner's wife greeted him when he walked in, you'd be suspicious too. She came out from behind the counter and threw her arms around him as if he was her long lost brother or something.

"I have no idea what their relationship might be, except that they're more than just casual acquaintances—of that I'm sure." She let out a long sigh, and when she spoke again I was relieved to find her sounding more like herself. "Maybe you're right. Maybe I'm just letting my imagination get the better of me. Anyhow," she continued determinedly, "Coffee, Tea and Destiny will be open again soon. And I'll make this shop so irresistible that customers won't be able to stay away."

"That's the spirit," Marnie said, giving the air a punch.

"Are you planning anything special?" I asked, relieved at the change of subject.

Her resolute expression of a second ago morphed into one of defeat. "I have no idea."

"I have one," Marnie said. "I've got dozens of cookies in my freezer. What you should do is hire someone to stand outside for your reopening and hand out free cookies and invite people to come in. I bet every person who walks in will also order a coffee and more of those cookies to take home."

"That's a brilliant idea," I said.

Marnie wasn't finished. "You know what else we should do? Instead of waiting until the day after tomorrow to open, why don't we aim for tomorrow, even if it means working right through the night? We all know that nothing drives business in this town like gossip. Tomorrow, every person in Briar Hollow will have heard about Swanson's murder and will be looking for a gossip session. We have to make sure those sessions happen right here."

Marnie was right. After the last local tragedy, Jenny's shop was packed. Customers sat at the tables, ordering cup after cup of coffee while reminiscing about the victim, grieving for the family, and speculating about who might have done the killing and why.

"Work right through the night?" I said.

"Great idea," Jenny said, holding my gaze as if begging me to agree.

I shrugged. "Let's do it."

"Well, then, what are we waiting for? We'll finish Della's shop in no time and then we can put all our energy into yours," Marnie said.

We returned to my shop and picked up where we'd left off. Soon, I was so engrossed in the painting that when the bell above the door rang, I almost jumped out of my skin. Two women walked in.

"Well, hello," one of them said. "I've been walking by here every day for two months. I'm so happy to see you're at the painting stage at last."

Her name was Judy Bates. I had met her a few months earlier at a county fair where I'd rented a booth to promote my shop and sell my woven goods. Judy had run the stall next to mine where she sold oil paintings. She was a pretty woman a few years older than me, with brown hair and a pixie smile.

"Della, meet my mother," she said. The woman looked like an older version of her daughter. I'd seen her around town a few times but had never officially been introduced.

"Nice of you to stop by," I said.

They walked around, *ooh*ing and *aah*ing, even though there was nothing to see except lots of plastic drop cloths and half-painted walls.

"Careful. I don't want you to get any paint on your clothes," I said. They scooted to the center of the room, away from buckets, brushes and rollers.

"Such a lovely shop," Judy said. "You have such a cozy space here," Judy continued. "I can't wait for it to reopen." The small talk having been done, she immediately changed the subject to what she'd really come in for. "I hear you found the body of the city inspector, Mr. Swanson. I can't imagine how you must have felt. Terribly upsetting, I'm sure."

"It was. Did you know him?"

Both women shook their heads. "But I almost feel as if I do," Judy said. "I heard so much about him from my neighbor, Susan. She didn't like him very much, I can tell you that much. He was a"—she blushed—"oh, dear. There I go again, opening my big mouth. I should not speak ill of the dead." She quickly overcame her embarrassment and continued. "But, in all fairness, the man did treat her shamefully when she redid her kitchen. She'd hired a contractor who did a beautiful job with the remodel. I saw the place myself. It was gorgeous. But that dratted inspector refused to give her a permit. For a while, it looked like she would have to tear the whole thing out and start over."

I could tell by the way Jenny had paused in her painting that she was listening intently.

"How awful," I said, hoping to keep her talking. "She must have been furious."

"Oh, you have no idea. I thought she'd kill the man."

Her mother looked shocked. "How can you say such a thing?"

Judy's eyes rounded as she realized what she'd just said. "I didn't mean literally. It's just a figure of speech."

"Of course," I said.

"Then, from one day to the next, everything was fine," she continued. "She got her occupancy permit without having so much as an outlet changed."

"Really?" Jenny said, coming forward. "That sounds exactly like what happened to me. It looked like I would have to change the electrical panel all over again. And then"—she opened her hands—"everything was fine. No need to change a thing."

Judy chuckled. "What did you do? Sleep with the man?"

Shock flashed over Jenny's face, but she quickly covered it with an amused smile. "Good grief. I would have preferred to redo the electrical instead."

Judy guffawed. "Now that is funny."

"Who are you talking about?" I asked.

"Susan Price. Maybe you know her?" I shook my head.

"In my case," Jenny said. "Swanson told us we needed two permits, one for Della's shop and one for mine. Then, once everything was ready, he told our contractor that we'd have to redo the electrical on my side." She explained how we had then discovered that, since we shared the same civic address, we'd only ever needed one permit. "We can't figure out why he would have lied."

Judy leaned in. "I don't know about your case, but in Susan's, I suspected she slipped him some money under the table."

As soon as she said this, I knew extortion had to be the answer. It explained everything. Why else would a city inspector hold back a permit unless it was for some kind of personal gain? That also explained how a city employee could afford a luxury home.

"Honestly, Judy," her mother said, sounding shocked. "The things that come out of your mouth."

"Did Susan say anything to suggest that?"

Her mother gave her a gentle nudge. "Don't you think we should get on our way?"

Judy threw her an apologetic look. "Just one second." She turned back to me. "Actually, she said, and I quote, that the solution had been expensive, but not nearly as much as if she'd had to redo the whole thing. When I asked her what she meant, she refused to elaborate." She leaned forward and whispered, "If you ask me, a payoff is the only explanation. I mean . . . one minute she can't get her permit and has to redo the whole thing, and then just a short time later everything is just fine. You tell me—how else would you explain it?"

As she said this, another idea occurred to me. Could Syd have been in cahoots with Swanson? It made sense. Syd would slow down a job until the owners became desperate. And then he could be the one to suggest possibly bribing the inspector. It would look less like a shakedown that way. And since the contractor supposedly offered the bribe in the owner's name, the chance of him going to the authorities was practically nil.

I nodded. "I have to admit, you make a good point. But I can promise you one thing. Nobody here paid off anybody."

"Oh, I never meant to suggest—"

"No offense taken. I might have come to the same conclusion."

Judy breathed a sigh of relief. "You know, I never met Mr. Swanson. But I did see him from a distance a couple of times. He used to drop off his wife at my place. We were in the same book club."

I had to ask. "Are you talking about his ex-wife?"

"Yes. I never met his new wife, but I have seen her around town."

"What is she like?"

"The ex? She's very nice. Just a pleasant, middle-aged lady. The new Mrs. Swanson is another story. For one thing, she's young—no more than twenty-five or so—and gorgeous." She tittered. "The first time I saw them together, I thought he was her father. I was shocked when I heard she was his new wife. I don't know how in the world he got her to say yes."

"I guess love is blind," her mother said.

"How are you feeling?" Judy asked me, suddenly solicitous. She shook her head. "If I'd found a dead body, I'd probably be home, having a nervous breakdown."

Her mother glanced at her watch. "Can it already be two o'clock? My goodness, we'd better get going, Judy." And just to make sure she followed, she took hold of Judy's arm and guided her toward the exit.

"Good grief. Can you believe that woman?" Jenny asked as soon as the door closed behind them.

"She was just looking for a good gossip session," I whispered back, as I watched mother and daughter going by my window. "And hopefully you'll have a shop full of people just like her tomorrow. Now let's get back to work."

Except for a short break for pizza, we continued painting until late into the night. By the time we finished putting everything away, it was almost two o'clock in the morning. Jenny called a cab and I stumbled up the stairs to my apartment. Five minutes later I was in bed. But as tired as I was, my mind was doing the whirlies. That's what I call it when my thoughts keep going around and around. So I got out of bed and padded to the kitchen where I made myself a cup of hot cocoa.

I loved my old kitchen. I had fallen in love with it the moment I'd laid eyes on it. And it was, as much as anything else, one of the reasons I'd bought the building. It was modestly sized, but it had antique glass cabinets that went all the way up to the ceiling. The counters were black Formica trimmed in nickel. Along one wall was an old farm sink complete with drain board. But what I loved most about it was the 1930s Chambers stove. It was my pride and joy.

Rather than climb into bed and wait for sleep to come, I dragged my loom from my bedroom to the dining room and settled down for a few hours of weaving. And as my hands threw the shuttle through the shed, I replayed in my mind the conversation I'd had with Judy Bates. If she was right, that Swanson was indeed extorting money in exchange for permits, no wonder the man had ended up dead. In my book, extortion was the same thing as blackmail— just another form of getting money from victims by using threats. A person could make a lot of enemies doing that.

From there, my mind wandered on to Syd Shuttleworth and how he might be implicated with Swanson, and possibly with the owners of Good Morning Sunshine, as well.

In the middle of the night Jenny's suspicions of him didn't seem nearly as crazy. She had made a few good points.

After ruminating about all of that for a while, I put away my shuttle and padded back to bed. By then fatigue had crowded out the stress and the only thing left was a desire for sleep. I crawled under the blankets thinking about Matthew. I hadn't heard from him all day. Maybe I should call him in the morning, and then dismissed the idea as quickly as I'd thought of it. It had been wrong of him to tell me what to do. So why should I be the one to make the first move?

Eventually I must have fallen asleep, because next thing I knew it was morning. I got up with the alarm, shocked at how stiff and sore I was. The long hours of painting had done their damage. There wasn't an inch of my body that wasn't screaming in pain. I hobbled over to the washroom and stood in the shower, letting the scalding needles of water massage my sore muscles until I felt almost normal again. I was halfway through my first cup of coffee when my house phone rang.

"Mom," I said, recognizing her number on the call display. "How are you?" I already had a pretty good idea what this call was about and sure enough, after the customary greetings, she got straight to the point.

"Honestly, sweetheart. I don't know how you do it. I heard there was a murder in Belmont and that you found the body. Are you all right?"

"I'm fine, Mom. Don't worry."

"Did you know the victim?"

"I'd seen him a few times, but never officially met him. He was the building inspector in charge of the permits for my store. That was why I was going to meet him."

"Please tell me you're not going to let yourself get tangled up in another investigation," she said.

"Don't worry, Mom. I promise I won't let anyone push me around."

There was a short silence, during which, no doubt, she was trying to figure out if I was being cute.

"I'm happy to hear that," she said, deciding I wasn't. "You know how I worry." *That,* I certainly did. "So let's talk about something more pleasant," she continued. "How is Matthew?" *Uh-oh.* Any discussion of my relationship with Matthew would be fraught with minefields. The last thing I wanted was for her to learn about our argument. I'd never hear the end of it.

"Matthew is good," I said. "I just saw him yesterday. He's hard at work on his second book and making good progress."

"That's nice, but that isn't what I was asking. How are the two of you doing? Are things moving forward nicely?"

"We're doing fine. We see each other regularly—three or four times a week."

"Has he used the 'L' word yet?" My mind went blank for a moment. "The 'L' word," she repeated. "You know, as in has he said, 'I love you' yet?"

I laughed. "I didn't know what you were talking about."

"In my experience, when a man tells a woman that he loves her, it doesn't take much longer until he proposes."

"Is that right, Mom? Where, in your experience, did you learn that?" My mother had married her childhood sweetheart—my father—and they were together for nearly forty years until he passed away of a heart attack five years earlier. "As far as I know, you only ever had one boyfriend and that was Dad. One man doesn't exactly qualify you as an expert."

She heard the amusement in my voice and laughed good-naturedly. "Okay, I'll grant you that. But I have lots of women friends who have lived more than me. Also, I used to read Ann Landers and Dear Abby religiously."

I burst out laughing. "Mom, you are something else. Please don't ever change. I'd love to talk longer, but I have tons of work today. Today is my official reopening day."

"Oh," she said, sounding disappointed. "Well, I won't keep you. Good luck. Big kisses to Matthew."

I dropped the receiver back in the cradle, relieved that I'd been able to field her questions and end the conversation before she got to her usual subject—grandchildren.

She hardly ever called without reminding me about my biological clock. And if I dismissed those comments, she'd rejoin by admonishing that I should remember that she was no longer young and that all she wanted before she died was to have grandchildren.

Talk about a guilt trip.

I swallowed the rest of my coffee in one gulp and hurried downstairs to my shop, wondering again if Jenny might have been right about Syd Shuttleworth, and how in the world I could find out?

Chapter 9

Anybody who knows me would tell you that I am a person of habit. Every morning, like clockwork, I walked the short distance to the nearest newspaper dispenser to pick up a copy of the *Belmont Daily*. This one happened to be conveniently located no more than ten yards away from Good Morning Sunshine, giving me the perfect opportunity to walk by and do some spying. I debated briefly and then decided, as I always did, that—what the heck—why not? I strolled by, casually glancing inside, while really scanning for every smallest detail.

Since reopening, the new owners had done little to change the interior decor. It was still furnished with the same dark leather armchairs, coffee tables and bar tables. Along the back wall was an old glass counter that had probably been there for decades. The only changes I could see was that the walls had been changed from what Bunny called contractor beige to a soft shade of blue. This morning, I noticed that they had decorated the side wall with ten or twelve childlike drawings of the sun. The effect was charming. It occurred to me that, other than a fresh coat of paint, Jenny and I had not come up with any ideas about wall decor.

Marnie's suggestion of giving out free cookies was pure genius, but there had to be something Jenny could do to create a warm and inviting decor.

"Morning, Jenny," I called out, popping my head into Coffee, Tea and Destiny. "Sorry I'm so late. How's it going?"

"Where have you been?" she said. "It's almost eight o'clock. We have tons of work to do."

"I don't know how much sleep you need, but unless I get a good hour or two, I can't function the next day."

"Hour or two?" she said. "That sounds like the kind of sleep Marnie usually gets. What happened?"

"It must have been three thirty by the time I fell asleep."

"So what are you complaining about?" she said in her best teasing voice. "You slept for a full three hours."

"Don't I get any sympathy around here? I'm also sore all over."

"No more than I am," Jenny replied.

"Hi, Della," Margaret called out from the top of a stepladder.

Margaret was in her early twenties and had been renting the second apartment in this building since I'd bought it. She and I had met around that time, when she'd posted one of her looms for sale on Craigslist. We'd become friends and, soon after, when Jenny's shop got too busy for her to handle by herself, she had hired her.

"Hi, Margaret."

The girl had a spray bottle in one hand and a rag in the other and was dusting the shelves behind the counter. "The place is really starting to come together, don't you think?" she said, spritzing lemony wax on the antique wood and giving it a wipe.

"Good grief. How long have you two been here? I can't believe how much work you've already done."

"Ed was waiting for me when I got home last night," Jenny said. "I couldn't sleep after hearing about his day. So I finally gave up and drove over around five o'clock."

"And I came in around seven," Margaret said. "I got

a message from Jenny that we were reopening today. I'm so happy to be getting back to work."

"I heard you were shopping up a storm in Charlotte the other day," I said.

"Yes. Thanks to my mother. She spoils me." Margaret's birth mother and she had only recently met, and were making up for time lost.

I turned back to Jenny. "Why did Ed have a bad day?"

"It's the little Williams girl," she said. I recognized the name of the family whose house had burned down.

"Oh, no," I said. "Don't tell me she didn't make it."

She nodded grimly. "She passed away last night."

"That's terrible," I said, thinking of the father. He had now lost his wife and his daughter. "I hope the boy makes it."

"Oh, haven't you heard?" Jenny asked. "He passed away two days ago."

"Oh, my God." I'd been so busy working on my new collection, trying to finish it in time for the opening that I had a pile of unread newspapers on my counter. "I didn't know."

"Folks took up a collection to help defray the cost of all the medical expenses," Jenny continued. "Now . . ." She gestured vaguely.

"Have they found out what caused the fire?" I asked.

"Not as far as I know," Jenny said. We were both quiet for a moment, humbled by the extent of the tragedy. "I saw him in church on Sunday," Jenny continued. "He looks like he aged two decades."

"His wife's funeral was just a couple of days ago, and now he has to arrange for his children's burial. It's a wonder he's still functioning."

I changed the subject. "By the way, I was just walking by Good Morning Sunshine and I peeked through their window."

Jenny turned away. "Do I really have to hear this?"

"All I wanted to tell you is that your shop looks way nicer than theirs. They have the same old leather arm-chairs and coffee tables every coffee shop in the country has—totally boring. The only thing they have that gives their place a bit of atmosphere is a wall of colorful draw-ings. It made me wonder if there's anything you could do to add some ambiance."

"You don't think my penny-arcade gypsy woman is enough?" She was talking about the shop-warming gift Marnie had given her last year. Considering that Coffee, Tea and Destiny also offered readings, the mechanized fortune-teller was the perfect touch. "Also, I thought I might hang the beaded curtain along the far wall, if you don't mind."

Before our renovations, we'd kept our shops separate by way of a wall of shelves with a doorway screened with an antique beaded curtain.

"I don't mind in the least. It really isn't suitable for my shop, so I'm only happy to see it being used."

She flapped a tablecloth onto a table and paused. "Other than that, I have no idea. Got any suggestions?"

"Remember when we opened last year? You went around taking snapshots of everyone who came in that day. Do you still have all those pictures?"

"Of course. Why? Do you think I should do that again?"

"That wouldn't be a bad idea. But I was thinking of something else. Why don't you have all those shots en-larged and framed, then cover a wall with them, as a sort of customer wall of fame?"

Her eyes lit up. "I love it. It'll get people talking, and everyone will come in to see if their picture is up."

"And any customer whose picture is not already on the wall will want their photo taken," added Margaret.

"Why don't you go get them now?" I said. "I can take them to be enlarged. Mason's Camera Shop in Belmont has a one-hour service. That way you'll have the wall set up for your opening."

She looked at her watch. "I'd better get going if we want to put them up today." She grabbed her jacket and bag, and stopped. "But you have your own shop to prepare. I'm sure it won't matter if we wait a day or two."

"I have a solution for that. I thought of calling Mercedes and asking her to come in and help. That way I'll be ready at the same time you are."

Mercedes was a seventeen-year-old girl who had taken some weaving lessons from me when I first opened my shop. From the start she had shown a surprising ability with the craft. Now, she'd become so proficient, that she occasionally brought in some of her own projects to sell. And she was thrilled to come in and help once in a while. I pulled out my cell phone and punched in her number.

"She's coming right over," I said, slipping it back into my pocket.

"Cool. In that case, be back in fifteen," she said heading for the door.

She hadn't been gone five minutes when Marnie walked in, carrying a stack of boxes. "Where do you want me to put these?"

"How about right here?" Margaret said, whipping a stack of cloths off one of the small café tables. Marnie dropped the box. "I brought six dozen assorted cookies for the promotion. Do you think that'll be enough?"

"I'm sure it will be plenty," I said.

"Where's Jenny?"

I explained about my idea to her, and said, "She's picking up the pictures so I can run out and have them enlarged and framed."

"That'll look great." She opened one of the boxes. "By the way, I also brought us a treat. I tried a new recipe last night—crème brûlée muffins. I want everybody's honest opinion."

"Crème brûlée? Oh, my God. That sounds sinful," Margaret said. "I think those muffins call for a pot of coffee." She poured beans into the grinder.

I went over to the box that Marnie had just opened and took a deep whiff of sweetness. "They smell divine."

"I've got another dozen boxes of assorted pastries in the car."

"I'll help you with that," I said.

"Della, do you want a cup?" Margaret called from behind the counter.

"Desperately. I've only had one this morning," I said.

"Good grief. And she hasn't turned into a werewolf," Marnie said. "Quick, get her a cup before she does."

"Very funny," I said, noticing Jenny's car pulling over to the curb. A moment later she came in, brandishing a box.

"I've got them all in here. There are way too many. You'll have to go through them."

"I almost forgot," I said. "Be right back." I dashed over to my apartment, returning a moment later with a small wrapped box. "A shop-warming gift," I said.

"That's so sweet. But I didn't get you anything," Jenny said, unwrapping the box, carefully peeling off the tape so as not to tear the paper.

"That's not how you do it," Margaret exclaimed. "This is how." She took the box out of Jenny's hands and tore off the paper. She handed the box back to Jenny.

She opened the box, lifting the cover carefully and peeking inside, she burst into laughter. "This is great." She pulled out an old-fashioned brass bell, and held it up. It was the same as the one I had in my shop—the type merchants installed above the door to let them know when a customer came in.

"Now you have one just like mine," I said. "And as soon as I can get my hands on a screwdriver, I'll put it up for you."

Margaret picked up the trash bag in which she'd just thrown the paper. "Today is garbage day," she said. "I'll be glad when we get the last of the mess out of here. If we don't get rid of it now, this garbage will sit around until the next pickup day."

"That reminds me," I said. "I'd better get rid of my trash too." I dashed upstairs again, grabbed my waste basket and dumped it inside one of the bins behind our stores. Then I helped Marnie carry the remaining boxes from her car, and while Margaret opened them, I started setting up the rest of the furniture. Half a dozen café tables and a dozen or so chairs were stacked against the far wall.

"Let me help you with that," Marnie said. Together, we got all the furniture in place. We dragged and pushed the antique gypsy woman penny arcade to the far corner and stood back to gauge the effect.

"It's perfect," Marnie said, still huffing and puffing from the exertion. "It adds just the right touch of mysticism to the place."

Soon, the glass display counter was filled with pastries and the place looked ready to open.

"It already looks wonderful," she said. "All it needs now is a bit of decor."

"And some customers," added Marnie, holding up her hand with her fingers crossed.

I was in my Jeep, on my way to the photo shop in Belmont, when I drove by Good Morning Sunshine and spotted Syd Shuttleworth's truck two doors down. I checked my rearview mirror to make sure there were no cops around, and made a fast U-turn. I went by again, this time slowing to a crawl, trying to catch a glimpse inside. But with the sun shining on the window, I couldn't see anything but glare. I turned around again and was about to speed up when I noticed a couple at the side of the shop, by the entrance to the house. They seemed to be in a serious conversation. I pulled to the curb and stopped.

I didn't recognize the blonde, but she bore a remarkable resemblance to the attractive brunette who co-owned the coffee shop with her husband. Her sister perhaps, I thought. But what really caught my attention, was the man. He was none other than Syd Shuttleworth himself.

I must have sat there for a good minute, watching them. Syd was talking animatedly, while the woman inched away from him, shaking her head. Suddenly, Syd grabbed her by the arm, hard enough to cause her to grimace. She twisted out of his grasp and ran into the house, slamming the door shut.

What was that all about? I might not have attached any importance to the argument I'd just witnessed if not for the look of fear in the blonde's eyes. Then, a moment later, when Syd turned around, I could see, even from my distance, that he was clenching and unclenching his hands furiously. I put the Jeep in gear and drove off slowly so as not to attract his notice.

During the rest of the drive, I couldn't put the picture out of my mind—Syd grabbing the blonde roughly, and her escaping into the house. I had seen a side of Sydney Shuttleworth I had never suspected. The man had a temper. I could easily picture him hitting someone over the head.

Chapter 10

It was almost noon when I got back. "Sorry. It took them a lot longer than I expected. Some problem with their equipment," I said, setting the parcel on one of the tables. "So I decided to pick some frames while I was waiting. All we have to do is slide the photos inside."

"I like them," Margaret said, running a finger over the wood of one of the frames. "Simple but elegant."

"They were the least expensive I could find."

"Let me do that," Jenny said, shooing me away. "You've already done too much. Now go get your place ready. I'll feel terrible if your opening is delayed because of me."

I had debated whether or not I should tell Jenny about the scene I'd witnessed between Syd and the blonde, but considering the degree of obsession she'd already displayed on the subject, I'd decided to keep it to myself. Besides, today was her grand reopening. I wanted her to enjoy it.

"Okay. Good luck," I said, and crossed over to my side.

"Surprise," Mercedes shouted as I walked in. She opened her arms wide. "So what do you think?"

I looked around, amazed. My shop looked wonderful. Still very bare, but sparkling clean.

"Jenny wants to open at one o'clock. If we hurry, you can reopen at the same time," Marnie said, and turned to Mercedes. "Sugar pie, you've got strong, young legs. Why don't you run up and help Della carry her merchandise back down?"

"Sure," she said, already dashing to the entrance. Over the next half hour, she ran up and down, from the shop to my apartment, moving box after box of my merchandise, and never so much as breathing hard. Meanwhile, all Marnie and I did was set up the displays and we were both exhausted.

"Oh, to be young again," I said.

"Oh, to be *thin* again," Marnie said. "Maybe I should get my heart broken once more."

"Not worth it," I said. "You look lovely just as you are."

She gave me a grateful smile and continued. "I don't know about you two, but if I don't have something to eat, I think I'll pass out. I'll pick up something from Jenny's. Anybody else hungry?"

She returned a few minutes later, carrying a tray with cups of steaming coffee and plates of sandwiches. "You'll never believe who I just ran into," she said, setting the food on one of my counters. "My neighbor, Norma Pratt. She was just walking by."

I must have looked confused because she explained. "Don't you remember? I was telling you about her just yesterday. Swanson nearly drove her to a nervous breakdown last year. After it was all finished, he refused to give her an occupancy permit. Then"—she snapped her fingers—"out of the blue, a couple of days later she had her permit."

I put down the box of place mats I'd just picked up. The same thing had happened to Judy Bates' neighbor.

Marnie lowered her voice to a stage whisper. "When I told her that Swanson had been murdered, she very sarcastically said, and I quote, 'It couldn't have happened to a nicer guy.'" She nodded importantly. "And then I said, 'Considering the way he's been extorting money from people in return for occupancy permits, it's a wonder he wasn't killed a long time ago.'"

"What are you talking about?" Mercedes said. "Who's extorting money?"

Damn. That was the one thing I didn't want to happen. If our theory ever got out, it would travel faster than light in this town, and possibly get us in a lot of trouble.

"Nobody's doing anything of the kind," I said. "Marnie is letting her imagination get away from herself again."

Marnie opened her mouth as if to say something, and then closed it.

Mercedes looked from me to her and back again. "I hate it when grown-ups stop talking around me. I might be just a teenager, but I am not stupid."

"If I thought you were stupid," I told her, "I wouldn't leave you in charge of the store the way I do."

That seemed to mollify her. We took a break and had our lunches, then went back to work as soon as we were finished.

"Mercedes," Marnie said, "could you do me a favor? I left some banners on the kitchen table in my house. I wonder if you could go get them."

"Sure." Mercedes pocketed her key and left.

As soon as the door had closed behind her, Marnie went back to her story. "About what I told Norma. I was just bluffing of course, but I wanted to hear what she'd say."

"And?"

She grinned. "She said, and I quote, 'That bastard cost me a fortune. I would have happily done away with him myself.'"

"So, it was true. He *was* extorting money in return for permits," I said. "I wonder if the police know about this."

Marnie crossed her arms and stared at me.

"Don't look at me like that," I said. "I am not planning to call the police. I'm simply asking a rhetorical question."

Marnie relaxed.

"But," I continued, "I think *you* should. That's the kind of information that could help solve the murder."

"Fine. You do it."

"Not me," I said. "I can just imagine how Lombard would react. You're the one Norma told. Why don't you call and tell her?"

Emotions flew over her face as she weighed the pros and cons. "You're right," she said at last. "And I'll do it right away, before I chicken out. Mind if I go up to your apartment and use your phone?"

I handed her my key. "I swear, you must be the only person I know who doesn't own a cell phone."

"I need a cell phone like I need a third ear," she muttered and marched out.

"Wait for me," I called. I locked the shop door and chased after her. "I want to dress up a bit for the reopening. This is a special occasion after all."

We went upstairs together. I pointed her to the kitchen phone, and went to change into dressier pants and a light sweater. After doing a two-minute makeup job, I came back out, just as Marnie was hanging up.

"What did the police say?"

"I spoke to the dispatcher, and then I had to wait until she connected me to"—she quirked an eyebrow—"Officer Lombard."

"Uh-oh."

"You can say that again. She took my information, but I could tell she was irritated as all hell."

"Then I'm doubly glad you made the call and not me. She would probably have bitten my head off. Before we go, I have a couple of boxes in my bedroom. Do you mind helping me with the last two?" These were all the pieces of my new collection. I could hardly wait to hear what everyone thought of it.

We returned to the shop with our arms full and dropped

the boxes in the center of the store. "Have you thought of anything you could do as a reopening-day promotion?" she asked.

I looked around the store for inspiration, and my eyes happened to fall on a basket of small woven lavender bags. I imported them from China, more as decorative items in the store than for resale. But I had a large box full of them, and they cost barely more than pennies apiece. "What about these?" I said, picking one up. "I could give them away with every purchase."

"Great idea," Marnie said. "And I was thinking that I might give weaving demonstrations. What do you think?"

"You wouldn't mind?" I said. "Are you up to it?"

"Of course I am."

"In that case, please do. It's a great idea. I bet we'll get people to sign up for weaving classes."

"That's what I'm hoping."

Jenny walked in at that moment. She too had changed, and was now wearing a pink bohemian top over a pair of black leggings. She looked gorgeous.

"Della just had a great idea," Marnie said, and told her about it. "With both shops having promotions, I'm sure the customers will be flocking in."

"You know, for the first time since Good Morning Sunshine opened, I'm beginning to think maybe you're right," Jenny said. "My business will flourish again."

"Of course it will," Marnie said.

"I have something to show you both," I said, lifting the cover of one of the boxes. I pulled out a piece from my new collection. It was a lovely Navajo-inspired rug in shades of black, red and tan. "What do you think?"

"That's gorgeous," Jenny said. "I love Native weaving. Where did you get it?"

"I made it." They both stared at me openmouthed.

Marnie was the first to speak. "You can't be serious. I

always knew you were good, but this is absolutely stunning."

"I have more," I said, taking out all the pieces one at a time, until they were spread all over the tables, chairs and even the floor. "I thought I'd decorate my window with a Native theme. What do you think?"

"Perfect," Jenny said. "People will be glued to your display."

"After being closed for two months, they'd better do more than stay glued to the window. I hope they come in and buy."

Chapter 11

After hanging all the photos on the wall, Jenny decided her store needed more color and switched her usual white tablecloths for red gingham ones. She put the long GRAND REOPENING banner that Marnie had made, we opened our doors wide, and Jenny sent Margaret outside with a gingham-lined basket of cookies. And then we waited for the crowds. It didn't take long for the lineup to form.

As expected, Jenny's wall of pictures was a huge hit. Patrons soon gathered round, pointing and laughing, and phoning friends to come check out their photos. Meanwhile, in between serving customers, Jenny took new snapshots.

My shop looked equally inviting. Margaret and Marnie had helped me drag my old-fashioned country counter by the door. And on top was my pride and joy, a shiny nickel candy-store cash register. It had been a gift from Matthew on my opening day last year. Next to it was a silk flower arrangement in a blue-and-white Chinese vase. The scene was as pretty as a picture.

"This makes so much more sense," Marnie said, admiring the results. "Now, customers have to walk by the counter as they leave."

Against the opposite wall, I'd set up my century-old pine armoire. Inside, I artfully displayed my more traditional items. Over the open cabinet door, I had draped a lovely monk's cloth tablecloth with hand-embroidered edges. On one shelf were luncheon and dinner napkins, on another, my latest addition — bread cloths. And on the lower shelf were sets of place mats. It made for a charming country presentation.

I had carried through with the theme by filling an apple crate with rolled-up rugs, and covering assorted tea tables with other woven pieces. And right by the front door, I'd set a basket with a FREE WITH EVERY PURCHASE sign on a plant stand. Inside the basket were the lavender-filled bags. Now, the entire room was perfumed with a lovely scent.

"For your lingerie drawers," I told my customers. I hoped every morning as they got dressed, they would think of my shop.

And last but not least, I had filled my window with pieces of my new Navajo-inspired collection. As I watched, two women walked by, then stopped to admire them. And then another two paused to look. My heart did a somersault. *Yes!* It was a hit.

"Marnie, come and see," I called out. She came round from the back of the shop, where I'd set up all my looms to create a private area for the weaving studio. "Look. My windows are creating a lot of attention. People love the collection."

"Well don't stare at them. You'll scare them away," she whispered. I turned away, still giggling like a little girl. "They like it."

"You're not really surprised, are you?"

Maybe not surprised as much as relieved. "Now let's just hope they sell."

I was in such a good mood, I resolved to give Matthew a call. I hadn't heard from him since our argument. Even though I'd sworn to myself that he would have to give in, it made sense that unless one of us made the first move, the bad feelings between us would fester, and things would only get worse.

"Hey," he said, sounding cheerful. "I was wondering when I'd hear from you."

If he wasn't going to bring up the way we'd left things yesterday, then neither would I. "Does that mean you finished your word count for the day?"

"I not only reached it, but doubled it. I was just about to take Winston for a walk. Want to join us?"

"I'd love to, but we just reopened"—I looked at my watch—"half an hour ago. I barely finished setting up the shop. You should come by. Marnie made some amazing cookies and Margaret is outside handing them out for free."

"Marnie made cookies? Can't say no to that."

"And I'll find a treat for Winnie too."

Just as I was slipping the phone back into my pocket, the door flew open. The bell above the door went into a tinkling frenzy as a woman walked in. "I simply had to stop by and tell you how impressed I am," the ultra-thin blonde said to Marnie. "I ran into Margaret and I tried one of your cookies. Your baking is to die for, simply to die for. I just bought a dozen for poor Philip Williams." It took me a moment to connect the name to the tragedy I had recently read about. "He's such a nice man. Of all the people for this kind of tragedy to happen to. It's simply not fair." She continued in a stage whisper. "I've been dropping off casseroles and treats for him, so he doesn't have to cook."

"He's not still staying in his house, is he?" Marnie asked.

"Oh, goodness no. The Bradfords across the street are away for a few weeks. When they heard what happened, they contacted the vicar and asked him to get in touch with Philip and offer him their house. He's been staying there since. Just between us, I don't think it's good for

Philip to be alone at a time like this." Even though there was nobody else in the store, she looked around to make certain no one could overhear. "Day before yesterday, I thought he was going to have a nervous breakdown. He left the house looking as if he was in agony. I think he was out of his mind with grief. Then he raced out of the driveway with his tires squealing. Later I found out his little girl might not make it. He was probably on his way to the hospital."

"You may not have heard," Marnie said. "But the little girl passed away."

"Oh, no," she said, a crease appearing between her brows. "You know what he should do is come stay with me. That way I can keep an eye on him and make sure he stays out of trouble." She leaned forward and whispered. "He's such a cutie. I've always had a thing for bald men." She raised the bag of cookies in her hand. "And this one needs somebody to take care of him. I'll keep him company and make sure he eats right." With that, she pivoted and sashayed to the door, calling out a cheerful, "Toodle-oo."

"Well," Marnie huffed. "His wife hasn't been buried more than three days and already the vultures are circling."

The door swung open again and this time Matthew walked in, followed by Winston. My heart skipped a beat.

"Winnie, sweetheart. I missed you," Marnie said. Winston gave her hand a lick and then came wiggling and snorting over to me. "What's the matter, Winnie? Don't you love me anymore?" she asked, putting on her hurt voice.

"Don't worry," I said. "It's not that he loves you less. It's that he loves the liver treats I keep in my drawer." I riffled through and threw him a dog biscuit. Winston caught it in a jump worthy of Kobe Bryant. He crunched twice and swallowed, and then gave me a pleading look, hoping for another.

"You already got your treat," I said. "Next time don't eat it so fast."

"Where my treat?" Matthew said, wrapping his arms around me. He gave me a quick peck. "I swear you pay more attention to that dog than you do to me."

"Didn't you know?" I said. "It's Winnie that's really got my heart. You're just part of the package."

"Ah, that explains it," he said. He gave me another quick kiss and released me. He took a step back and looked around. "Nice job. I have to admit the place looks more upscale with the new floor plan. Having your own entrances will be good for Jenny's business. And now that you don't have to get up quite so early in the morning, maybe I'll have the pleasure of your company for breakfast once in a while."

Marnie covered her ears. "Oh, this is getting too personal for me. I think I'll go back to my weaving."

As soon as she was out of sight, Matthew gave me a serious look. "So tell me. You found the body of the city inspector—what—a bit over twenty-four hours ago? Have you discovered the killer yet?"

"Don't be ridiculous."

"Surely you've picked up a few clues."

"I heard some gossip, but that's all."

"Really?" he said, sounding suspicious. "I'm surprised you haven't been snooping around."

I decided to ignore that. "One of my customers stopped by yesterday and mentioned that her neighbor had renovations done in her home, and after all the work was completed, Swanson refused to give her a permit. And then a few days later, Swanson decided to issue it without making her redo anything."

"I don't get your point."

"The point is that my customer wondered if her neighbor didn't have to pay some kind of bribe."

Matthew's eyebrows jumped up. "You think Swanson was into extortion?"

I shrugged. "That's not all. Marnie ran into one of her neighbors, too. That woman also had a problem with Swanson about a year ago. Marnie decided to bluff, and she casually mentioned that, considering all the bribes Swanson had been taking, it was surprising that he hadn't gotten himself in trouble sooner."

"What was her reaction?"

I grinned. "She fell for it. She admitted that she'd had to pay him off in return for her occupancy permit."

He knitted his brows. "Were you or Jenny squeezed for a payoff too?"

"No, not at all."

"Well, then, how do you explain that?"

"I don't know. Maybe he was planning to squeeze us when he was murdered. Or, maybe he was choosing his victims according to their affluence. Or," I added, as a new idea came to me, "maybe he was demanding payoffs for permits for work that normally would not have passed inspection."

Matthew nodded, his brows furrowed. "So, rather than have their work redone, some people preferred paying him off."

To my surprise, Matthew wasn't giving me a hard time about my interest in the case.

"I hope you called the police and told them what Marnie's neighbor said."

My mouth dropped open. "Did I just hear right? Are you suggesting I get involved?"

He brought a finger under my chin, raising it until we were both staring straight into each other's eyes. "It's not that I don't want you to get involved. It's that you've been known to get yourself into some dangerous situations in the past. I don't want to have to worry about you again. The last time I nearly had a heart attack I was so worried." The way he looked at me as he said this made my insides melt. He continued. "I've been thinking about it, and you're right, you're an independent woman. I have no business telling you what to do or not do."

"Thank you." I threw my arms around his neck. "Did I ever tell you that you're the best?"

He laughed. "Hold on a second. I'd still like you to promise me one thing."

I pulled away. "Promise you what?"

"Please swear you won't put yourself in any danger."

"How about this? I promise I will do everything in my power not to get myself into danger."

He sighed. "I guess that's the best I can expect." He pulled me against him again and gave me another kiss, this one lingering a few seconds. "How about having dinner with me tonight?" he asked, changing the subject to one I much preferred. "It feels like we haven't seen each other in forever. Let's go out for a change. I'll take you to the Longview and we'll celebrate your reopening."

The Longview was the finest local restaurant. It belonged to a friend and former client of mine, Bunny Boyd, a famous interior designer and TV personality. Some years ago she had bought a local guesthouse. Then last year she'd spent a fortune turning it into a boutique hotel, complete with a fine-dining restaurant. It had been an instant success.

Before her place opened, the only other local restaurant was The Bottoms Up, a barnlike space complete with rough wood floors and a pool table. Briar Hollow had been in dire need of a more upscale place and Bunny had the vision to bring one to the community.

"Sounds great. I can get all dressed up," I said. "I don't often get the opportunity to do that around here."

He chuckled. "Pick you up at six," he said, heading for the door.

"If you want me to look great, you'd better make it six thirty."

He laughed, and left with Winston trotting ahead. The door hadn't quite closed when it opened again. This time two women walked in, nibbling at oatmeal raisin cookies.

"Hi, Della," the older one said. I drew a blank as to her name, but I remembered her being around Marnie's age, in her mid-fifties or so. She had taken a weaving class from me some months ago in the hopes of making a tablecloth and napkins. It was a rather ambitious project for a newbie, and just as I'd expected, before the end of that first session she had become overwhelmed and given up. A few days later she'd come in and purchased the items instead.

"I thought I'd stop by and see your new place." She looked around, admiringly. I snatched a lavender sachet from the basket and gave it to her.

"An opening-day gift," I said.

She brought it to her nose and took a deep whiff. "How lovely." She dropped it in her bag. "I like what you did with the place." She pointed to the studio area. "That's good, having it in a separate area. And I love that Jenny's coffee shop has its own entrance now. So much better this way."

Her friend, an attractive blonde around my age, stepped forward, hand extended. "I'm Susan," she said. "Susan Price." We shook.

Susan Price. I had heard that name recently. And then I remembered. "Why, a friend of yours was just telling me about you yesterday—Judy Bates."

"Oh." Her smile faded. "I wouldn't exactly call her a friend. She's my next-door neighbor."

"She told me you had some trouble with the building inspector," I said, hoping to get her talking about it. "That man drove me crazy. I thought the renovations would never end."

"Mr. Swanson?" she asked.

"Who else?" I replied.

"He's the same one I had to deal with. I hope I never see that man again."

"Well," Marnie said, returning from the studio. "I can assure you, you won't."

"Why? Was he fired?" Susan asked, sounding hopeful.

"I'm afraid the man is dead," Marnie said.

Susan's eyes widened. "That's terrible. How did it happen?"

"All I know is that he was murdered," I said quickly. "I went by his office yesterday, and found him dead. Somebody hit him over the head with a bookend."

"His office?" Susan said, her face suddenly tense with fear. "You mean it happened at city hall? Yesterday? At what time?"

"I found his body around ten thirty," I replied. "Why?"

Her friend looked startled. "Why, isn't that exactly the time you—" Susan gave her a quick jab with her elbow. The woman closed her mouth.

Susan gave me a look that reminded me of a trapped animal. "Er . . . I was supposed to meet with him around that time, but in the end, I got caught up with errands and never made it there." She turned to her friend, who was staring at her, befuddled. "Let's go." The older woman came out of her trance and followed Susan out of the shop.

Chapter 12

"What did you make of that?" I asked Marnie once the door was shut.

"I got the distinct impression the lady has something to hide," she said, still staring at the closed door.

"My thoughts exactly. And I bet I know what it is. She probably saw Swanson shortly before I found him." Suddenly, I remembered the silver car that had shot out of the lot. "Marnie," I said. "Do me a favor. Run out and see what kind of car Susan Price drives. I'm curious to know the color."

Her eyes widened. "Do you think she could be the killer?" she asked as she dashed to the door.

"I have no idea. But one thing I do know is that killers generally look like your next-door neighbor. And they sometimes do turn out to be your next-door neighbor."

A few minutes later, she was back, shaking her head. "They got into a car, but her friend got behind the wheel. It was a blue Volvo. Now, explain to me why you wanted to know about her car."

"Maybe it had nothing to do with Swanson's murder, but when I drove into the city hall parking lot yesterday, a car came screeching out of there and almost crashed into mine. Later, I wondered if the driver might have been the killer making his getaway."

"Did you see the person's face?"

"It all happened so fast, all I know is the driver was wearing a light blue baseball cap and large sunglasses."

"A baseball cap you say? It must have been a man."

"Not necessarily," I said. "Women wear them nowadays. And if somebody wanted to disguise their appearance, what better way than to cover their eyes with sunglasses and pull up their hair under a cap. It's as good as a mask and won't attract any undue attention."

She gave me a teasing smile. "In other words, the driver may or may not have been the killer, and might have been a male or a female. That sure narrows it down."

"You're giving me as much grief as Lombard."

"Just teasing."

"I'm getting nowhere fast on this investigation, aren't I?"

"Good thing this isn't your investigation, Sherlock," she said, laughing. "It's the police's."

For the remainder of the day, customers dropped by to watch Marnie's weaving demonstrations or simply to see the changes to my store. Meanwhile, I busied myself by completing my displays.

"I guess that's it," Marnie said, coming forward at five thirty. The last customer had left about half an hour ago. "All in all I think we had a good first day."

I opened my cash register. There wasn't much money inside, but I had made a few credit card transactions. "Not bad," I said. "Let's find out how Jenny did." I locked the door and we went over.

Jenny was sprawled out on one her chairs.

"You look like someone who has just finished a marathon," I said.

"That's because she did," Margaret said from the next table. She looked just as weary.

"Good God," Jenny said, pulling herself to her feet.

"If I'd had to serve even one more cup of coffee, I think I would have collapsed."

"And just yesterday you were crying that your customers might not come back. Now you're complaining? Make up your mind."

"Don't get me wrong. I'm thrilled. Thrilled but exhausted." She made her way behind the counter. "I think I can summon just enough energy to make us all a cup. How about it? You can tell me about your day."

"I have a better idea," I said. "Why don't we give you a break, and Marnie and I can make the coffee?"

"I'll take you up on that," she said, returning to her chair and letting herself fall into it. She waved toward the glass display. "I think we might have a few cookies left. Help yourselves."

"Sorry," Margaret said. "We're all out. I think we still have some carrot cake, but that's about it."

"Thanks," I said, spooning coffee into the coffee-maker. "But I'm having dinner with Matthew tonight. I don't want to spoil my appetite."

"Well, I might regret it when I get on my scale tomorrow, but I'm not saving my appetite for anything or anyone," Marnie said, helping herself to a large slice. "So, you had a great day?" she asked, joining Jenny at her table.

"An amazing day. Giving out those cookies made the difference. Marnie, what would you say, we do this once in a while, especially when we want to test out some new pastries?"

"Great idea."

I set mugs on the table. "Nothing for me," Margaret said. "I hope you don't mind but I'll just take off now."

"See you tomorrow," Jenny called out as Margaret let herself out.

"Marnie and I had a good day too. I didn't sell much, but a lot of people stopped by."

"And we already have a few people signed up for classes," Marnie added.

Jenny took a sip of her coffee and put her mug back down. "I'm sorry, guys, but I'm completely wiped. Would you mind terribly if I called it a night, too? Maybe we can get together tomorrow instead."

"No problem," Marnie said. "I'll take my cake and coffee next door and finish it there."

"Before you go," Jenny said, "one of my customers was telling me that she had renovations done in her house and she and her husband used Syd Shuttleworth too. She said Syd and the city inspector hated each other. She thinks that might be why our renovations were taking so long. It wasn't Syd stretching out the job. It was Swanson. And it wasn't because of us. It was because of some conflict they have with each other."

"Great," I said. "Now we find out—once the work is all done. I wish someone had told us before. The work might have been finished a lot sooner."

"Does that mean you don't think Syd was plotting against you with the owners up the street?" Marnie asked.

"Who knows?" Jenny replied. "I'm too tired to think about anything but sleep right now."

I made a mental note of that tidbit as we left her shop. If Jenny's customer was right, chances were that Syd and Swanson were not working the scam as partners. Marnie and I had just returned to our side and I was calculating the total of my sales and preparing my bank deposit slip, when the door opened and Johanna Renay, the lady from city hall, popped her head in. Her hair was a darker shade of blond today. And the cut was shorter and more modern.

"Johanna, you look wonderful," I said. "I love what you did to your hair."

"Oh, er, thank you," she said, bringing a hand to her

hair. At that moment it hit me that the woman was wearing a wig. My heart went out to her. She was probably a cancer patient. No wonder she wore such thick foundation. Underneath the heavy makeup, she was probably deathly pale.

"I was in the neighborhood," she continued, "and decided to drop by and say hello. Are you still open?"

"For you, of course. Come in."

She closed the door behind her, giving me a wide smile. "A few of my friends told me about your place and it wasn't until you left yesterday that I made the connection that you're Della Wright, the owner of Dream Weaver. I've heard so much about your shop."

"How nice of you to come by. This is my friend and right-hand woman, Marnie Potter."

Marnie looked at her through narrowed eyes. "You look familiar. Haven't we met before?"

"Not unless you came by city hall. I'm sort of a floater. I work in all the departments at some time or other."

Marnie snapped her fingers. "That's it. You were the lady who served me when I stopped by to pay my house taxes."

"I hope you won't hold it against me," she said, laughing. "Working in that department doesn't always make me very popular."

I cut in. "Let me show you around." She followed me as I pointed out the different areas of the shop, ending with the studio. "And this is where I give classes. I've had to put those off during the renovations, but I'm about to start again."

"Really? I wonder if I'd like weaving," she said. "I've been thinking of adopting a new hobby. I've been lonely since my husband and I divorced."

Marnie, who had followed along, said, "Let me show you how it works." She sat at my dobby loom and picked up the shuttle, demonstrating the way the bobbin fit inside. "This is what we use to weave the warp through the weft."

"It looks so simple."

"As you can see," Marnie continued, "I've already started working on a project. This is a place mat I'm half-way through." She worked the loom for a few minutes and Johanna watched as row after row of yarn was added to the piece. Within a few minutes the place mat had grown an inch longer.

"I think even I could do that," Johanna said.

"I'm sure you could," I said. "Although it does take some dexterity. Most beginners have trouble keeping the tension even."

She nodded. "I knit. And it's the same thing."

"The dressing of the loom is a lengthy process. Not everybody likes that part."

"When are your next classes?"

"I'm planning a new beginners' course in about two weeks. I'll need that much time to register enough students."

She asked the price, and then said, "Put my name on that list, would you? I'd like to give it a try."

We made our way back to the counter, where I took down her name and telephone number. "I'll give you a call when I have a definite date."

Before she left, she asked me if I'd heard anything about the murder case.

"No," I said. "How about you?"

"The police kept at us for hours after you left. They kept asking us the same questions over and over—if we saw anybody go to, or leave, his office—whether or not we heard any unusual sounds. That sort of thing."

"And did you?"

She wrinkled her forehead. "We came to the conclusion that he must have been killed very shortly before you found him—no more than a few minutes."

"What makes you say that?"

"A few of the other employees saw him when the snack truck came by at ten o'clock. He always gets himself a coffee and doughnut." So the victim had been alive half an hour before I found his body. I stored that little piece of information in my head.

"Was anybody seen going in or out?"

"I'm afraid not." She looked at the floor, as a flash of worry crossed her eyes.

"What is it?"

"Well . . . I don't want to alarm you, but somebody told the police that he saw you trying to wipe blood off your jeans, and that when you couldn't wipe it off, you ran to the car and put on a raincoat to hide it."

My mouth dropped open. "You can't be serious." I thought back, trying to remember. "I was trying to wipe off vomit. I might have had some red paint on them. I repainted my front door a couple of days ago." I marched over and opened it. "See?" I said, pointing to the outside.

"Of course, I believe you. And I'm sorry if I've upset you," she said. "I didn't want to worry you for no reason, but then"—she shrugged—"I figured I'd want to know if I were you."

"Thank you." It suddenly occurred to me that after receiving that kind of a tip, the police would surely want to question me again. "When did this happen?"

"About half an hour ago. He only remembered it this afternoon. The police came by again just before closing."

I felt as if I'd just been punched in the stomach. The police would probably show up at any second. I could bet my life on it.

"Is there anything else I should know?"

She sighed. "One of the clerks who wasn't questioned yesterday spoke to the police today. She claims that she heard an argument coming from Mr. Swanson's office shortly before you ran out of the building."

"What?"

She nodded, looking miserable. "And she insisted that the second voice was that of a woman." She smiled apologetically. "I'm sorry, dear. I feel as if I have nothing but bad news for you." And with that, she gave an apologetic smile and left.

I stood paralyzed. What was I supposed to do? Call a lawyer? I'd seen enough cop shows to know that the police would twist anything a person said during an investigation. My pulse was galloping.

Marnie looked at me strangely. "Are you all right, Della? You're very pale."

"I'd better call Matthew." I snatched my cell and pushed the SPEED DIAL button for his number. "The police are on their way to question me," I said, not giving him the chance to so much as say hello. "One of the city employees told them he saw me wiping blood off my clothes, and that when it wouldn't come off, I got my coat from the car to hide it. What do I do?"

"Where are you?"

"I'm in my shop. I was just about to close."

"Go home. Lock the door and don't open it until I get there. I'm coming right over. And don't say a word. You hear me? Not. One. Word."

"I'll lock up," Marnie said. "You go."

I ran straight upstairs—and paced. Who would have said those things to the police? Could it have been Mr. Goodall? No. It must have been some other employee. I tried to remember the faces of all the people working behind the counter, but other than Tom Goodall, I could picture only women. Had there been any other men? I could have sworn not. But Johanna had definitely said "he." So that meant kind old Mr. Goodall, was not so nice after all.

Besides, no one other than he, Ronald Dempsey, and

Johanna had come close enough to see the splotches of red on my jeans. They were so close, in fact, they should have clearly seen that those stains were paint, not blood. The color was more raspberry than red.

I had all but pinned this on Tom Goodall, when I reminded myself that I had not paid much attention to the bystanders the entire time. A number of people had left the building, gathering around to watch. For all I knew, one of them might have stepped closer at some point. I would never have noticed. It could have been anyone.

Another thought occurred to me. Marnie had told the police about Swanson extorting money. In fact, she had spoken to Lombard personally. Knowing that, how could they possibly imagine I had anything to do with his death?

I knew the reason, and her name was Lombard. The only crime I was guilty of was getting her nose out of joint. And she was going to make me pay dearly for it.

Chapter 13

The buzzer rang. "It's me," Matthew's voice came through the intercom. I let him in and he came bounding up the stairs, Winston galloping behind him. He closed the door and wrapped me in a hug.

"Don't worry. It'll all work out. I promise."

"How can you be so sure?"

"Because I won't let anything bad happen to you." I melted in his arms.

He released me. "Now, first things first. Go get those clothes you were wearing when you found the body—everything," he repeated. "Even the shoes."

I dashed to my bedroom and was going through the clothes hamper, when I remembered. "Oh, shit."

"What is it?" he asked from the doorway.

"I don't have the jeans anymore. They were so splattered with paint, and then when I threw up there was spittle all over them. They were disgusting. I ditched them."

I had to hand it to him. He didn't stress easily. He gave me a reassuring smile. "That's okay. Maybe it's not too late. Where's your garbage?"

Whatever hope I'd had, vanished. "Yesterday was garbage day. They're at the dump by now." A fresh problem occurred to me. "Oh. Now the police will accuse me of getting rid of evidence."

"Let's not panic." This time, he didn't look quite so calm. And his next words didn't reassure me one bit. "You know as well as I do that the police are only doing their job. They have to follow every lead, no matter where it goes. They're probably questioning a number of people at the moment. I'm sure you're not their only suspect."

I swallowed hard and nodded just as the buzzer sounded again. Winston, who had been napping in the corner, jumped to his feet, barking. "Quiet, Winnie," I said. He tilted his head, as if questioning my order. "Down boy." He returned to his cushion and watched, ready to pounce, as I went to the door.

"Police. Open up." I recognized Officer Lombard's voice as it boomed through the intercom. I pressed the buzzer to allow her in.

Lombard and her partner Harrison stepped in. She was wearing a victorious smile that disappeared as soon as Winston let out a low, menacing growl.

"Quiet, Winston," Matthew ordered and he stopped immediately. The moment she noticed Matthew, Lombard stuck her hands in her pockets, shuffling uncertainly. "Mr. Baker. I didn't know you would be here."

"Matthew is my boyfriend," I said. She turned to her partner, mumbling something I couldn't make out under her breath.

"I'm sorry to have to do this, sir," she said, apologizing to Matthew rather than to me. "But this is a search order signed by Judge King." She handed him the paper to examine. "You're free to stay while we search the premises, but you can't touch anything or stand in our way." Suddenly she and Harrison split up, each heading for a different part of my apartment.

"Sorry, but that's not how you're going to conduct this search," Matthew said. They looked at him, surprised. "I am going to keep an eye on you every second. So the way we're going to do this is: you will both search one room at a time, and I will be right there with you. I don't want either of you out of my sight. Do I make myself clear?"

"Are you inferring that we might plant some evidence?" Lombard said.

"No. I just want to make sure everything is done according to the book."

There was some grumbling, but they headed for my bedroom together.

Matthew turned to me. "Della, you stay here." And he followed them.

I let myself drop onto the sofa and patted the seat next to me for Winnie to join me. He hopped up and sat, watching me with large mournful eyes. He looked as frightened as I was.

"Don't worry, Winnie. You heard what Matthew said. He won't let anything bad happen to me." I wrapped an arm around his shoulders and drew him close for comfort.

There came the sound of drawers being opened and then slammed shut, then the grating noise of hangers dragging along the closet rod. This was followed by footsteps, then a squeaking I recognized as the lid of my laundry hamper. My cheeks flushed hot. Were they going through my dirty clothes? The thought of strangers going through my things, all my most personal items, was more than just a little disturbing. It was embarrassing—a violation of my privacy.

The footsteps started again, going from my bedroom to the laundry room, followed by the clang of the washer door banging shut, then the dryer. There were other softer noises, like clothes being dropped to the floor. What kind of a mess were they making? How much cleaning up would I have to do? I sat glued to the couch with Winnie, my heart hammering against my ribs.

After what seemed like an eternity, Officer Lombard

and Harrison reappeared. "Why don't you make it easier on yourself and tell us where you hid them?"

I had no idea what they were talking about. "Hid what?"

She gave me a look that cried of disbelief. "The shirt and the jeans you were wearing when you"—she made air quotation marks—"*found* the victim's body."

I glanced at Matthew and he gave me the slightest of nods. "I don't have the jeans anymore. They were old and covered in paint. I threw them away."

"Are you telling me you got rid of material evidence? You could be in big trouble for that."

"Why would my clothes be evidence? They had nothing to do with the murder."

"A witness saw you wiping blood off your clothes."

"Claims," Matthew said.

She looked at him and then corrected herself. "*Claims* to have seen you wiping blood off your clothes. According to this witness, you then ran to the car and hid the blood under a raincoat."

I held on to my calm. "I was wiping off vomit. After finding the body, I was upset. I threw up. Some of it splattered on my jeans." She nodded, her mouth a straight line. "If you don't believe me you can ask Mr. Goodall." I was taking a chance naming him as my witness since he might have been the one who made up that story. "Or Johanna Renay," I added quickly. "They were right behind me when I ran out of the building. They'll tell you I threw up. They came over to make sure I was all right. As for the *blood*," I said, this time making my own air quotations, "that was red paint I'd recently used on my front door. If you don't believe me, you can go downstairs and see for yourself. My door is freshly painted."

A single corner of her mouth stretched into a smile. "I think I'll do just that." She marched off toward the door and walked downstairs, followed by the faithful Harrison.

"Don't let her intimidate you," Matthew said, giving my shoulder a little squeeze. "She's only posturing."

A minute went by, and then Lombard returned. "Do you have any of that paint left? I'll need to take it with me."

I looked at Matthew again. This time he answered for me. "I'm sure Della won't mind at all."

I went to the laundry room where I'd stored the half-empty quart of red paint.

"Here you are. Anything else I can get for you?"

Ignoring me, she handed it to Harrison. "Mark that as evidence and put it in the car."

"I'll get you my running shoes and the raincoat I wore over my clothes yesterday. I'm sure you'll agree that if there was any blood on my clothes, some would have transferred to my raincoat." Just as I expected, my offer was met with a calculating look. She no longer seemed so sure of herself.

"What are you standing there for? Get me those items now."

I went to my bedroom with both cops on my heels. Going straight to my closet, I retrieved the coat and shoes. Then riffling through the same clothes hamper they had already searched, I pulled out the shirt. "I guess you were looking for clothes with bloodstains. As you can see, it doesn't have any."

"How can we be sure that's the same shirt?"

"I'm sure you already got a description from the witnesses."

Officer Lombard snatched it from my hands and handed it to Harrison, who carefully placed it in a large paper bag. At that point, I expected them to all leave, but no.

"We have a couple of questions for you," she said.

"Go ahead. I have nothing to hide."

Next to me, Matthew squeezed my arm. "Is Della under arrest?" he asked.

Lombard shook her head. "All we want is some information. If she's innocent, as she claims to be, what's the problem?"

"The problem is that you can use anything she says and twist it out of context," he said.

"Don't worry," I told him. Knowing they would find nothing on my shoes or my coat had restored my confidence. "I'm okay."

"Sorry," Matthew said, "but I'm not going anywhere. If you want to question Della alone, you're going to have to charge her with something. If you want her to talk, I'm going to stay right here."

Lombard scowled. "According to another witness, a heated argument was overheard coming from the victim's office only minutes before you were seen running from the scene."

"Whoever that was, it wasn't me. I told you yesterday that, just as I was driving into the lot, another car came screeching out of there, like a bat out of hell. It almost rammed into me. If you're looking for suspects, I'd start there."

"Oh, right. The mysterious man—or woman—you saw driving a silver car. With that kind of information, the pool of suspects is just about every other person in town. I find it strange that you can't even tell us what make of car it was."

Matthew spoke up. "Della couldn't tell you the difference between an American made and a Japanese import. She's not making that up. You can take my word for it."

She kept her expression impassive, but her attitude was gone. "After leaving the scene, did you happen to remember anything you might have forgotten to mention?"

"No. Not a thing. Sorry. However, there is one thing I think you should know. My employee, Marnie Potter, heard something from a friend. It seems that Mr. Swanson was conducting a little extortion business on the side." I already knew Marnie had reported this, but it didn't hurt to remind her.

Her eyes narrowed. "That's right. And didn't you tell me yesterday that you went to city hall to get Swanson to sign your permit, after"—she made air quotations again—"he came by your shop that morning?"

"That's right," I said. Too late, I realized the trap I'd just fallen into. Lombard probably thought Swanson was trying to extort money from me, and that was my motive for killing him. "He'd already approved my permit," I added quickly. "If you don't believe me, ask my contractor. He'll confirm it."

"I think I'll do just that. What's his name?"

"Sydney Shuttleworth. I'll give you one of his cards." She followed me to the kitchen where I rummaged through my catchall drawer until I found one.

She slipped the card into her pocket. "If you think of anything else, give me a call."

And just like that the interrogation was over.

Chapter 14

The door closed behind the officers, and all at once my knees wanted to give out. Now that it was over, all the stress I'd been holding back came bubbling to the surface. Matthew must have sensed it, because he wrapped an arm around my waist and walked me to the sofa.

I let myself collapse into it and Winston plodded over, laying his chin on my knees. I patted him absently. "I thought she'd never leave." I took a long breath. "How did I do?"

"You did fine. I couldn't have done better myself. You came across as open and honest."

"That's because I was telling the truth."

"As I'm sure they know. When they get a tip, they're obligated to follow it. As soon as they test your clothes and see that there's no blood, they'll eliminate you as a suspect."

"Thank goodness you were here. I don't know what I would have done without you."

"You handled it all by yourself." He sat next to me and patted my knee. "Still up to going out?"

I'd completely forgotten about our dinner date. I checked my watch. "It's already six thirty. Isn't it too late to make our reservation?"

"A quick phone call will fix that. Come on. We still have to eat."

"Give me fifteen minutes. I won't look as nice as I'd planned, but I can still clean up pretty good."

Half an hour later, Matthew and I walked into the Long-view reception. Bunny Boyd, the owner, came forward from behind the reception desk to greet us with her arms open wide.

"It's been so long," she said. "Too long. I saw your name in the reservations book and wanted to be here to say hello."

"It has been too long," I said. "Margaret sends her love." Bunny was Margaret's birth mother. The two hadn't met until the previous fall. And what started as a conten-tious relationship had soon turned into a loving one.

"Did she tell you that she and I went shopping day before yesterday? We had a great time."

"She did. She was very excited about all the new clothes."

"I'm glad. But you two aren't here to chat with me. You're here for dinner. Let me walk you to your table."

We followed her down the hall to the dining room, a generous space with art-covered walls and different an-tique chandeliers, one hanging over each table. She guided us to "the best seat in the house for two of my favorite people." The table was set directly in front of the fieldstone fireplace. She pulled a chair for me and then one for Matthew, and gestured to the waiter, who hur-ried over with the menus.

"Please take special care of these two," she told him. "And whatever drinks they order are on the house." She leaned forward and whispered into Matthew's ear. "If you want a truly romantic dinner, I recommend ordering a bottle of Cristal Champagne."

"That's very generous of you, Bunny. But we can't ac-cept. It's too much."

"In that case, let me order it for you. My friends will

have a bottle of Cristal," she told the waiter. "Now, I'll leave you two to your dinner. Enjoy."

"I love this place," I said, leaning back. "As far as I'm concerned, it's every bit as good as any restaurant in Charlotte."

The waiter reappeared with the bottle of champagne. He popped the cork expertly, offered a half-inch in a glass for Matthew to taste, and then poured.

As soon as he had left with our food orders, Matthew raised his glass and looked me in the eye. "To you."

I felt myself melting under his gaze. "To you," I said, and took a sip. It still amazed me that after knowing each other all our lives, and after harboring a major crush on him for so long, Matthew had developed romantic feelings for me. Sometimes, I had to pinch myself. But, as thrilled as I was, his mother and mine were even more so. It had become obvious to me over the last year or so, and very possibly to Matthew too, that our mothers had been hatching a plot to match us up. Unfortunately, the more his pushed him, the more he dug in his heels. No man worth his salt wants his mother to dictate his love life. It was only after I pointed this out to my mother, and she relayed the message to his, that they retreated. Now that we were officially an item, the pressure was mounting for us to get engaged. I dared to hope he'd be asking me before the year was out.

"Penny for your thoughts," he said.

"Oh, sorry. I was just thinking about the shop," I said, not wanting to so much as utter the word marriage. Pressure from mothers was bad enough. But from a girl-friend, that would be disastrous.

"I should have asked you sooner. How was your first day?"

"Encouraging. Today we saw mostly lookie-loos, but there was a lot of interest. Tomorrow will be better."

We were still making small talk when I noticed a

beautiful woman sitting with a man, a few tables over, trying to attract Matthew's attention. I leaned in.

"I think there's somebody over there who knows you."

He turned in her direction. "Well, what do you know? Excuse me for a second, will you?" He made his way over wearing a grin the size of Texas. I glanced at the woman's hand and was relieved to see she wore a wedding ring. Matthew chatted with the couple for a moment, and they came over to join our table. It was only when she came closer that I recognized her. It was Susan Price. She had been in my shop no more than a few hours ago, and now she was completely transformed. She looked like a movie star. Her blond hair was styled in an elegant cut, and she was all dressed up in a sleek black dress with a beaded neckline.

"I invited them to join us for a glass of champagne," he said, as they sat. "This is Della, my girlfriend." My heart did a somersault, as it did every time he referred to me that way. "Della, this is John and Susan Price. The three of us went to college together."

"How are you?" I said. "Nice to see you again."

"You two know each other?" Matthew asked.

"We met this afternoon," Susan said. Matthew gestured for the waiter to bring two more glasses. Soon, we were all sipping champagne. While the men caught up, Susan and I chatted about fashion for a few minutes, and then changed the subject to how wonderful the food was here, and then to the art in the room. Through it all, I couldn't help but notice that Susan seemed nervous. Her chatter was quick. She flitted from one topic to another, as if she couldn't allow a moment of silence. After exploring a number of subjects, the discomfort that had hung over our conversation returned. At last I decided to ask her directly.

"I hope you're not uncomfortable with me."

"Why would I be uncomfortable?"

"I got the impression that you were annoyed with me about the conversation in my shop this afternoon."

She opened her eyes wide, an attempt to look confused, no doubt. "I have no idea what you're talking about."

"Mr. Swanson's murder." At her blank look, I continued. "He was apparently overheard arguing with a woman just a few minutes before I found him."

"If you think—"

"No, of course not. The problem is that, now, the police seem determined to prove that woman was me. So, if you know anything, please tell me."

Her attitude went from defensive to sympathetic, in a heartbeat. "How perfectly awful." Emotions flew over her face until she seemed to arrive at some decision. "You're right. I did feel awkward this afternoon. You see, I had an appointment with him that morning. I was going to tell him that I'd decided to lodge a complaint against him, but in the end I decided against it. He'd been with the city for decades, and I know others had made complaints and nothing ever came of them. When I heard he was killed around the same time I was supposed to meet with him, I was worried that if it got around, people would think I'd killed him. You know how people are."

"Believe me. I do."

"And I don't trust the police," she said. I silently agreed with her there. "Lately all we hear about are cases where some person is released after years of serving a sentence for some crime they never did." She nodded toward her husband. "John thinks I'm being paranoid, but, if it can happen to others, it could happen to me."

"You said others had gone to the city about him? Do you know who?"

"No. I called the city and the woman I spoke to told me others had tried before me. The way she said it, I got the impression she was warning me that nothing would come of it. She went on to tell me that he'd been at the same job forever and that he had an excellent reputation."

"Do you remember who you spoke to?"

"No idea. Except that it was someone in the permits department." I made a mental note to ask Marnie if she remembered who she had spoken to when she called about my permit.

"What I can't figure out is, if he was so disliked—"

"So I've heard."

"—then why was he still at the same job?" She huffed. "And how he managed to land himself a beautiful young wife like Mona is beyond me."

This was the second time someone remarked on how attractive his new wife was. "Did they go out for a long time before getting married?"

"No, not at all. She was dating somebody else for a long time. And when that relationship suddenly broke up, she started seeing Swanson and almost overnight, the two of them were married. I don't think it was more than a few weeks after they met." I stored that tidbit of information away.

"That must have been hard on her ex."

She frowned. "No, I think they remained—I wouldn't say friendly—but on good terms."

"You wouldn't happen to know who that was, by any chance?" I said.

"Of course I do. Sydney Shuttleworth is an old friend of ours. As a matter of fact he was at college with John and me too."

"You're kidding." I turned to Matthew and waited for a break in his conversation with John. "Did you know that my contractor, Syd, was at college at the same time you were?"

"Really?" he said. "I don't remember him there."

"Maybe that's because he was a couple of years ahead of us," John said. "He graduated our first year."

That explained it.

Before I could react, her husband stood. "I think it's about time we returned and give these people their table back. Besides, I think the waiter is bringing over our food." They both said good-bye and left.

A few minutes later our own food arrived, and I lost myself in the heavenly flavors of my salad *caprese*—my all-time favorite—followed by *spaghetti alla vodka*. We were relaxing over coffee when I noticed the Prices leaving, and a question came to me.

"I suddenly get the feeling you're a million miles away," Matthew said.

"Oh, er, sorry. I have to run to the washroom." I made a dash for the exit, but instead of going to the ladies' room, I turned right and darted to the back entrance, which gave me a view the parking lot. I opened the door just as John and Susan were getting into a silver luxury vehicle. The car was the right color, but was much larger than the one I'd seen speeding away. All at once I remembered a detail that until now had slipped my mind. The silver hatchback had a sticker on its back bumper—something about death or the hereafter.

I returned to the restaurant feeling relieved. Susan Price was a nice woman. And I instinctively felt she had nothing to do with the murder.

"Are you feeling all right?" Matthew asked as I sat.

"Of course. Why?"

"You took off so fast I was afraid you felt ill."

I gave him a beaming smile. "It's sweet of you to worry, but I'm fine. Just had to powder my nose."

Matthew stared at his coffee for a few minutes, smiling to himself. "It was great running into John after all this time. It brings back so many memories." He chuckled. "We both tried out for the Carolina baseball team. He made it. I didn't. He never let me forget it."

He launched into a recital of old stories, but I didn't hear a word of what he was saying. How could I not have thought of it earlier? Light blue was not a common color for baseball caps. It was, however, the color of the UNC baseball team. At the same time, another idea occurred to me. Syd Shuttleworth often wore a light blue T-shirt under his overalls. I was convinced it was a T-shirt from UNC. And I was willing to bet he also had a college baseball cap too.

On the way back to my place, Matthew brought my hand to his mouth and kissed it.

"Now that your shop is running again, are we going back to the old routine of me dropping off Winston in the morning?"

"I hope so. I like having him around. He's good company on quiet days, and I always feel safer having him in the shop. Although" — I chuckled — "if I had to count on him to rescue me, I might as well take lessons in self-defense."

He gave my hand a squeeze. "In that case, should I leave him at your place for the night?"

"That's a good idea." We were both quiet for a moment, and then he added, "You know, you'd probably feel a whole lot safer in your apartment if I was to spend the night too." He glanced at me sideways, the streetlights flashing over his handsome face as we drove by. My heart skipped a beat.

"I think you make a very good point."

The next morning, I came downstairs at a quarter to ten, Winston trotting happily after me. Matthew had taken off around eight thirty, to get an early start on his writing.

"You're here early," I said, finding Marnie already in.

"I had to drop off Jenny's order. So there was no point in going back home for just a couple of hours. Besides, I was sure you'd be here no later than eight, but then I saw Matthew leaving an hour ago." She gave me the eyebrow. "That explains why you look so happy this morning."

I felt the blood rising to my face. "Nonsense. The whole point of the remodel, in case you've forgotten, was that I would no longer have to be here before ten every morning."

"Of course," she said, rolling her eyes. Much to my relief, she changed the subject. "How did it go with the police last night?"

"They showed up with a search warrant and ransacked my house, looking for the clothes I was wearing when I found Swanson's body."

"Oh, for crying out loud. Don't they have better things to do than to harass innocent folk?"

"My thoughts exactly. But unfortunately, I'd thrown away the jeans I was wearing. So now they think I got rid of them because they would have incriminated me. The only good thing is I still had my shirt, my coat and running shoes. Matthew says that as soon as the lab report shows there is no blood on them, the police will drop me as a suspect." I sighed. "But who knows how long that'll take. They're never in such a rush when they think the evidence will exonerate a suspect as when it will convict him."

"You? A suspect? It's just plain ridiculous." She changed the subject abruptly. "I made cranberry-lemon muffins. Want one?"

I'd just had a big breakfast, but I could never resist Marnie's baking. "Sure."

From his cushion behind the cash register, Winston growled. Sometimes I could swear he understood. "It's okay, Winnie. I have a treat for you right here." I rummaged through my catchall drawer and threw him a liver treat. He snapped it in midair and chowed down.

Marnie reappeared from Jenny's shop, carrying a tray with two coffees and a basket of pastries. "You should see her place. It's packed."

"Again? I'm so happy for her."

"There isn't an empty seat in the place. Jenny was just telling me she's going to have to find a way to add seats. She's thinking of putting in a bar with stools in front of the window. She could get another five or six places that way."

"You know what else she could do," I said. "During the summer she could put café tables on the sidewalk. Of course she'd need a permit for that."

"A permit? Are you crazy? I don't think any of us ever wants to deal with the city for permits again."

The door swung open and Margaret came in. "I just wanted to tell you," she whispered. "I overhead one of the customers talking about the owners of Good Morning Sunshine. It seems they're related to the city inspector's wife."

A bell sounded in my mind. "Related in what way?" I asked.

"Lori Stanton is Mona Swanson's sister."

"Well, isn't that interesting?" Marnie said. "No wonder Swanson was doing everything in his power to slow down Jenny's reopening."

"I hadn't thought of that," I said. "But it makes sense. Swanson might have wanted to please his wife's family by crippling their competition. But I also found out something interesting. Syd used to date Mona before she met Swanson. That gives him one more reason to hate the city inspector. Also, he went to UNC, and you know what their official color is—light blue—the same color as the baseball cap the driver was wearing when he sped out of the city hall parking lot. I'm more and more convinced that Syd is the killer."

"Makes sense," Marnie said.

"By the way," I said. "Yesterday I happened to see Syd and a blond woman having an argument. She looked so much like Lori Stanton, I'm sure they're related. And, now, knowing he used to date Mona Swanson, I'm sure that was her."

Marnie frowned. "They were arguing?"

"Yes, and it looked like a doozy. He grabbed her by the arm, hard. She twisted out of his grasp and ran inside the house, slamming the door behind her. I wonder what that argument was all about."

"Wait till Jenny hears about this."

"Maybe you shouldn't tell her about any of this. She's got enough on her mind," Marnie said.

Margaret scoffed. "But, what if she wasn't being paranoid after all? There really could have been a plot to keep her shop closed as long as possible. I wonder if we should mention this to the police."

"Let's think about it before we say anything," I said. "With my luck, Lombard will probably twist that into another reason why I might have wanted Swanson dead. Besides, what's to tell? Jenny thinks there was a plot, and I saw Syd and a blond woman, who may or may not have been Swanson's wife, talking. That hardly counts as evidence. Lombard will laugh me right out of the station."

Chapter 15

From my spot behind the counter, I watched a steady stream of customers going in and out of Jenny's shop. I was happy to see that her business had picked up. But in the meantime, no one had so much as popped their heads into my shop all morning. This left me somewhat disconcerted.

After a while, I left the front counter and joined Marnie who was busy at my dobby loom in the back. She was walking the pedals at a ferocious speed.

"It's so quiet up front, I think I'll do some weaving for a while," I told her. "What are you working on? More place mats?"

"Since you keep complaining that you never have enough of them, I thought I'd make you as many as I can. That way you won't run out so quickly. What about you? What are you going to work on? Some new project on the Navajo loom?"

"Right on."

After my decision to try this ancient form of weaving, I'd ordered two specialty Navajo looms, a large one for the shop and a smaller one I'd been using in my apartment. I'd already completed a number of projects on the smaller one, but this would be my first time working on the large one. I looked at it now—such a simple contraption—a four-sided frame with manually operated sheds. I'd brought in a cushion so that I could work the traditional way, sitting on the floor to start. Then, as my project progressed, I'd move higher and higher, to a stool, then a chair, a barstool and so on as the weaving progressed up the warp. I'd even seen pictures of Navajo women with their chairs on top of a table so that they could reach the top toward the end of their project.

I picked up a spool of the yarn I'd chosen for the weft and began the dressing, which, with this type of loom, took a fraction of the normal time — one more reason to love this technique. Half an hour later I had just finished when the doorbell chimed.

"Wouldn't you know it?" Marnie said. "All you have to do is get busy, and a customer is sure to stop by."

"I am not complaining. I can use the business." I hurried up front to greet Judy Bates.

"Judy, hi. What good wind brings you?"

"I love the Native American-looking collection in your window. The pieces are gorgeous. You never carried this type of merchandise in the past. Did you just make those?"

"I did. I decided to try my hand at something completely new. And with the shop being closed for so long I had lots of time on my hands. So I gave this a try."

"That's renovations for you. It always takes twice as much time and three times as much money as you expect. My friend Susan went through hell when she remodeled her kitchen." She frowned. "I think I told you about her, didn't I?"

"Yes. Funny you should mention her. My boyfriend and I went out to dinner last night and we ran into her and her husband. She also mentioned what a frustrating experience the remodeling turned out to be."

She snapped her fingers. "I did tell you about her. I remember now." I was sure our conversation hadn't slipped her mind. She'd been eagerly looking to pick up some gossip when we'd talked about it yesterday. "You know, something came back to me last night," she continued. "Susan's renovations were last fall. Being livid as she was with that inspector, Mr. Swanson, I'd never have thought I'd see him at her place again. But, just the other day, there he was, large as life, leaving her house in the middle of the afternoon." She wrinkled her brow. "I wondered what he would be doing at her place six months after her remodeling."

"Maybe she's having something else done?" I suggested.

She nodded emphatically. "That's what I thought too. But the next day, when I ran into her, I asked her if she was having more work done. She said, 'I'd rather get a root canal.'" Judy folded her arms, as if waiting for me to comment.

"That is odd," I said warily. Chatting with someone like Judy was a bit like walking a minefield. I had to be careful what I said, in case my words found their way back to Susan. Gossip lovers often enjoyed nothing more than to set people against each other. It made for great spectator sport. There was, however, one thing I might find out without risk of it being interpreted the wrong way. It had occurred to me that a financially comfortable couple might own more than one car. "I saw her and her husband drive away in a really nice car last night. I'm thinking of changing cars myself, but I'm so bad when it comes to makes and models. You wouldn't happen to know what they drive, would you?"

"Were they driving his or her car?"

"I have no clue. So they each have one?"

"Actually, they have three, a new Lexus, which he drives. Then they also have a midsize car that she uses most of the time. But they also have a sports car. Some fancy European make—probably worth a fortune."

"The car I'm talking about was silver."

She chuckled. "That doesn't help. They must have a thing for silver cars. The only one that isn't silver is the sports car. That one is red."

"I think it might have had a hatchback."

She shook her head pensively. "No, that doesn't sound like anything they drive. Anyhow, enough talk about cars. I want to know more about your new merchandise. I just love those rugs and blankets in your window. I'm looking for a decorative throw for my living room. We just redid our kitchen, opened it up onto the living room. We put in a rustic floor and a fieldstone fireplace. And just last week we bought a new living room set—genuine leather, a beautiful tan color. Don't you think some Navajo-inspired accessories would look wonderful in there?"

I could picture it in my mind. "It sounds wonderful. You must invite me. I'd love to see your home. It sounds beautiful."

"Sure. Just as soon as I'm finished with the decorating. I was wondering if you'd let me borrow one of the blankets to try out. If it works, I'll be back tomorrow to pay for it, and maybe get a couple of the cushions too."

"Of course we can do that." I climbed into the window while she went outside and pointed out the pieces she liked. Back at the cash register she signed a loan receipt for two throws and three cushions—five pieces instead of the one she'd originally mentioned.

After she left, I returned to the studio with a spring in my step. "I think I might have just sold two of my newest blankets and three cushions," I told Marnie.

"Great. I was looking at the ticketed price. Those aren't cheap."

"They're very popular right now. If this collection sells well, it'll bring in a lot of money."

"I overheard you and Judy talking, and it gave me an idea. You should redo your window display to make it look like the corner of a real room. You could put in a rustic floor—some laminate flooring that snaps together. And borrow a leather chair to use as a display piece for your collection. It would pull in the customers like mad."

It was a great idea. "And you know who has brown leather furniture? Matthew," I said. "Maybe he won't mind lending it to me for a couple of weeks." I snatched my cell phone and called him.

When he answered, I went straight to the point. "I have a small favor to ask you." I told him about Marnie's idea.

"No problem," he said, without hesitation. "Want me to drop it off when I pick up Winston?"

"That would be wonderful."

"I'll do that. If that's all, I'll say good-bye and go back to my writing."

"I take it he said yes?" Marnie asked when I returned to my loom.

"He did."

I had been working at my loom for a few minutes when I remembered something Judy had said. "You know, I didn't pay attention to it at the time, but Judy mentioned that she saw Swanson at Susan's place just a few days ago. Don't you think it's odd, considering how much trouble he gave her last fall when she did her renovations?"

"What are you thinking?" Marnie asked.

"I wonder if she had more work done, this time without a building permit. If Swanson found out, he could have put the squeeze on her pretty hard."

"How can you find out?"

"I have an idea." I marched off to the front, picked up the phone and dialed the number for city hall.

"May I speak to Johanna Renay?" I said.

"Della. This is a surprise," the woman said, hearing my voice.

"Johanna?" I said. "Is that you? I didn't expect you to answer."

"I work in whatever department needs me most. After so many years working here, I can do everybody's job. The only one I do all the time is answer the phone. You'd be surprised at how many times I can take care of a problem without having to transfer the call. What can I do for you?"

This gave me another idea. "I have a couple of questions I'm hoping you can answer. Someone mentioned calling the city to lodge a complaint against Mr. Swanson. But the clerk she spoke to apparently discouraged her from formalizing it. All she could tell me is that the woman worked in the permit department. Would you happen to know who the clerk might be?"

"In the permit department?" she said, sounding confused. "But . . . there's never been anybody but Howard in that department." There was a pause before she spoke again. "I think maybe whoever told you that might have been lying."

Could Susan have made up the story? I wondered. And if so, why?

"You had another question?" she said.

"Oh, right. I was wondering whether you could find out if there was any building permit issued to somebody with the last name of Bates."

"Will knowing this help you find out who killed Howard?"

"It might."

"I really shouldn't be giving out that kind of information." There was a pause. "But, if it will help bring the killer to justice . . . As long as you promise never to tell a soul."

"I promise."

"How far back would you like me to go?"

"No more than a year," I said.

"Let me write this down so I don't forget it." I couldn't believe she had agreed so easily. "All right. I'll give you a call back as soon as I have the information."

I was about to return to my weaving when the store phone rang. A glance at the call display told me it was my mother.

"Mom. Hi. What's new?"

"I'm all right," she said. "Considering my age."

Oh, dear God. Here it was. The guilt trip. "Mom, you're not old. Didn't you hear? Seventy is the new fifty."

"You know what would really make me feel young again? Grandchildren. Are you really doing everything you can to encourage Matthew?"

"Any more encouragement and he'll be feeling cornered," I said.

She sighed. "Well, I suppose we don't want that."

As we chatted, I absently unfolded the morning newspaper, which was still on the counter, untouched. CITY EMPLOYEE MURDERED, the headlines read. And then my eyes fell upon the color photograph accompanying the article. I gasped. I was looking at the picture of a woman standing in the doorway of a silver hatchback. She was the blond woman I'd seen arguing with Syd. So that confirmed my suspicion that the blonde was Mona Swanson. But what really caught my attention was the car. As ignorant as I was about makes and models, I was pretty sure it was identical to the one I'd seen in the city hall parking lot the morning of Swanson's murder.

"Sweetheart? Are you still there?"

"Sorry, Mom. A customer just walked in. I'll call you later. Love you," I said and hung up.

If the car I'd seen racing away that day belonged to the victim's wife, that meant . . .

Whenever I watched true-crime television dramas, the murderer always turned out to be the spouse. And it might turn out to be the case now too.

Marnie joined me at the cash register. "I'm ready for a coffee break. How about you?" She went out, returning a few minutes later with two mugs.

"You look preoccupied," she said, handing me one.

"I think I might just have solved the crime."

"What? Who killed him? And why?"

I showed her the picture in the paper. "I think this is the car I saw speeding away from city hall, minutes before I found the body. It belongs to her, Mona Swanson."

"His wife?" she said in disbelief.

"It makes sense. In the last twenty-four hours, two people have remarked on how beautiful and how much younger she is than him. People are mystified as to why a gorgeous girl like her would marry someone like him."

"They think she married him for his money?"

"She wouldn't be the first."

"True. Except that he was a city employee, not a millionaire. Nobody knew about his lucrative little sideline."

I thought about this. "Well, let's think about this. What do men do when they want to attract a woman who is beyond their reach?"

"Er. Take her out to dinner? Buy her gifts?"

I nodded. "He'll try to impress her—show her what a good catch he would be."

"Of course," she said, her eyes lighting up. "You think he flashed his money around her."

"He might not have told her how he was making his money, but you can bet your booty he was showing off."

"So what are you going to do? Call the police?"

"Maybe. But not until I have some proof."

Chapter 16

The next few hours went by fast. The door opened and closed nonstop as customers came in. Before I knew it I'd made a number of sales and placed half a dozen orders for Native-style rugs.

"How are you going to fill all those orders?" Marnie asked, after the last order.

"I'll do what I always do—get my ladies to help." From the day I first opened, I had accepted pieces on consignment, and over time I'd occasionally hired a few of my local weavers to help on larger projects. "The only problem is that I doubt any of them has the proper loom." I walked over to the back and, tapping an index finger to my chin, I studied my large loom. "I wonder . . ."

"What?" Marnie asked.

"It looks so simple," I said. "I bet a carpenter could build one of these. It might be cheaper than buying them from a retailer."

"That's a great idea."

Armed with my cell phone I snapped a number of pictures, making sure I had close-ups of every feature and from every angle and pulled out my measuring tape. Returning to the counter I spread out a sheet of paper on which I drew the basic design, adding the measurements. Then I got on the phone.

By midafternoon, I had lined up three of my regular

weavers, and I had also found a local carpenter who claimed to have made looms in the past, and quoted me a reasonable price.

"I have an appointment with him at eight o'clock tomorrow morning," I told Marnie. "All in all, I've had a really good day."

"And it isn't over yet," she said.

Suddenly, there was a fresh burst of activity. The door was opening and closing nonstop with customers attracted by my window display. I got busy racking up more sales. By the time the rush quieted, I had sold quite a few items, and had also signed on two students for my next beginners' weaving class. I now had a total of four students. That reminded me, Johanna Renay had asked to join my next class. I made a mental note to ask her about it when I next spoke to her. The thought had just crossed my mind when the phone rang. And when I checked the call display, I saw the number was from city hall. *Johanna.*

"You already have the information?" I said. "That was fast."

"It was no trouble at all. I asked the young lady who's temporarily taken over for Mr. Swanson. She went through all the permits and there haven't been any requests from anyone with that last name."

It was pretty much what I'd expected—not that it mattered anymore. I was pretty sure I knew who the killer was. Then, out of curiosity, I asked her, "Would you happen to know if the police have bothered to look into the permits?"

"Not as far as I know," she said. "But . . . hold on. I'll find out." She put me on hold for a few minutes before coming back. "No," she said. "Except for going in and out of Howard's office a couple of times, they haven't spoken to anyone at all. But why would they want to do that?"

"It was just an idea. Being a building inspector, I imagine Mr. Swanson might have made some enemies."

"That makes sense," she said. "I hadn't thought of that."

"Also, it's come to light that he was extorting money in return for permits."

"What?" She choked on the word, and then lowered her voice. "Impossible! I simply won't believe that. He may have had his flaws—he stepped out on his ex-wife while they were married—but he was an honest man."

Strange, I thought, that she would describe a man who cheats on his wife as honest. "I'm sorry if I upset you. But I'm pretty certain it's true."

"It's just that . . . that I thought he was a nice man. I feel like I would have sensed if he was so dishonest."

"Maybe you're right."

She seemed to regain her calm. "I've been meaning to ask you. Did the police question you about the blood on your clothes?"

"It wasn't blood. It was paint," I said. "But, yes. They did show up about twenty minutes after you left. I can't thank you enough for warning me. It was unpleasant enough when I was expecting it, but it would have been much worse if I'd been unprepared."

"Well, let's hope they don't keep pestering you."

"They wouldn't have questioned me to begin with if it hadn't been for whoever made up that story about me wiping blood from my clothes."

"I know. It was really awful of Ronald Dempsey to say something like that. I don't know where his head was at the time."

"It was Mr. Dempsey?" I said.

She gasped. "Oh, dear. I wasn't supposed to name names."

"But . . . didn't you tell me it was a city employee?"

"I was trying to be discreet. I failed pretty miserably, didn't I?"

I was still trying to wrap my head around this new information. "I don't understand. Mr. Dempsey had already left by the time the police arrived."

"He'd left his card, you see. And the police called him. So he had to come back. By then you were already gone."

"I suppose it doesn't matter anymore. I think I've already figured out who killed him."

"What? Who do they think did it?"

I told her about recognizing Mona Swanson's car as the same one I'd seen speeding out of the lot.

"Mona?" she said, sounding surprised. "Of course. It makes perfect sense. I tried to tell him he was making a mistake by marrying that piece of trash." She stopped. "Oh, dear. I can't believe I just said that. I suppose it's the shock of finding out that she killed him."

"Please don't repeat this to anyone yet. I shouldn't have said anything. This is all speculation on my part. I have no proof, you understand."

"Well, I, for one, am sure you're right."

"While I have you on the phone," I said. "I just scheduled a beginners' weaving class." I gave her the date and the time.

"Let me check my calendar." She was back in a minute. "I'm free. I'll be there. You can count on it. Before you go, dear, would you do me a small favor?"

"Gladly."

"If you hear anything else about the investigation, would you let me know? I realize it's none of my business, but the man was a friend. I won't sleep until his killer is brought to justice."

"I'll be happy to." We said good-bye and hung up.

"You won't believe this," I told Marnie, joining her in the back. "I was under the impression that it was Tom Goodall who told the police he saw me wiping blood from my clothes. But I was wrong. Johanna just told me it was Ronald Dempsey. I can't figure out why he would say such a thing, unless he lied on purpose."

"Why would he do that?"

I shrugged. "The only reason I can think of is if he was trying to throw suspicion on me."

Marnie rolled her eyes. "Good God, woman. You're beginning to sound as paranoid as Jenny. Let's just forget about this murder. Put it out of your head. It's history. Over and done with."

"You're right. Let's forget about it."

The door opened, throwing the bell into a tizzy. It was Matthew.

I checked my watch, surprised that it was already closing time. Winston, who'd been snoozing on his cushion behind the counter, hopped to his feet and ran to greet him.

"Hello, big boy. How are you doing?" Winnie was wiggling around excitedly and grunting with pleasure. "You look like you had a nice day." Matthew scratch him behind the ear, then came over and kissed me. "I love your window display. That's the new collection you were telling me about?"

"I'm glad you like it."

"I've got the leather chair in my car. Where do you want it?"

I told him and he brought it in. "How are you going to lift it into the window?"

I smiled. "I happen to know this big strong guy who comes around just about every day. I'm sure he'll give me a hand when I'm ready."

"I see your game," he said, and gave me another quick kiss. He nodded to Marnie. "So, what kind of a day did you ladies have? Solved any crimes lately?"

"Actually, I think we did."

His eyes widened. "Really? I was just joking. But, tell me."

I told him, with Marnie filling in the details whenever I stopped to take a breath.

"Good for you," he said. I detected more than a little relief in his voice. Knowing the way his mind worked, I knew he was happy that the murder was solved. "Now promise me that your only involvement will be in supplying the police with the clue to solve it."

"I can't say a word to the police with no more than an idea."

"I hope that doesn't mean you're planning anything dangerous."

"I'm not planning anything," I said.

"That's good, because, chances are you're wrong. The police always look at the spouse first. If there was any evidence his wife killed him, they would have likely brought her in by now."

"Maybe they don't have proof yet."

"You might be right. But it seems to me that you're jumping to conclusions. You don't even know if her car is the one you saw leaving city hall."

I knew everything he was saying was true. Maybe spending so much time with Jenny was beginning to rub off on me, but I had a feeling about this. Mona Swanson was not innocent. It was her car I'd seen that morning. I was certain . . . or almost.

"I had an idea," he said, turning to Marnie. "I was going to invite Della over for dinner, but why don't you join us too? I made chicken curry—my specialty."

"I can vouch for his curry," I said. "I've had it a few times and it is delicious."

"I'm sure it is," Marnie said. "But I've already got plans for the evening." Knowing her, she was making herself scarce to give Matthew and me some privacy.

When it came to wanting Matthew and me to get married, she was almost as bad as my mother.

"Are you sure? You're more than welcome to join us," I said.

"No. You kids have fun. You don't need me as a third wheel," she said, confirming my suspicions.

When no amount of convincing made her change her mind, I closed up shop. Marnie went on her way and Matthew and I drove to his place.

Matthew's small Victorian house was only a few blocks down the street. During the drive, which took no more than a couple of minutes, I was acutely aware of his presence just a few inches away. The confined space made our closeness all the more intimate. He drove slowly, as if to extend these lovely moments and I leaned back against the headrest and breathed in the spring air.

It was mid-April. The days had finally started getting longer, and the sun was just beginning its descent in the west. It was almost six thirty, a time when most people were getting ready for dinner. This left the street nearly deserted, as if Matthew and I were alone in the world.

Matthew took my hand. "How was business on your second day? As good as you expected?"

"Better. Much better. I sold a few of my classic pieces, but, more important, my new collection is taking off. I've got pieces out on approval and three orders for rugs. Luckily, a few of my weavers have agreed to help me fill the orders. I think that collection will turn my business around."

"I had no doubt you would do well."

We arrived at his house, and while he took the curry out of the oven, I filled Winston's bowls and set the table. Soon he poured us some wine and we sat down to eat.

"Heard from your mother lately?" he asked.

"She calls me at least three or four times a week. And

now that there's been a murder in town, she's upped her quota. How about you? Speak to your mother?"

"As a matter of fact, I spoke to her this afternoon. She called to make sure I'd be here all day tomorrow. She sent me a package—something special, according to her, and I have to be here to sign for it. The way she was carrying on about it, you would have thought it was the *Mona Lisa*."

"Any idea what it might be?"

"None. I just hope it's not some old floral rug or something equally frilly."

"If it is, you can give it to me. I love that kind of stuff."

We lingered over dinner, and the conversation turned to the case. "So tell me everything you've learned about the case," he said.

I searched his eyes. "You honestly want to talk about it?"

"Of course. If you're interested, I'm interested." That was so sweet, I could have kissed him.

"The thing is, if Mona Swanson is innocent, the suspect pool will be huge. There could be hundreds of them. The man was extorting money in return for permits. Anybody who had any remodeling done in the last year or two could have a reason for wanting him dead."

"Well, then start with those you know."

"My main suspect at the moment is Mona Swanson. Next on my list is Syd Shuttleworth. It turns out that he and Mona used to be involved before she dropped him to marry Swanson."

"So you think he killed him out of revenge, or jealousy?"

"Maybe. Somebody—I forget who—mentioned that Shuttleworth hated him, and that Swanson was giving Syd a hard time on all his jobs."

Matthew nodded. "Sounds like some egos got bruised. Hopefully, this isn't a game of bloody knuckles gone out of control."

I took a sip of wine and put my glass back down. "If Mona married him for his money, as some people seem to think, she probably killed him in order to get her hands on it. Is there any way we can find out if she had a policy on his life?"

He shook his head. "Insurance policies are not public domain. However, Swanson was a city employee. He definitely had insurance through his work. It was probably worth a couple of times his yearly income. Are Syd and Mona your only two suspects?"

"No. I'm also keeping an eye on one of my clients who had a problem with him a few months back," I said. "But it isn't as if I have any real evidence against her. And even her motive is weak. Then there's Ronald Dempsey who told the police he saw me wiping blood from my clothes."

"Dempsey said that?"

"He did. And whenever somebody throws suspicion on somebody else, it always makes me wonder what their motive is."

"A few suspects, but no real evidence."

"That's all I have at the moment."

"It's a start," he said—his way of telling me I was no-where close to solving it.

Chapter 17

The evening had been lovely and I was tempted to stay the night, but a part of me still resisted spending too much time with Matthew. Our romance was new and I feared that, unless I gave him a regular opportunity to miss me, he'd soon lose interest.

"You don't have to go, you know. You can stay."

"Thanks, but I have an early day tomorrow—an eight o'clock appointment with a carpenter in Belmont."

"In that case, let me walk you back."

"No, you stay. I'll take Winston. That way you won't have to drop him off in the morning."

"Are you sure?" He looked so disappointed. That was good, I told myself. *Absence makes the heart grow fonder.*

"I am." To be honest, I also wanted to think over everything I knew about my suspect and make certain I was on the right track. I clipped on Winston's harness.

"Ready to go, big boy?"

He threw me a grateful look. Going for walks was Winston's favorite thing, along with eating, cuddling, playing catch and a dozen other things. After a kiss and a hug from Matthew, we set off, Winston heading toward my apartment. The walk should have taken five minutes tops, but Winston dawdled, sniffing and baptizing every fire hydrant, lamppost and bush along the way.

"You never met a tree you didn't like, did you, Winnie?"

He threw me an irritated look.

"Let's go, Winston. Don't you want to go to sleep?" His ears perked up. Sleep was another of his favorite things. He barked a comment, which I interpreted as, "Hurry up."

I got home, set a cushion on the floor in my room for the dog and went straight to my loom.

Ever since I'd picked up weaving as a teenager, my loom had become my go-to place whenever I had a puzzle to solve. I'd sit and weave, sometimes all night, and more often than not, by the time I climbed into bed, I'd made some headway in solving my problem. Unlike Marnie, I was never a fast weaver. She could produce in an hour what took me half a day to do. But that was fine by me. I enjoyed the activity itself and had no wish to rush it. I savored every moment the way a reader might enjoy each word of a good book.

There was something soothing about the rhythmic motion of throwing the shuttle from hand to hand, of walking the pedals. Weaving is the kind of mindless activity that leaves one's brain free to wander. After a few minutes, my mind wandered to the question of the moment. Did Mona kill her husband? I was still convinced she had. But how could I prove it?

I reviewed what I knew so far. Mona was years younger than her husband. She was in her early to midtwenties, and if Swanson was in school with Johanna Renay, the two had to be close in age—around fifty or so. Had she married him for his money? There was no way to prove that, and even if she had, that didn't mean she killed him. The only proof I might be able to get was to somehow show that the car she was driving was the same one I'd seen speeding out of the lot that day.

What about my other suspects, like Susan Price? She had admitted that she never wanted to see the inspector again. Yet, according to Judy Bates, he had been at her house just a few days before he was killed. Had Susan done more renovations on her house that forced her to pay off Swanson, again? Or was that just conjecture on Judy's part?

Then, there was Ronald Dempsey, who had been doing some deflecting of his own and throwing suspicion on me. Why clse would he have reported seeing me wiping blood from my clothes? Other than that, I had no real evidence against him, but upon reflection, I could think of a few reasons he should be on my list.

The first reason was that he had opportunity. He happened to be at the scene of the crime when I found the body. What I didn't know was the exact time he'd gotten there that morning. I made a mental note to ask Johanna Renay. If anybody could tell me, she would.

The second reason I should seriously consider Dempsey as a suspect was that he was a developer, and as such, he needed permits too. If, for any reason, Swanson refused to provide them, he'd stand to lose whatever amount of money—a fortune no doubt—that he'd already poured into the development. His entire business could go down the drain. On the other hand, I reminded myself, Swanson was buying a house from him, so that would indicate that he approved of his building practices.

Then, of course, there was Syd Shuttleworth. Syd used to be involved with Swanson's wife, and she had dumped him for Swanson. On top of that, Swanson was sabotaging his career. Those were two strong reasons he could well be the killer, and considering there had to be at least a dozen cars like Mona's in Belmont, she could well be innocent.

I mulled all of this over while adding more rows of weaving to the saddle blanket on my loom, until eventually my eyes were too tired to stay open. Only then did I drag myself to bed.

*   *   *

The next morning, I felt surprisingly alert considering I'd
had only a few hours of sleep. At seven thirty I was already dressed and ready to set out for Belmont. I had
Googled the carpenter's address and had the directions
to his place.

I had also copied Mona Swanson's address. I wanted
a close-up look at her car. If it had the same sticker on
the back bumper, there would be no doubt about it being the one I'd seen driving away. Then, as an after-
thought, I took note of Syd Shuttleworth's address too.

I hopped into my Jeep, and hit the highway. Fifteen
minutes later, I pulled over in front of a white clapboard
structure with an attached garage sporting a sign. It read
CARPENTRY AND WOODWORKING BY BEN BROWN. I was at
the right place.

"Mr. Brown?" I said, walking into the man's large garage.

"That's me," he replied. "You must be my eight o'clock
appointment. The weaver."

"Della Wright." We shook hands and I looked around.
His workshop was filled with tools and machinery. Along
one wall was an assortment of furniture—tables, dress-
ers, chests, chairs. All of them of fine workmanship.

"Let's take a look at what you've got," he said, plant-
ing his worn hands on the counter as he stared at the
pictures I spread out before him.

"I've got the measurements too," I said and handed
him the paper on which I'd jotted them.

He studied these in silence for a few minutes, looking
at each picture carefully. "I can do that no problem," he
said at last. "It's not complicated at all. Like I told you,
I've made a couple of looms in my time, none exactly like
this one. But this one looks simpler." He wrote out the
order. As I wrote him a check, my eyes fell upon the newspaper. It was an older issue of the *Belmont Daily* showing
a picture of a house fire on the front page.

"It's a damn shame what happened to that Williams family," he said. "I was just reading about it in the paper when you got here." He glanced at it as he spoke. "That man lost his whole family. No wonder he was out of his mind at the funeral yesterday."

I had no idea what he was talking about. A few seconds later, he continued.

"His kids' funeral was yesterday. I didn't know him, other than seeing him around town. But I thought I'd show my respects, you know. Hundreds of people showed up."

My ears perked up. "What are you talking about?"

"I'm surprised you didn't hear. The burial was over and the crowd was beginning to thin out when Williams went berserk."

"Why did he do that?"

He shook his head. "I couldn't really tell you. I was too far away to hear anything but the general commotion."

Mr. Brown picked up the check. "You can expect the first loom to be finished in a couple of days. I won't start working on the other two until you've checked the first and made sure it's right." We said good-bye and I left.

Back in my Jeep, I consulted the directions to Mona's address and took off. A few blocks farther and I slowed to a crawl for a good look.

The house was just the kind of home I'd expect a city employee to own. It was a yellow bungalow with a green tile roof, a black front door and a well-kept front lawn— pretty in a modest way. Nothing about it shouted money.

On the other hand, they had been planning to move into a new house in Dempsey's development. And, if this little house was fully paid for, it would amount to a tidy little sum when sold, and as his widow, chances were that it now belonged to Mona. Not a bad payout after a six-month marriage. I was about to drive on when my eyes came to rest on the silver hatchback in the driveway.

I stopped the Jeep and hopped out. After a quick look around, I dashed over to the back of the car. Sure enough, right there on the back bumper was a sticker that read ARE YOU READY FOR JUDGMENT DAY?

This was it. The very same car I'd spotted as it sped out of the parking lot. I had absolutely no doubt in my mind that Mona Swanson was guilty of her husband's murder. But, proving she was the person behind the wheel was another story. Could she have lent somebody her car? I wondered. If she had, she *had* to have been involved. I was standing there, staring at the car, when my eyes traveled up to the living room window. Mona was there, staring daggers down at me.

Startled, I dashed back to my Jeep, and as I did, I happened to touch the hood of the hatchback with my hand. I hadn't planned to do it. But as soon as I did, I knew the car had not been in the driveway for more than a couple of minutes because it was still hot. I drove away, wondering where Mona had been so early in the morning. Could she have just returned from spending the night with Syd?

I stopped at a corner a few streets over and breathed deeply for a few minutes. The woman had given me the creeps with that cold stare. I had no difficulty imagining her conking her husband over the head with a marble bookend.

I consulted my directions again and made my way over to the other side of town, to Syd Shuttleworth's address. During the two months the man had worked for me, he showed up at seven sharp every morning. I could have set my clock by him. It was now past eight thirty. There was no chance he'd still be at home at this time.

Though he'd worked on my shop for two months, I knew little about Syd. He'd come in, say hello and get right to work. That was the extent of our relationship. I had no idea what kind of a life he led, and I wanted a peek at his house. I was curious to see how comfortable his lifestyle was, compared to Swanson's . . . or at least compared to the lifestyle Swanson and Mona were about to adopt once they moved.

I turned onto his street and as the numbers got closer, I slowed to a crawl. To my surprise, as I drove up, I recognized Shuttleworth's truck in his driveway. I stepped on the gas again and, as I sped by, I noticed the driver's door was ajar. Syd was sitting inside with his arm sticking out—probably about to back up. I turned my head, hoping he hadn't noticed me. Halfway down the block, I pulled to a stop and waited.

Ten minutes later his truck hadn't so much as budged. A sick feeling came over me. Syd should have left his house two hours ago. Something was not right. I waited a bit longer, now watching in my rearview mirror for any movement. The minutes ticked by and my feeling of dread grew, until at last, I couldn't take the suspense anymore. I stepped out of the Jeep.

"Hello?" I called out as I approached his vehicle. I came around to the driver's side and saw that his arm was still hanging out of the window. Now, I could also see that his head was slumped over on his chest, as if he was asleep.

"Syd? Are you all right?" I tapped his arm, and when he still did not respond, I pulled open the door. Syd's body tumbled out of the truck, coming to rest on the pavement. That's when I noticed the handle of a knife protruding from the center of his blood-soaked sweater.

My heart was beating so hard it might have been broken free of my chest. I dropped to my knees and grabbed his wrist.

"Syd! Speak to me! Say something!"

But his skin was cool. I dropped his hand and scurried back. That's when I noticed the trail of blood leading all the way inside the garage and to a mess of tools that seemed to have been dumped in the center of the space. Then I noticed the overturned tool cabinet. There had been a struggle. He'd fought his attacker before being stabbed. And from there he had managed to drag himself all the way to his truck, only to collapse once he'd climbed in. A wave of sorrow for the man swept over me. I'd pegged him as one of the suspects for Swanson's murder, but now, it was clear he had nothing to do with it.

After what seemed like a long time, I snapped into action, grabbing my cell phone and punching in 9-1-1.

And for the second time in the space of just a few days, I reported a murder.

Chapter 18

Seeing me standing next to Syd's body, Lombard's face registered a flood of emotions—shock, disbelief, anger and finally disgust. She turned to her partner.

"You go talk to her. I'll bust an artery if I have to deal with that woman again." Then, instead of walking away, she came charging over. "I find it very strange that you just happen to be the one to find a second murder victim. Others may believe your innocent act, but I don't. Not for one minute." She strode away.

"Sorry about that," Officer Harrison said. "You look a bit pale. Are you feeling all right?"

I swallowed hard. I felt light-headed and nauseated, and frankly I would have gladly sat down. But all I said was, "I've been better."

"Do you need to sit down?" he asked. I nodded. "Follow me." He led the way to the front door, which now stood open.

"It wasn't even locked," Lombard said, stepping aside.

From the outside, Syd's house was lovely—a light stucco with stone trim—and considerably larger and more modern than Swanson's. And, now, stepping inside, I could see that the interior design was equally as attractive. Its charm, however, did not extend to the decor. The house was furnished with odds and ends—a chrome-and-glass coffee table, a light maple dining room table surrounded by inexpensive garden chairs, and in front of the large-screen television, a recliner that was ready for retirement in the local dump.

It looked like the worse kind of bachelor's lair. As we walked through to the table, I noticed a bookshelf with a couple of framed photos, but it was too far away to recognize any faces.

"Be careful not to touch anything," Officer Harrison said, indicating for me to sit. He pulled a chair across from me. "I'm sure you don't feel much like being questioned right now," he said, surprising me with his consideration. "I promise to get this over and done with as quickly as I can."

"I know the procedure," I said. "Unfortunately." He gave me a glimpse of smile, gone as quickly as it had appeared. But it had been there long enough for me to notice. Did that mean he did not view me as a suspect? I dared to hope.

"Tell you what," he said. "Why don't you tell me in your own words what happened here?"

"I couldn't sleep last night," I said. "I kept going over Swanson's murder, and the only two people I could imagine had a real motive for killing him was his wife, or Syd Shuttleworth. And now that Syd is dead . . ."

"You think it can only be Mona Swanson." I nodded. "And you're wondering if we considered her."

I looked at him sharply and glimpsed another quick smile. I chuckled. "I suppose I am."

"We are still investigating." That answer was so vague it told me nothing. "Explain to me why you're here."

"Yesterday, there was a picture of Mona Swanson on the front page of the *Belmont Daily*. She was standing next to a car that looked exactly like the one I saw speeding from city hall. Since I had to come into Belmont on business this morning, I thought I'd drive by and take a look at her car from up close. Well, it turns out that her car *is* the one I saw." I told him about the bumper sticker.

"You never mentioned that sticker when you first described it."

"I know. It came to me afterward."

"And it didn't occur to you to let us know?"

"I should have. I'm sorry."

"The problem is that now, after you've seen her car, one could argue that you made up the sticker story to incriminate her." I hadn't thought of that. "So why did you drive by this house after recognizing Mona's car?"

"It occurred to me that she may not have been the driver." A new thought occurred to me. "Do you think it's possible that Mona and Syd were in on it together?" I strung my thoughts together out loud. "She and Syd were involved before Swanson came along."

"You know I can't discuss the case with you."

"Yes, but there's something else. When I walked by Mona's car this morning, I put my hand on the hood and it was hot. Oh, my God," I said, shocked at the new thought that had just popped into my mind. "What if she and Syd were in on it together? Maybe she talked him into killing her husband and then she killed him. That way, nobody can testify against her." This seemed to register with him, and he pulled out his notebook and jotted something inside. As I glanced outside, I noticed the coroner stepping out of his car.

"At what time did you drive by Mona's house?"

"No more than five minutes before I got here."

Harrison was silent for a few moments. Then he shot to his feet, mumbling something about being right back.

I ran to the window to see where he was going. Just as I'd expected, he walked over to Lombard. They spoke for a few minutes. At one point she turned, spotted me in the window and threw me a dirty look. Whatever he was telling her, was not making her happy. He spoke a few more words and then made his way back to the house. I dashed back to the table, this time detouring by the bookshelf. Of the three photos, two were of a woman I was sure was Mona. I pointed this out to him as he sat down.

"You should take a look at those pictures, over there." He turned. "I believe the blonde in the photos is none other than Mona. Wouldn't most men take down pictures of a girlfriend after she's dumped him and married another man? Unless they're still involved, or, maybe he was still carrying a torch for her?"

He stared across the room. And when he turned back to me, there was respect in his eyes. "You're free to go," he said. "If I have any more questions I'll give you a call."

The questioning had taken the better part of an hour, leaving me emotionally drained. After the events of the morning, all I wanted was to hightail it back to the safety and security of my store.

"Where've you been?" Marnie asked as I walked in. Her face was red and she looked ready to blow a gasket. "I've been worried sick about you. It's almost eleven o'clock. At ten thirty, when I still hadn't heard a peep out of you, I went upstairs to see if you'd overslept. I rang and rang and all I got was Winnie scratching at the door."

"Oh, no. Poor Winnie. He's probably peed all over the apartment by now." I dashed out, taking the steps two at a time and unlocked the door. Winnie greeted me with sad eyes. "I'm sorry, pumpkin. I got busy." I gathered his food, one of his toys and took him for a short walk.

"Here you go, Winnie," I said, walking into the store. I set him on his cushion behind the cash register, and within two minutes he was already snoring.

Marnie glared at me. "You still haven't given me any explanation. If you hadn't walked in when you did, I would have called the police. I was afraid you might be dead."

"As you can see, I'm perfectly fine," I said. "But somebody else isn't."

The anger melted from her face. "What happened?"

"Syd Shuttleworth was murdered this morning. I just found his body."

"Oh, my Lord." She grabbed on to the counter as if to steady herself. "Do you think his death is tied to Swanson's murder?"

"I'm sure it is," I said. "And I think Mona Swanson is probably going to be arrested for both murders. She might not have killed her husband herself, but she sure as hell killed Syd Shuttleworth."

The bell above the door tinkled and Jenny appeared carrying a tray with coffee and muffins.

"I saw you come in and figured you probably hadn't had breakfast yet."

"You *are* a mind reader. I'm starving." I grabbed a mug and a lemon-poppy seed muffin.

"Syd Shuttleworth was murdered," Marnie told her.

Jenny's face fell. "What? When did this happen?"

"Della just found his body."

I told them about my appointment with the carpenter and how I'd driven by Mona Swanson's and then Syd Shuttleworth's homes. "She stabbed him in the chest."

"What makes you think she killed him?"

"It had to be her." I told her about stopping by Mona's house, recognizing the bumper sticker and then touching the hood of her car. "She and Syd must have conspired to kill her husband. And then she got rid of him." Both women were silent as they thought this over.

"She wouldn't have to share any of her inheritance with him," Jenny said.

"And he could never testify against her," Marnie added.

"That's exactly what I think," I said. "But it's all just conjecture at the moment. Don't you dare breathe a word about this to anyone," I said. "I don't want Mona Swanson to come after me now."

"Not a word," Jenny said. "I'd better get back before

Margaret has a nervous breakdown. It's pretty busy this morning. Want a coffee?"

"I could use a refill," I said.

"It's crazy busy already," she said. "Once the news of Syd's death gets out, it'll be a madhouse."

"I'd better eat something," Marnie said, helping herself to one of the muffins. "I'll need my energy. When Jenny's shop is busy, we get busy too."

Chapter 19

"By the way," Marnie said, after Jenny had left. "I made two sales this morning."

"That's good."

"But one of them I suppose doesn't really count. Judy Bates came by to pay for the merchandise she borrowed yesterday. So technically that sale was yesterday. She says it looks amazing in her living room. In fact, she said your blanket and cushions pulled the entire decor together."

"That's great. Let's hope the rest of the day brings more good sales."

In between reorganizing my window display and waiting on customers, I couldn't help but notice the number of people going into Coffee, Tea and Destiny as the morning turned into the afternoon, and I wondered how Jenny was able to seat everyone.

"Marnie, do you mind keeping an eye on the shop for a minute? I'll be right back." I crossed over to Jenny's shop and made my way between the café tables to the counter where Margaret was counting out a customer's change.

"And here are your cookies," she said, handing the woman a bag, and turned to me. "Hey, Della. What can I get you?"

"I'll have a coffee," I said, watching Jenny rush from

table to table. "And I'll take one for Marnie too. Things are really swinging over here. That's good."

"I know. Isn't it wonderful? Although, I doubt it'll be this busy once the mystery of the murders is solved." She leaned closer to whisper, "This is the meeting place for the Briar Hollow Gossip Society."

I laughed.

"There is no such club," she said, "but there might as well be." She pointed discreetly with her chin. "It's the same group of biddies who always get together whenever there's a tragedy to dissect."

"I take it the tragedy is Syd Shuttleworth's murder?"

She handed me a cup of coffee, looked around the room. "Everybody is wondering what the link between the two murders is."

"What's the consensus?"

"You wouldn't believe the theories. Swanson, it seems, was quite the lady's man. Some people seem to think his ex-wife might have killed him, and that Syd Shuttleworth was killed because he figured it out." She rolled her eyes. "That's pretty lame if you ask me. Then there's this theory: Syd killed Swanson for God knows what reason and Swanson's wife killed Syd in revenge. And, of course, there are those that think they were both killed by organized crime."

"But of course," I said, jokingly. "Why didn't I think of that?"

"If I hear anything more, I'll let you know."

I picked up the second coffee and left.

When I got back to my shop, Marnie was on the phone. "Here she is now," she said, and covered the mouthpiece. "It's Mrs. Renay."

"Oh, Della," she said. "It's just terrible. I heard there was a second murder. What is this world coming to?"

"It's upsetting, I know."

"And, of all people, *you* had to find the body. How

traumatic for you. You were just recovering from the first murder and then you had to stumble onto this one. How are you feeling?"

"A bit shaken up," I said. "But otherwise all right."

"Do the police have any idea who did it?"

"Not that I know of," I said, deciding on discretion.

"I still think Mona Swanson killed Howard," she whispered. "But I can't figure out why she would kill that contractor—unless . . ."

"Unless what?"

"Do you think maybe he found out she did it and she had to silence him?"

"That's one theory," I said. "But I got the feeling the police aren't taking that one too seriously."

I could hear the disbelief in her voice when she spoke again. "They think she's innocent? I hope they checked to see if she has an alibi."

"I would be shocked if they hadn't," I said.

"But," she said, "do you think it could be Ronald Dempsey? He had the opportunity. He was here when—" Suddenly there was another voice in the background. "Oops. I'd better go," she whispered into the phone. "I'll call you later."

I hung up, thinking about Ronald Dempsey. I looked at my watch. One o'clock. Still four hours till closing.

"Marnie," I called, heading toward the back. She was measuring a warp, wrapping yarn around the rack I'd had installed directly on the wall. "Are you starting a new project?"

"I thought I'd try my hand at Native-style weaving too," she said. "But since I don't have the right loom, I figured I could copy the design, using finer yarns, and maybe make some place mats to match the rugs and cushions."

"That's a great idea. And once you finish the first set, I'll give Judy a call. She might like to get some to continue with her decor theme."

"You were about to say something?"

"Yes. How would you like to go for a drive with me after work?"

Her eyes lit up. "Are we going to break into anybody's house?"

"That's not even funny," I said. I'd once done exactly that, and had almost been caught. The experience had been terrifying and I was in no hurry to repeat it. "I just want us to visit Ronald Dempsey's development, Prestige Homes."

"Sure," she said. "I've always wanted to see how the other half lives. Does that mean you're going to do some detecting?"

"I just want to see the place, and get an idea of the prices. Since Swanson was planning to buy in that development, knowing how much he was spending will help determine the scope of his little extortion game."

The phone rang and I returned to the counter. It was Matthew.

"I just heard there was another murder. I can't believe you didn't even call me."

"I didn't want to disturb you while you were writing."

"Sweetheart," he said in a tone that made my knees turn to jelly. "There are times when you should call. I've been worried sick since I found out."

"How did you find out?"

"The chief called. He wants me to come in to the station, so I can give him my opinion on some evidence they've got. He feels this latest murder might be linked to the city inspector's."

I could have told him that. But all I said was, "They want you to join the investigation?"

"No, nothing like that. He only wants to show me something, hear what I have to say about it. I was worried it would take away from my writing, but he promised it was a onetime thing."

"I wonder what he wants to show you."

"He wouldn't tell me on the phone." Being ex-FBI, I knew Matthew often missed the challenge of catching the bad guys. "I'm heading over now, so I won't be picking up Winston until later. I figure around seven or so. Want me to bring a pizza when I come over?"

"Sounds great," I said. "See you then."

Seven o'clock was perfect. It gave me time to check out Prestige Homes and be back before Matthew showed up. "Did you hear that, Winnie?" He opened his bleary eyes and stared up at me. "You're going investigating with me, big boy." The prospect did not seem to excite him in the least. He closed his eyes and went right back to sleep.

By the end of the afternoon, we'd sold a few more pieces, making for an excellent day. I counted the cash and checks, and slipped them into the overnight-deposit bag.

"Ready when you are," I called out to Marnie in the back. She hurried forward, slipping on her jacket.

"I was just waiting for you."

We locked up and climbed into my Jeep. "Come on, Winnie." He jumped in. After a quick stop at the bank, we headed for the highway with Winston riding shotgun on the console between the two front seats.

"Get back, Winnie," I said. "That's dangerous." He threw me a dirty look and resentfully hopped to the backseat.

"Where is this development?" Marnie asked.

"On the outskirts of the other side of Belmont. I looked it up on Google Maps."

"Tell me again why we're going there?"

"I'm just curious. If Mona was responsible for her husband and Syd's deaths, the only question I still have is how lucrative was Swanson's extortion business. And how much would she have to gain by offing her husband?"

"He could have been doing it for years," she said.

"And if he was, he could have been hiding a lot of money."

"And what better place to invest it than in a brand-new home?"

"I doubt he would have done that. Paying cash for a house would be a sure way to attract the attention of the IRS."

Twenty minutes later, Marnie and I pulled up in front of an imposing black iron gate. Above it in large letters read PRESTIGE HOMES, EIGHTY PERCENT SOLD.

"He built it as a gated community," she said. "That was smart of him. It adds another level of status to the place."

We drove through the entrance and followed the signs to the sales office, passing a dozen homes, each larger than the other.

"Now *that's* what I'd call a McMansion," she said, looking at a huge two-story home with two chimneys and an attached garage. "Can you imagine how long a place like that would take to clean?" She clucked her tongue. "I'm happy in my tiny little house."

"It's hard to believe there are enough people around here with the money to pay for such houses," I said.

"How do we know eighty percent are really sold?" she pointed out. "He could be posting those numbers just so it looks good."

I peeked at the windows of the houses we drove by. Cars were parked in the driveways, curtains in the windows, perfect landscaping. I even spotted a swing set in one of the backyards. "Most of them look like people are living there."

We followed the arrows marked SALES OFFICE until we got to a large white-stone house. We stepped out of the Jeep and took it all in. There must have been a dozen windows on the facade alone, every one of them with black shutters. The effect was almost overwhelmingly elegant.

"I think we'd better leave Winston in the car," she said. "They'd probably frown on bringing a dog into that fancy place."

"Good idea," I said.

We made our way to a tall black wrought-iron door.

"Well," Marnie said as we climbed the steps. "So far, I gotta admit I'm impressed."

So was I. Everything in this development screamed expensive. "From what I've seen so far, it looks as though Dempsey spared no expense." I'd secretly harbored a suspicion that Dempsey might have also been extorted. If he'd been cutting corners on his project, Swanson could have milked him for a bundle. So much for that theory.

We stepped inside to a magnificent foyer that opened onto a second-floor mezzanine. I looked down to a brown marble floor edged with a narrow trim of black marble. Farther in, I caught a glimpse of a ballroom-sized living area with plush white sofas and mirrored furniture.

"Wow," Marnie whispered.

From an area right of the living room, came the sound of voices. We headed in that direction, and as we rounded the corner, a young woman came forward.

"Hello," she said. "Welcome to Prestige Homes. My name is Karen. Is this your first visit to our community?"

Marnie nodded, looking tongue-tied.

"It is," I said.

"Are you looking to buy in the near future?" she asked.

"My fiancé and I are getting married in the fall," I said, deciding to play the role of a prospective buyer. "I'm just starting to look. I wanted to get an idea of what's available in the area."

"That's very wise of you," she said. "Why don't I start by telling you about this development?"

She guided us to the dining room, where the long elegant table was being used as a desk. Behind it was a man dressed in a business suit—another sales person no doubt. I looked around the walls covered with floor plans. On an easel was a map of the development, with dozens of tiny squares. Each represented a house. I noticed that most of them had a small round sticker.

"What do those dots mean?" Marnie asked.

"The red ones are properties that are already sold. The blue ones are reserved by clients, pending financing."

"You don't have very many left," I said.

"That's true, but phase two is scheduled to begin this summer, with the first properties due to be finished by Christmas. The timing might be perfect for you. Would you like to look at the floor plans? We have three bedrooms, four bedrooms and five bedrooms."

"Maybe I can take some brochures home, so I can show them to my fiancé," I said.

"Certainly."

"A friend of my family was buying in this project. Unfortunately he just passed away."

She frowned. "Who was that?"

"Howard Swanson."

"Yes, I heard about that. Such a tragedy. I feel awful for his poor wife."

"It's very sad," I said. "What's going to happen to that house? He told us all about it. It sounded wonderful. I was wondering if it's going to go back on the market."

"I have no idea. Until we get instructions from his widow, we can't do anything."

She picked up a stack of glossy brochures, and after going through them for a few minutes, selected one. "This is the model Mr. Swanson was buying." She handed it to me.

My eyes went straight to the price. "Wow. I never imagined he was buying such an expensive house."

"Well, he got a very special price," she said. "He and

the builder were very good friends. Also he was the first person to buy."

I could tell, from the information she had just revealed, that she loved to gossip. I leaned in. "How much did he pay?"

"I'm sorry. I'm not allowed to give out that sort of information," she said, looking chagrined. I knew that she'd spill the beans at the slightest encouragement.

"But now that he's deceased, doesn't that change things?"

She looked thoughtful for a half second. "You're right. But you have to promise not to tell a soul I told you. He got it for half the asking price."

"Half?!" I asked, stunned. I'd expected it to be no more than ten, maybe fifteen percent. "Wow! I wish I could get that kind of a deal."

"I know. I can't figure it out." She gave me the remainder of the brochures and changed the subject. "If you decide to purchase from phase two, there are discounts to be had, but they get smaller as we get closer to the delivery date."

"I'll keep that in mind. Could you do me a favor and let me know what Mrs. Swanson decides to do about the house? Maybe she won't want it anymore."

"I'll be happy to," she said. "But if it does go back for sale, it will be at its regular price."

Instinct took over, and rather than write my name I gave her Jenny's, but added my own home number. We thanked her and returned to my Jeep where Winston greeted us like long lost family. "Yes, yes," I said between wet doggie kisses. "I love you too."

Before taking off, we flipped through all the brochures. There wasn't one under a million dollars. And the one that Swanson was buying was just under one million five.

"He was going to pay over seven hundred thousand

for it. No matter how great a discount he got, that's still a lot of money," Marnie said as we took off.

"It answers one question," I said. "Instead of extorting money from Dempsey, I suspect he got his payoff in the form of that discount. Either that, or he paid the first half in cash."

"That would be one way of laundering dirty money."

Marnie was right. But as I started the drive back, another idea was taking shape in my mind. Now that Dempsey was about to begin a second phase to his project, it would have been just like Swanson to demand a second payment. That could explain the fifty percent discount. If I was a builder and somebody blackmailed me into giving him a seven-hundred-and-fifty-thousand-dollar price reduction, I'd be mad as hell. That gave Dempsey one heck of a motive for murder.

The thought had just flashed through my mind when I stopped myself. I already knew who the killer, or killers, were . . . or did I?

Chapter 20

I hadn't been back more than five minutes when the bell rang. I buzzed Matthew up and greeted him with a glass of wine, while Winston all but did somersaults for his attention.

"Down boy," he ordered, and Winnie sulked away.

"Where's the pizza?" I asked.

He slapped a hand to his forehead. "Oh, I completely forgot. I'll call and have it delivered. It won't take long."

"That's okay. I can make pasta if you'd rather. It will be ready in fifteen minutes." But he had already dialed and was placing the order.

"Double cheese," he said and gave them the address. He turned off his phone. And that's when I noticed the tenseness around his mouth.

"Something's wrong. What is it?" He took the glass from my hand and drank a long swallow, then without a word, headed for the living room and let himself fall back into the sofa, wearing a grim expression. I sat across from him.

"Matthew, you're scaring me. Tell me what's going on. Is it about the case? Did somebody else get killed?"

He shook his head. "Nothing like that. The chief called me to come down to the station because they found traces of blood on your shirt and on your running shoes."

"What!"

"He only contacted me out of courtesy. It's come to his attention that you and I are in a relationship and because he respects me for all the help I've brought the department over the years, he wanted to let me know so that I could talk with you myself."

"Talk about what?"

"Turning in the clothes you were wearing when you found Syd's body yourself—to spare you the distress of having your apartment searched again."

"Oh, my God. They're building a case against me," I said, jumping to my feet, tears threateningly close to flowing. "I don't know how they could have found blood. I never even went close to the man. Please tell me you believe me."

"Of course I do," he said, and I almost wept in relief. "And that's exactly what I told them—that I've known you my entire life and that there is no way you could have killed someone." He steepled his fingers under his chin and leaned forward deep in thought. "Come to think of it," he said at last, his expression relaxing slightly. "All he said was 'traces of blood.' He never once mentioned DNA. That blood could have been anybody's."

I sat back down, trying to remember. "I suppose I could have stepped in some of Swanson's blood. That could explain the running shoes. Did he mention whether the blood was on the sole or on the top?"

"Good question. I must have been really out of it to not even ask that."

"As for the shirt, I have no idea how I could have gotten blood on it."

"You used to get nosebleeds when you were younger," he said.

"I haven't had one in years. But I have been known to cut myself cooking."

He laughed, the last of his stress seemingly gone. "That I can believe. You in the kitchen with a knife can

be a dangerous situation. It's a good thing I don't love
you for your cooking."

I gasped. This was the first time he'd used the "L"
word, as my mother called it. But it hadn't sounded like
a declaration of love. The way he'd said it, the word love
could just as well have been replaced with "like."

"But," he continued, "I suggest you gather the items
you were wearing this morning when you discovered
Syd's body and we'll drop them off after we eat."

He got off the sofa, pulling out his cell phone and punching in a number. "Put me through to the chief," he said,
walking out of the living room. At that moment the bell
rang and my heart went into a gallop. Was that the police,
come to arrest me? I went to the foyer and pressed the intercom button.

"Pizza," a voice called from downstairs. I pressed the
door buzzer and scurried for my purse, catching the end
of Matthew's conversation.

"We'll be by to drop them off in an hour or so." He
dropped the cell in his pocket. "I'll get the pizza," he said
and hurried to the door.

Soon, we were at the kitchen table. I still felt like hell,
but was able to get a few bites down. But I had another
worry. "You don't think they could have planted that
blood, do you?"

"No."

I should have felt better, but I couldn't get the image
of Lombard's angry eyes out of my mind. It only made
me more determined to find the killer myself.

"Sweetheart," he said. "Stop worrying and eat."

I made a halfhearted attempt to eat, but after a few
bites, I gave up.

"I don't understand what's going on. Mona had the best
motive to kill him. Why are they even looking at me?"

"They're just following the evidence. They found
blood and they have to test it. And they'd be remiss in

their duties if they didn't also test the clothes you were wearing when you found your contractor's body."

"The whole thing is just silly."

"Think of it this way. They have to cross you off as a potential suspect, if only to tighten the evidence against the real killer."

I thought this over. "Okay. I understand."

After clearing away the dishes, I gathered the pants, shirt and jacket I'd been wearing earlier and stuffed them into a bag. Then I took off my shoes. "I hope they don't keep these forever. I like them. I wear them all the time."

"Providing they don't find anything on them, I'm sure they'll return them as soon as they're done."

We climbed into Matthew's antique Singer Roadster. As a car hobbyist, this was the oldest one he'd ever owned or worked on.

We got on the highway to Belmont, the silence stretching until it felt like lead. He glanced at me and, as if reading my mind, he reached across the gear shift and gave my hand a light squeeze. "Don't worry. Everything will be fine."

At the station, I stopped at the front desk, turned in my clothes and signed a number of forms. And then we headed back to Briar Hollow.

"Are you going to be all right by yourself?" he asked. I wasn't sure if that was his way of asking if he could stay over, but I felt like being by myself. I was planning on a good sulk and long bath.

"I'll be fine."

He walked me to the door, took me in his arms and told me one more time not to worry. Then he picked up Winnie and left.

By five o'clock the next morning, I was already in my weaving studio. I studied the Native-style weaving Marnie had started. It was gorgeous. I was almost tempted to pick up her shuttle and do a few lines myself, but I knew that was a bad idea. Weaver's tend to work at slightly different tensions. I could always tell when more than one person had worked on a project.

I left that loom and settled at mine to continue my own project. This rug would be the fifth I'd made. And with each one, I was becoming better. I checked the bobbin—still full—and got to work.

Before I knew it, it was light outside. I had been so deep in my concentration that I hadn't noticed time going by. At that moment, there was a knock on the door.

"I saw your light on, so I figured you were already here. You're in early today. How come?"

"Insomnia," I said. "The police found blood on the shirt I was wearing the day Swanson was killed. And they asked for the clothes I was wearing when I found Syd's body." Just talking about it, brought a lump to my throat.

Jenny studied me in silence for a moment. "Let me get you a cup of tea."

"Make that a coffee," I said as she walked out. A few minutes later she was back. I looked at the cup she handed me. "You know I don't drink tea."

"This time you will," she said. "I want to read your tea leaves."

I was not in the mood for this kind of nonsense, but I couldn't say that without wounding her feelings, so I drank the cup, turned it upside down in the saucer as she instructed, and then turned it three times while asking my secret question. *Will I be arrested for murder?*

Jenny took the cup and stared inside. To me it looked like nothing more than a few clumps of wet tea leaves.

"I see a dagger near the rim," she said, showing me. "The closer it is to the rim, the nearer in the future this event will happen. I think this is imminent. Do you see it?"

Looking at the spot she was pointing to, I had to admit that the shape of the leaves did look a bit like a dagger. "I guess so."

"And see, over here there's a snake. This one is a bit lower. I'd say in a few days or so."

"A dagger and a snake. Neither of those sound very good."

"Actually, the dagger is a good omen. It represents a favor from a friend. As for the snake, that represents an enemy, but also wisdom. And down here I see a banana. Any fruit indicates prosperity." She put the cup down, and gave me a cheerful smile. "I didn't see anything terrible."

"What about the enemy? That sounds ominous," I said, even though I didn't believe in this stuff.

"That's the good thing about having your fortune told," Jenny said. "It can act as a warning. Now that you're aware, you'll keep your eyes open. And chances are you'll thwart whatever malicious intent an enemy may have."

"Thank you," I said. "That was nice of you to do that."

She chuckled. "I know you don't believe a word I just told you. But I bet the reading will stay with you, and because of it you'll be on your guard. So whether you admit it or not, the reading will have helped." She went to the door. "Now I'll get you that coffee you asked for."

She was right about the reading staying with me, because even after she left, I found myself wondering if that enemy was Officer Lombard.

I was halfway through the article in the *Belmont Daily* about Syd Shuttleworth's murder, when Marnie showed up.

"I just dropped off Jenny's order for the day." She set a basket of apple turnovers and a fresh cup of coffee on the counter. "Thought you'd welcome one of these." Marnie's turnovers were the best, and I hadn't had one in months.

"Delicious," I said, taking a bite.

"Jenny told me about how they found blood on your clothes."

"There's not much I can do about it but wait for the DNA report to exonerate me."

"How long is that going to take?"

I shrugged. "Your guess is as good as mine." As I said this, the door swung open and Matthew walked in followed by Winston.

"Morning, sweetheart," he said. "Marnie."

"Don't mind me; I'm going straight to the studio," she said, scurrying away.

I rolled my eyes. "I think she might be happier than both our mothers combined that you and I are dating."

He came close and gathered me in his arms. "Not happier than I am—that's for sure." He always said the sweetest thing.

"Speaking of mothers, did you get that parcel she sent you?"

"Yes . . . er . . . It wasn't anything important."

I frowned. He was hiding something. I could tell. "What was it?"

"I'll show you some other time." And then he changed the subject. "I was thinking about it last night, and a possibility occurred to me. Do you remember if anybody at the scene of Swanson's murder touched you that day?"

"You think somebody might have transferred blood to my clothes?"

"It's a possibility."

I closed my eyes, trying to picture the events. "Tom Goodall, he's one of the city employees, I bumped into him as I ran through the main room." I shook my head. "But he was wearing a white shirt. I would have noticed if he had blood on it." I thought more. "Ronald Dempsey was wearing a dark sweater, but I don't remember him coming anywhere near me. Though, Dempsey went and got me a glass of water and he handed it to me. He got pretty close then." I stopped. "Does this mean the police have eliminated Mona as a suspect?"

"All I know is they haven't arrested her."

"They must know something we don't," I said.

"Anybody else come close to you that morning?"

I blanched. "Uh-oh."

"What is it?"

"Officer Lombard," I said. "She asked me to go to Swanson's office with her, and at one point she bent down to look at the body and then she came to stand right next to me. She could definitely have touched me without my noticing." I looked at him. "You don't think—"

"No, of course not." And then he paused. "Well, at least not on purpose," he added. "But that gives me an idea. I left my cell at home. Can I use your phone?"

"Of course." I handed it over and he punched in a number.

"This is Matthew Baker. Please put me through to the chief." A moment went by. "Chief, Matthew here. Something just occurred to me. I know you haven't got the DNA results on Della's clothes yet, but, as I told you, I know her. There is no way she killed anybody. But if the blood turns out to be the victim's, which I very much doubt, it might have gotten there when somebody at the scene touched her. I think you should get the clothes that everybody at the scene was wearing," he paused and then added, "including the police officers."

Even standing four feet away, I could hear every word the chief was screaming. "Are you implying that one of my officers—"

Matthew cut him off. "I'm not suggesting anything of the sort. What I'm saying is that sometimes these things can happen by accident. Besides, think about it. If you're going to arrest somebody you want to make damn sure you've dotted all of your I's and crossed all your T's. I'm only bringing up something a lawyer might." They talked for another few seconds and then hung up.

"What was that about arresting someone? Did you just tell him how to make the case against me airtight?"

"Of course not. All I did was point out the flaws in his reasoning. If he was to charge anyone with murder, any defense attorney could shoot holes the size of cannonballs through his case."

"I forgot to ask you yesterday. What about motive? Why do they think I would have wanted to kill Swanson any more than anyone else?"

He sighed. "They seem to think that Swanson refused to give your store a permit, and when you went to his office, the discussion turned into an argument and in the heat of the moment you lost control and hit him over the head with a bookend." He looked at his watch. "I'd better get going. See you later."

I plastered on a smile and gave him a quick kiss. As soon as he left, Marnie came forward.

"Did I just hear right? The police are looking at you as a suspect?"

I nodded and fought the sudden surge of tears.

"Take this," Marnie said, handing me a tissue. "All I can say is they must be pretty desperate if they're considering you. I think you and I are going to have to solve this case for them, if we want to keep you out of jail."

Those were my thoughts exactly. I snatched the landline and scrolled through my in calls until I found the city hall number and pressed REDIAL.

"Well, hello, Della," Johanna said. "What can I do for you?"

"I have a problem, Johanna, and I hope you can help."

"Sure, whatever I can do."

"The police found blood on the shirt and the shoes I was wearing the day I found Swanson's body. And I was wondering whether Ronald Dempsey might have touched me that morning. Do you remember?"

"You think Ronald . . . Oh, my. Let me see. I remember the blouse you were wearing. It was pretty paisley with lots of colors. No wonder nobody noticed if there was blood on it." She was silent for a few seconds. And then, "I think I do remember him coming close to you. He got you a glass of water and he came right up to you when you took it. But whether he touched you? I don't know. He might have."

"Thanks, Johanna. You've been a great help." I hung up. Marnie was looking at me worriedly.

"So, did he or didn't he?"

"She doesn't remember him touching me, but he got close enough that he might have."

"Hold on. I think, no matter how upset I was, I'd remember if a man touched my blouse."

"I guess it depends on where the blood was found. If it was a chest level, he'd have gotten a slap in the face." I picked up the phone again. This time I dialed Matthew's number.

"I was just wondering something," I said. "Did the police happen to tell you where on my blouse they found the blood?"

"It was on your left sleeve," he said. I gave Marnie a thumbs-up signal. "Why do you ask?" he continued.

"Because, if it had been on the front, I would have noticed."

"Good point. And since it was on your left sleeve, it could have been transferred there by somebody's right hand when they were facing you."

I smiled into the phone. "That's exactly what I was thinking. And that's the kind of everyday gesture that nobody would notice." We said good-bye and hung up.

"Okay, so now we know that the blood could have been transferred there by a third party," Marnie said.

"And you suspect it was that Dempsey fellow. So I have a question. Does that mean Mona Swanson has been cleared by the police?"

I shrugged. "Your guess is as good as mine."

"Do we start looking for other suspects in case?"

"I think I'd be crazy not to." I thought for a second. "If the killer is Dempsey, I wonder if I could get him to admit it."

"And pray tell, dear, how in the world would you do that?"

Chapter 21

My plan was simple. I would confront Dempsey at his home and record our conversation on my cell. And then I'd do what all good poker players do. I'd bluff.

Now that I had decided, I could barely wait for the day to end. Marnie, of course, was finding flaw after flaw with my plan.

"Five minutes ago you were sure Mona was the killer. Now, all of a sudden you think it's Dempsey."

"I told the police about the bumper sticker on Mona's car. I told them her motor was still hot, five minutes before I found Syd's body. If they still think I'm a suspect, they must have eliminated her."

"Or they simply don't believe anything you tell them."

I sighed. "Maybe you're right. Maybe Dempsey had nothing to do with either murder, but what else am I supposed to do? Sit and wait for them to arrest me? There's nothing wrong with checking out Dempsey. I sure as hell know *I* didn't kill anyone, and if the police don't think Mona is the killer, then the next best suspect is him. If someone was blackmailing me into giving him a fifty percent discount on a one-point-five-million-dollar house, I think I'd like him gone—not that I'd kill anyone, but seven hundred and fifty thousand dollars is more than enough for a lot of people to commit murder for."

"I suppose. And who knows how much he would have

wanted if there'd been a phase three. But I can't believe you're even considering going to his home and confronting him. That's the kind of plan that could get you killed. And if you're right, and he's already killed two people, what makes you think he won't kill a third time?"

"That's where you come in. I'll leave my cell phone on with you at the other end. You'll be waiting in the car. You'll hear every word he and I say. If at any point you think I'm in danger, start honking the horn like crazy and call the police."

"Good plan, Einstein, except, I don't have a cell phone."

"Ask Jenny if you can borrow hers. She'll say yes."

She groaned. "What makes you think he'd admit it? Ronald Dempsey didn't become so successful by being a stupid man. He'll never say the words, 'I killed him.' And that's what you need if you want a confession that sticks."

"It doesn't matter. This tape could never be used against him in court."

"So why are you doing this?"

"For the police. If they hear it, they'll know I'm innocent and leave me alone."

"I'm not so sure about that," she grumbled.

"Will you come with me?"

Before she could answer, the door swung open and Judy Bates walked in, and a second later Jenny appeared carrying a tray with coffee and muffins.

"Yum, that looks good," Judy said as Jenny set the tray on the counter. "Wish I could join you, but I'm just dropping by to let you know that the *Belmont Daily* is doing a style page featuring my home. Isn't that exciting? They're sending a photographer over in a couple of days and he'll be taking pictures of my living room. The reporter fell in love with your pieces. I told her you made them and made her promise to mention you in her article."

"You did that?" I asked. "I don't know what to say. Thank you so very much. That'll be a huge coup for me."

"That was so thoughtful of you," Jenny said.

"Think nothing of it," Judy said. "It's so nice to have somebody offering the kind of quality home goods that you do, it's my pleasure to do whatever I can to help spread the word."

I was overwhelmed. Marnie stepped closer. "I'm working on place mats to add to the collection," she said. "Would you like to see?"

"Absolutely," Judy replied, and followed her to the back.

"See?" Jenny whispered. "I told you that a friend would do you a good turn. That was the dagger in your cup." She gave me a satisfied little smile and left. A moment later Marnie and Judy returned.

"Please reserve the first four you finish for me. Is there any chance I could get them before the photographer comes?"

Marnie thought for a moment. "I can definitely promise you two or three by then. I'll try for all four, but it might be tight."

"I'll take whatever you have."

"Let me give you a discount," I said. "You've been so kind to tell the reporter about my work."

"I won't hear of it," she said. "Call me the minute they're done."

She walked out, leaving me overcome with guilt. "I can't believe how nice she is," I said.

"I'm surprised you're not considering her a suspect too."

"What's that supposed to mean?"

"I'm just saying. One minute it's Syd, then Mona, then it's Dempsey."

"For your information, I still think Mona is guilty. But I'm just covering all my bases. Especially since the police don't seem to suspect her of anything. I must be missing something that they know already."

"You may be right about Mona. Whenever I watch those televised true crime dramas, the killer is always somebody close to the victims."

I nodded. "That's been my observation too. If the killer isn't the spouse, then it's somebody else close—a lover, a sibling, a child. I still think Mona Swanson is the one person with the most to gain through both deaths." I stopped as a new idea came to me. "You know who I never considered? Swanson's *ex*-wife. I wonder what happened to her after they divorced."

Marnie rolled her eyes. "Good grief. Next you'll be suspecting me."

I ignored that. Sometimes Marnie just liked to get my goat. I opened my laptop and typed in Sondra Swanson in the online Belmont phone book. Nothing. I typed it again, this time in Briar Hollow. Still nothing. "I know who could tell me—Johanna," I said, already grabbing the telephone.

"Me again," I said. "I just have one quick question. Do you know what happened to Swanson's first wife after they divorced?"

"You mean Sondra?" She paused. "You think she might have killed him?"

"All I know at this point is that *I'm* innocent. So I'm looking at every possible suspect. And, generally speaking, most murders are committed by spouses or lovers."

"Hmm. I never thought of that. But you might be right. Sondra was very upset when Howard left her. She had a fit in his office, accusing him of being a two-timer. And she happened to be right about that. He *was* having an affair."

"With Mona?"

"Why, yes, dear. Who else could it be?" she said.

"Would you happen to know where his ex-wife lives now?"

"Last I heard, she moved away from Belmont. But don't ask me where. I have no idea."

"Oh. That's too bad," I said. "Thanks anyway. If you happen to think of anyone who might know, give me a call."

"What are you going to do? Try to find her?"

"Possibly. But it won't be easy without at least a general idea. I might check out Charlotte. Most people around here have relatives living there."

"I'd remember if she'd moved to Charlotte. I'm sure she said it was somewhere else, but I can't, for the life of me, remember where. I remember she had some sort of breakdown after the divorce. She wouldn't leave her house and wouldn't even pick up her phone. I wouldn't be surprised if she didn't even bother getting connected in her new place."

"It sounds like the divorce devastated her."

"It did. She sort of lost her mind for a while. I hope she's better now, poor thing."

I thanked her, said good-bye and hung up. I returned to my laptop and typed in a search for the entire state of North Carolina. Dozens of listings with the name Swanson popped up, but none had the first name Sondra, nor even the initial S.

"Maybe she reverted to her maiden name," Marnie said. "I bet Johanna'll know."

"I just called her two minutes ago. I hate to be a pest. I'll give her a call tomorrow."

"Unless you get a confession from Dempsey before then," she said with a teasing lilt to her voice.

"Go ahead. Laugh all you want. I just want to make sure I look at all the possibilities."

At four thirty Matthew called. "I just found out I have to drive into Charlotte to meet with my agent. Would you mind keeping Winston overnight?"

"Of course not. You know I love having him over. Besides, I always feel safer with Winnie around."

"I wish I could stay with you and make you feel safe," he said in a teasing voice. And then, "What's making you nervous?"

"Maybe I'm just being silly. I felt uncomfortable on my own after finding Swanson's body. But now, after a second murder, I'm really spooked."

"You're not being silly. I worry about you too. That's why I keep telling you to be careful," he said. "By the way. I have some good news for you. The blood on your clothes was not human. It was from a dog."

All at once I remembered. Winston had scraped his paw and I'd washed it and dressed it. I must have gotten blood on my clothes at the same time. My heart skipped a beat. "Does that mean they don't consider me a suspect anymore?"

"I wouldn't go that far, but it sure didn't hurt." He paused. "Listen, I have to get going."

"Before you do, I just remembered I'm out of dog food," I said. "Would you mind if I dropped by to pick some up when I take him for his walk?"

"Sure. I might already be gone by then. Just make sure to lock it when you leave."

"No problem. And thanks."

I turned to Marnie after hanging up. "We're good to go, and Winston is coming too."

I calculated my daily sales—which were more than twice the usual amount—and prepared the deposit. Marnie had borrowed Jenny's cell phone. I had mine in my pocket and it was equipped with a recording app.

"We're as ready as we'll ever be," I said as we locked up.

"Let's use my car," Marnie said. "It'll be less noticeable." We climbed into her small Honda with Winston in the back. "By the way," she added once I'd dropped off my daily deposit, "I don't know how to use Jenny's cell phone. What if I have to call the police?"

"Give it to me," I said. I punched in 9-1-1 and handed

it back. "All you have to do is press the little green telephone. Think you can handle that?"

"My, but we sure are touchy, aren't we?"

"Sorry. I guess I'm a bit nervous. I shouldn't be taking it out on you."

"Don't worry about it. I've known you long enough to know that you get snippy when you're nervous. All that tells me is that maybe you're not so sure this is a good idea, and that maybe it's not too late for me to change your mind."

"I'm not turning back," I said, hoping I wasn't making a huge mistake.

After about twenty minutes of driving up and down the street, we finally located Dempsey's house. It was set back from the road, and was so well hidden, most people would never guess there was anything there but a small wooded area.

"This doesn't make me feel much better," Marnie said. "He could have you killed and buried before anybody finds the house."

"Now you're letting your imagination run wild. Just keep that phone glued to your ear."

She pressed it to her ear.

"Can you hear me?" I asked, speaking into my own phone.

"Loud and clear, both on the phone and in person."

"Good." I climbed out. "Wish me luck."

"Break a leg," she said.

I followed the path until the house came into view. It was large and modern—lots of glass and dark tile.

"Can you hear me, Marnie?"

"Sure can."

"Okay, ready or not, here I come." I pressed the RE-CORD button, dropped my cell into my jacket pocket and rang the doorbell. My heart was beating so loudly I wondered if Marnie could hear it from her phone.

I pressed the bell twice and had just turned to walk away when the door suddenly flew open and I found myself face-to-face with Ronald Dempsey. He looked at me blankly for a moment, and then recognition flashed in his eyes.

"I know you," he said. "You're that girl who found Swanson."

"Della," I said.

"What can I do for you, Della?"

"I have some news you might be interested in," I said.

He frowned. "Really?" he asked, and stepped aside. "Come in." He closed the door behind me. I heard him turn the dead bolt and my knees almost gave out.

"I'm only going to be here for a moment. You don't have to lock the door."

"Force of habit," he said, but I couldn't help noticing that he didn't unlock it.

Please be listening, Marnie.

"So what is it you wanted to tell me?"

I took a deep breath. "I know what you did," I said, trying to keep my knees from shaking.

His eyebrows jumped up. "What did I do?"

"Swanson was blackmailing you. You had to sell him a house for hundreds of thousands less than the listed price. You might have been able to swallow that, except now, with the second phase of your project ready to start, he wanted more. You knew he was going to be a problem that would never go away." The blood had drained from his face. I had hit a nerve, and I knew it. "And that's why you killed him."

Dempsey stood frozen in shock. Then, I watched the fear in his eyes turned into something else—rage.

"You have a lot of nerve barging in here and accusing me of murder."

"I'm not through," I said. "You thought you were being so smart, telling the police you saw me wiping blood from my clothes. You were trying to throw suspicion on me, but that backfired. That's why I first began to suspect you. I figured the only reason you would do that was if you were guilty."

"So, you're the reason the police showed up wanting my clothes earlier," he said, his eyes narrowing. "Let me make myself perfectly clear. If you think you're going to pick up where Swanson left off, you have another surprise coming." He suddenly took a step toward me.

He's going to strangle me. I yelped and ducked.

A moment later I felt foolish. All he'd done was walk around me to unlock the door.

"Don't forget what happened to Swanson. The same thing can happen to you," he said as I walked out on gelatin legs.

"Are you all right?" Marnie asked as soon as I got in. "I heard you yell as if you were being choked, and I tried to do what you said—push the green phone. But it wouldn't get off the line."

I stared at her. "You were supposed to hang up before you push the green phone."

"Oh," she said, looking puzzled. "How do I do that?"

"You push the red phone, right next to the green phone," I said, in disbelief. "I came *this* close to being murdered, all the time imagining you were my lifeline."

I started to laugh, and kept laughing until I cried.

Chapter 22

Marnie pulled to a stop in front of my shop, still smarting over my hysterical laughter. "I still don't get what was so funny about my not knowing how to use a cell phone."

"I'm sorry, Marnie. I didn't mean to offend you. It was just my nerves."

She mumbled something indistinct while Winston and I hopped out, and then drove off before I could say good-bye. Sometimes she got a bit irritable.

Winston followed me to my apartment. After I finished feeding him and was microwaving some leftover pizza—typical lazy evening at home—the phone rang. I glanced at the call display, expecting it to be my mother, but it was a blocked number. I picked it up.

An unrecognizable voice screamed into my ear. "Listen, bitch. You keep going around asking questions and you'll be dead just like the others."

I dropped the phone, shaking. Almost as if he could sense that I was upset, Winston came trotting over, looking at me with big mournful eyes. But I couldn't move. Hell, I could hardly breathe. The microwave beeped, stirring me out of my stupor, and I dashed to the front door, checking that it was safely locked. I raced back to the kitchen and punched in Marnie's number.

"What is it? Find some other great joke at my expense?" she said.

"Oh, Marnie. Somebody just called and threatened to kill me."

There was a quick intake of breath. "Did you call the police?"

"What's the point? They'd only tell me it's some kid's prank, and that I should keep my door locked just to be on the safe side."

"Are you at home? By yourself? Hold tight. I'll be right there." Less than fifteen minutes later, she was at my door, carrying a bag of frozen food.

"I was just about to heat up some chicken divan, so I grabbed a second portion for you. And I added a couple of mini chocolate cakes."

"That sure beats the leftover pizza I was going to have."

"Leftover . . . what?" She marched down the hall to the kitchen and opened the microwave. "Good grief. Were you really going to eat this? It's as dry as cardboard." She threw it in the garbage can under the sink. "All right. First things first. What we both need is a glass of wine." She opened a bottle of white and poured two generous glasses. After a few swallows, she put her glass down. "Now, did you recognize the voice?"

I shook my head. "It was disguised. I couldn't even be sure it was a man or a woman. And the number was blocked."

She knitted her brows. "Don't you think it's strange that you should get that call no more than an hour after confronting Dempsey?"

"Somebody is getting scared," I said. "That tells me I'm getting close. If he thinks he can scare me off, then he doesn't know me very well."

"He? So you *do* think it's Dempsey."

I thought about it for a moment. "I suppose it could be Mona Swanson. But how would she know I've been investigating? I'm with you. It is pretty suspicious that I got that call so soon after leaving his place." I snapped my fingers. "Speaking of which, I have that recording." I dashed to the foyer, snatching my jacket from the wall hook and breathed a sigh of relief. My cell was in my pocket exactly where I'd left it. I returned to the kitchen, brandishing it.

"Here it is. Wait till the police hear this."

While Marnie popped the chicken into the oven, I set it on the table and pushed the PLAY button. After a few minutes of intermittent silence and squeaks, came a muffled voice. It was me, but I could barely make out what I was saying. The voice changed to that of a man, but it was even more muffled.

"There's no way anyone will understand a word he says."

"Even if they did," Marnie said. "He didn't confess. So it's of no use, anyways."

"Maybe not directly, but he said something like, if I thought I could just pick up where Swanson left off, I had another think coming. And then he added that what happened to Swanson could happen to me. If that's not a direct threat, I don't know what is."

Before Marnie could reply, the telephone rang. We both froze. And then I sprang into action, snatching the phone.

"It's him," I said, seeing the name Prestige Homes on the call display. I grabbed my cell and turned on the recording app, holding it against the phone. But, to my surprise it wasn't Ronald Dempsey voice, but a woman's.

"May I speak to Jenny please?" she asked. I was about to tell her she had the wrong number when I remembered that was how I'd identified myself to the saleslady when we'd gone snooping at the development.

"This is Jenny," I said, garnering a confused look from Marnie.

"This is Karen, from Prestige Homes. When you came by the other day, you asked that I let you know Mona

Swanson's decision regarding the house she and her husband bought. If you had your heart set on that one, I'm afraid I have disappointing news for you. She's decided to move in."

"Oh," I said, surprised. "I thought, after what happened, that it might be a bit too expensive for her."

"It might have been, except that her husband had mortgage insurance."

"Really?" I said, storing that information along with all the rest of Mona Swanson's possible motives.

"Perhaps I could make an appointment for you and your fiancé to come in together?"

"Let me speak to him and I'll call you back." After a hurried good-bye, I turned to Marnie.

"You won't believe this. Mona Swanson is going ahead and moving into the house."

"All by herself in that great big honkin' house?"

"Maybe her original plan had been to move in with somebody else," I said, quirking an eyebrow. "Even if Dempsey did kill those men, I'm convinced she was planning on getting rid of her husband somehow. And listen to this: Swanson had taken out mortgage insurance."

She frowned. "What's that?"

"If the person who borrowed the money dies, the insurance covers the unpaid portion of the mortgage."

"So she gets the house free and clear?"

"A one-point-five-million-dollar home—all hers. Plus whatever else he left her—he probably had life insurance through his work, a pension plan—as his widow all of that would now go to her. He might have an IRA too. Then, there's the house she's living in now. All in all, Mona is probably laughing all the way to the bank."

"No wonder she's your number one suspect."

Another thought stirred. "What if she didn't kill Swanson herself? Maybe she hired someone to kill her husband? And what if that somebody was Syd? Let's not

forget that they were a couple before she got married."
Now the ideas were flowing. "Wouldn't you think that
most people would get rid of an ex's pictures? Or at least
put them away? Well, Syd didn't. There were pictures of
her all over his living room."

"So you think he was still in love with her?"

"And she could have used that to her advantage, like
maybe let him think that if he killed her husband, he and
she would get back together again. And then, once he
did the deed, she got rid of him?"

Marnie's eyes widened. "Not a bad plan. Except—"

"Except what?"

"I can't help but wonder. If she knew Syd was going
to murder her husband that morning, why would she go
to city hall? Don't you think she would have made sure
she had some unshakable alibi?"

"You're right." I puzzled over this for a moment.
"Maybe she does have an alibi. That could be why the
police haven't arrested her."

"And why they're still considering you a suspect."

"About that," I said. "I have some good news. Turns
out the blood on my shirt was Winston's."

"Not the victim's? That's great news. So you're off the
hook."

"Not completely, but at least they don't have DNA evidence against me." I returned to the subject of Mona. "If
she does have an alibi, she might have lent Syd her car.
His van, with his company name on the side, would have
been recognized in a New York minute, whereas half the
cars in town are silver. She probably forgot about her
bumper sticker."

Marnie nodded. "Okay, Sherlock. So who was it?
Mona by herself. Mona and Syd, or Ronald Dempsey?"

I dropped into a chair, exhausted by the endless speculation. "At this point I have no idea."

The oven timer beeped and Winston galloped over.

"Sorry, Sugar," Marnie said. "This is people food." He slunk away with his tail between his legs.

"Aw, poor baby. I should have stopped by Matthew's to get you some more kibble." I went to the cupboard, emptied what little dog food was left into his bowl. He stared at it, unimpressed. "What's wrong? Not good enough for you?" I opened the fridge and tossed him a piece of cheese. He threw me a grateful look and returned to his cushion, munching contentedly.

"You spoil that dog," Marnie said. But a few minutes later I caught her sneaking him a morsel of chicken.

"Who's spoiling him now?" I asked.

Over dinner we reviewed the possibilities until I came to the decision that we couldn't ignore any lead until we were certain who the killer was. "I should still try to speak to Swanson's ex-wife, just to rule her out. And if she isn't the killer, she's probably the one person who would willingly tell us more about Mona. But the problem is I have no idea where she lives."

"Have you checked the Charlotte listings?"

"I checked the entire state."

"Maybe she reverted to her maiden name after the divorce," Marnie said. "There must be somebody around here who would know. She must have had some friends who would know."

"You're right," I said, and suddenly remembered something. "Judy Bates might know. I think they were in the same book club together." I pushed away my plate and set my laptop on the table. "Here's her number," I said, already punching it in. A moment later I had her on the phone.

"Of course I know her maiden name. It's Andrews. Sondra Andrews. Why do you ask?"

I wasn't prepared for that question, so I said the first thing that popped into my mind. "She placed an order from my shop and I forgot to take her number."

"You want her number? I have it around here some-where. Give me a minute."

I covered the mouthpiece. "She's got her number," I told Marnie, giving her the thumbs-up.

"Here it is," she said. "Do you have a pencil?"

A few minutes later I was surprised when after two rings Sondra Andrews picked up.

"Hello," answered a pleasant voice.

I introduced myself. "You don't know me," I said. "But I'd like to ask you a few questions about a delicate matter."

There was a short pause. "Does this have anything to do with Howard's murder?"

"It does," I said, half expecting her to hang up.

"Well, it's about time somebody came around to speak to me," she said. We made arrangements to meet the next day, and I took down her address.

"I thought you said she was agoraphobic," Marnie said.

"I guess she got over it."

"Now that that's settled, come back and finish your meal," Marnie said, "or I won't ever cook for you again."

"Now, that's the kind of threat that really scares me." I put away my laptop and settled back to enjoy my meal. "You know what's really weird," I said. "I haven't heard from my mother. I was sure, after I found Syd's body, that she'd be calling me, worrying that I was getting myself into trouble again. I'm sure she must have read about the second murder by now. I hope nothing's happened to her."

"You have nothing to worry about. She's fine," Marnie said.

I stared at her. "How would you know?"

"Oh, er . . . I spoke to her," she said, suddenly looking very uncomfortable.

"You spoke to my mother? When did this happen?"

"She, er . . . called me when she couldn't reach you."

"What do you mean she couldn't reach me? I always have my cell phone with me."

"How should I know how come she couldn't reach you? All I know is she called and she seemed fine."

"What did she want?"

She hesitated. "She wanted to make sure you were all right," she said at last. "She'd read about your finding a second body and she was worried. I told her you were fine."

"Tell me the truth," I said. "She was angry at me for getting involved, wasn't she?"

"I didn't want to upset you," Marnie said.

"I knew it."

In bed, later, I tossed and turned for hours. Every little creak amplified in the dark, every shadow a killer waiting to pounce. I was so spooked I even broke my own rule and allowed Winston to hop into bed with me. He snuggled his back to mine, no doubt thinking I was doing him a huge favor.

In this case, however, the favor was mine. His presence felt reassuring, and eventually I fell into a fitful sleep. But at five o'clock I was wide awake. There was no point in trying to get any more sleep. I threw back the bed covers and padded to the kitchen with Winnie on my heels, flicking on all the lights along the way.

"All right, big boy, what would you like for breakfast? Kibble, or kibble?" I opened the tin container in which I kept it. "Oh, crap." I'd clearly forgotten that I'd given him every last bit last night. And since no store would be open for another four hours, I'd have to pick some up at Matthew's. "Oh, crap," I said again, remembering I'd made arrangements with Matthew to do just that, and to lock his door as I left afterward, which meant his door had been unlocked all night.

Normally I might have thought, "What could happen in Briar Hollow?" But with a murderer running around loose, one just never knew.

I jumped into my clothes, put on the coffeemaker and we took off, covering the two blocks to Matthew's place in something between a jog and a speed walk. And when I tried the doorknob, sure enough, it was unlocked. I latched it behind me as I went in, and turned on all the lights.

Sheesh. Yesterday's anonymous phone warning had left me more than just a bit shaky. Hopefully, I'd soon get over this giant case of the nerves. I got the bag of dog food from inside the pantry and then, looking around for a container, I opened and closed one kitchen drawer after another, until . . . *Hold on. What's this?* In the catchall drawer was a brown manila envelope addressed to Matthew. And after a lifetime of Christmas and birthday cards, I recognized the handwriting as his mother's. Could this be the "valuable" object she had sent him?

I opened it. Inside, was an antique sterling silver box—the kind used for engagement rings. I gasped. It couldn't be, I thought, my hands beginning to shake. I held it in the palm of my hand, staring at it, gathering my nerve. I opened it and gasped. I was looking at a beautiful diamond engagement ring. I knew this ring. I had seen it dozens of times on Matthew's grandmother's finger. During her life, she had often mentioned that it should go to the first of her grandsons to get married. I'd always expected Matthew's older brother to get it. But here it was now.

My mind scrambled to make sense of this. Could it mean that . . . No. It couldn't be. Or could it? Our romance had grown over the last few months, but he hadn't—as my mother called it—used the "L" word yet. I took the ring out and slid it on the third finger of my left hand. It was a perfect fit. It suddenly hit me that if Jenny was here, she'd tell me that trying on an engagement ring was sure to be bad luck. I tore it off, placed it back in the box and stuffed it in the envelope.

I went through the rest of the drawers until I found an appropriate bag, filled it, and returned to my apartment in a daze. There, I filled his bowl. "What do you think, Winston? Is he getting ready to propose?"

Winston threw me a get-real look and returned to his food.

At eight o'clock, I'd already been at my loom, weaving, for a couple of hours when Jenny tapped on my door. I dropped my shuttle and dashed over.

"Guess what," I said. "I just found an engagement ring at Matthew's."

Her eyes widened. "You mean . . ."

I threw my hands up in the air. "That's just it. I don't know *what* it means. All I know is he was expecting a package from his mother, and—" All at once it came to me, and I let out a long sigh. "False alarm," I said. "He had no idea what was in the package." I was so disappointed, I could have cried.

"You never know. Maybe he said that to make sure you didn't know," Jenny said. "Tell you what. I'll go turn on the coffee, and as soon as Margaret shows up, I'll come over with my tarot cards. If there's a marriage proposal in the near future, I'll see it."

Normally I would have scoffed at her offer. But this time I jumped at it. I wanted very much to be told Matthew was about to propose. After she left, the five minutes until she returned felt like hours.

"I'm back," she called out, setting a tray on my front counter. "I brought you coffee and something to eat." Next to the mug was a plate of muffins. "I don't have time to do a full reading, so I'll just give you the abbreviated version. Now pick up the deck and shuffle," she said.

I did as ordered, cutting the deck twice, while asking my secret question, and then handed it back to her. She spread out ten cards in the shape of a cross.

"Now pick one card from each position in the spread." I tapped those I chose. She turned them facing up and studied them. "Hmm. Interesting," she said.

"I hate when doctors do that. I always think I'm going to die."

"Well, you're not going to die, but somebody will come very close to death."

"Is it a woman? A relative?"

"A woman, yes, but she looks like an acquaintance." I thought of Johanna and wondered if it could be her. I knew nobody else who might be ill.

Jenny put that card aside and moved on. "And as far as your fortune, or business, things look excellent."

"Must be my new collection," I said. "It's been selling well."

She picked the third card. "Uh-oh. I see danger. It is lurking around you and you should be very careful. Somebody wishes you harm."

"Can you tell me who?"

"Sorry. It doesn't work that way." She studied the fourth card. "Somebody in your family is going to surprise you. And it will be a happy surprise."

"The only family I have is my mother," I said. "And if she wants to make me happy, she'll find herself a gentleman friend, so she can concentrate on her own life instead of mine."

Jenny laughed. "Now for your secret question." She picked the card from the center of the cross and turned it over. "Ah. The lovers," she said. "That's good—very good."

"What does it mean?"

"It means you're in a happy and healthy relationship and it looks like smooth sailing in the future."

"What about marriage?"

She shook her head. "Sorry. But I don't see it." She continued. "But it's all good. Your mother, your business and your love life."

"How can you say it's all good when somebody I know will get sick, and somebody wishes me harm?"

"I didn't see death, so the person will recover. And you keep living, so whatever happens to them, you'll survive."

"Gee, great. Just what I've always wanted—to survive."

"Come on," she said, putting away her cards. "Cheer up. Matthew is crazy about you. Just give him time. Everything comes to those who wait."

"Before you go," I said. "I forgot to tell you. I had an anonymous phone call last night."

"A heavy breather?"

I shook my head. "No. Somebody wants me to lay off investigating the murders—or else."

Her eyes filled with worry. "That's probably what I saw in the cards—the 'somebody' who wishes you harm. But as I said, you go on living, so they won't succeed," she said, already opening the door.

"By the way, I'm driving into Charlotte this afternoon. I have an appointment with Sondra Swanson. So if there's anything I can pick up for you while I'm there . . ."

"Sondra Swanson? As in Howard Swanson's ex-wife? Why in the world are you going to meet her?" Just as she asked this, I looked up to find Lori Stanton marching in looking like an approaching storm.

Jenny stepped forward. "How can I help you?" she asked.

"Which one of you is Della?" she demanded.

Jenny turned to me and the woman's gaze followed hers. She marched over. "Where do you get off telling the police that my sister killed Syd?"

"I never—"

She took another step toward me, jabbing the air with an angry finger. "Did you for one moment think about her feelings? She just lost the man she loves. And, if that's not bad enough, some nosy parker like you has to go poke her nose where she has no business. As a result, the police go over asking a million questions, upsetting her all over again."

I was shocked, not so much about what she was saying, but I couldn't imagine how Mona could have known that I'd shared my suspicions with the police. Maybe she'd noticed when I touched the hood of her car and instinctively knew that since I'd found Syd's body only minutes later, I'd naturally share the information with the police.

She wasn't through. "Just so you know, my sister would not even hurt a fly, let alone kill anyone. So, why don't you do everyone a favor and butt out? If you so much as mention my sister's name again, I swear I'll come over and . . . and . . ." Was she threatening to kill me? Just as suddenly as she'd barged in, she turned on her heel and marched out.

I was too stunned to speak. Jenny found her tongue first.

"Wow," she said, "that was some showdown. I guess that gives us a pretty good idea of who wishes you harm."

"Oh, crap," I muttered. Now, Mona's sister would know I was meeting with Swanson's ex-wife. If she suspected that I was planning to ask Sondra about her, she'd be mad as hell.

Chapter 23

"How'd you sleep?" Marnie asked the minute she walked in. "I don't know about you, but I couldn't sleep a wink all night, and I wasn't even the one who got that call."

"I didn't either. I've been up since five. And then I got a nasty surprise. Lori Stanton showed up and gave me an earful. Somehow, she blames me for the police investigating her sister."

"What? When did this happen?"

"Half an hour ago. She just stormed in here, made her speech and then left. It was over in a minute—thank God."

"Well, I spent the entire night baking. I made scones, and they're delicious. So, have one. Maybe it'll make you feel better." She set a small bag on the counter. "I dropped them off at Jenny's but kept a couple for us."

"I already had a cranberry-orange muffin," I said, eyeing the blueberry scones as she opened the bag. "But, that was a while ago." Marnie wrapped one in a paper napkin and handed it to me. "Oh, my, this is so good," I said, having a bite. I allowed myself a second one and put it aside. "You won't believe what else happened."

She made the sign of the cross. "Please don't tell me somebody else died."

"No, nothing like that." I told her about finding Matthew's grandmother's diamond ring in his house.

"Oh. Thank God." And then she planted her hands on her hips. "What were you doing? Snooping?"

"I was not. I was out of kibble for Winston, and went to get some so he could have breakfast. Matthew had okayed it." As if he knew we were talking about him, Winston jumped to his feet and looked at us. Then he plopped back down and went back to sleep.

Marnie gave me the eyebrow. "That's a likely excuse."

"It happens to be the truth. Besides, what's going on here? You're *my* friend. You're supposed to jump up and down and tell me you think he's about to propose."

"Is that what you want?" She did a sorry imitation of jumping, her toes never leaving the floor. "Oh, this is so exciting. I think he's going to ask you to marry him," she said in high chirpy voice.

I rolled my eyes. "You're spoiling all my fun," I said. "Anyhow, Jenny read my cards—" At this, Marnie's mouth dropped open.

"You're kidding. Jenny read the cards for *you*? And you *let* her?"

I shrugged. "It's not as if it means anything. It was all just in good fun."

"Goodness. You are full of news today. What did the cards say?"

"Not a whole heck of a lot. My business will continue to do well. My mother will surprise me. An acquaintance will be very ill, but will survive. And somebody wishes me harm but won't kill me." I opened my hands. "There, you've got it in a nutshell."

"We already knew somebody wishes you harm. That was the threatening phone call last night." Her eyes widened. "You know who it might have been? Lori Stanton. If she thought you gave the police information about her sister, she well might have picked up the phone and threatened you."

"Or Mona. It could also have been her. Whether it's Lori or Mona, I might be in even deeper doo-doo now. Lori Stanton happened to walk in at the exact moment I was telling Jenny that I was driving to Charlotte this afternoon to see Swanson's ex-wife. How much do you want to bet she got on the phone to her sister the minute she got home?"

"Uh-oh."

"There's nothing I can do about it now, except maybe keep Winston with me as much as possible and hope he looks scary enough to ward off any wannabe murderers."

"I wouldn't count on it."

The bell above the door went into a tizzy and I looked up to see Jenny walking in, carrying two mugs of coffee. "I figured you'd be having scones and that you might like another coffee."

"Yes, please," I said.

"I'll have one too," Marnie said.

"At what time are you planning to drive to Charlotte?" Jenny asked.

"I'd like to leave before one o'clock. I called Mercedes to come in and help."

"If you don't have a chance to have lunch before you leave, I can make you a sandwich to eat on the road."

"That would be great. Thanks."

"Don't mention it," Jenny said, already on her way out.

Marnie turned to me. "I just had a thought. Whoever made that anonymous call to you last night has to be the killer. Aren't you afraid that if it's Mona, and she hears you're going to talk to Sondra, she might come after you?"

"It occurred to me."

"So, what are you going to do?"

"Promise me you won't say a word of this to Matthew." I waited for her nod and continued. "There's nothing I can do except continue with my investigation. I have a feeling I'm getting close."

At ten o'clock, Marnie and I came up front from the studio to open and found Judy Bates standing at the door.

"This is a first," I said, as she walked in. "We've never had anyone waiting at the door for us to open before."

She laughed. "It's just that I'm in a bit of a rush. The photographer called and he's coming over to take those shots this morning instead of this afternoon. I was hoping Marnie might have finished a few of the place mats." She looked at her pleadingly.

"As a matter of fact I have. But only two," Marnie said.

"That's fine. I don't need all four. I'll set up the breakfast bar for two and it will look gorgeous." Marnie went to get them and placed them on the counter for her to examine. "They are perfect," she said, running her fingers over the weave. "Absolutely perfect."

I wrapped and bagged them. Before leaving, Judy picked up one of my business cards. "I'll give it to the reporter to make sure she gets your name and address right." Turning to leave, she almost collided with another customer coming in. It was Susan Price, who gave her a tight smile. Judy brushed by without so much as a hello.

"Good morning," I said. "How can I help you?"

"I noticed your window display," she said. "It's gorgeous."

"Thank you. We've been getting a lot of compliments for it. I have a few items from the collection on the rocker in the corner." Susan went over and picked up one of the decorator cushions.

"I love this." She stopped, her smile disappearing into a sullen expression. "Please tell me my neighbor didn't just buy pieces from this group."

"If you mean Judy, I'm afraid she did."

She dropped the cushion. "Just my luck." She sighed. "Oh, well. The colors weren't right anyhow."

"What are your colors?" I asked.

She shrugged. "I have a pretty blank slate at the moment. The space is open. My kitchen is white with white marble counters and backsplashes. The floors are all sunbleached oak. My sofas are slipcovered in white linen, and the dining room table, coffee tables and buffet are all light acacia—a sort of light sandy color."

"It sounds gorgeous."

"I was always more of a beach type than a mountain type, so this is my husband's way of compromising. I don't have the beach, but I've got the beach decor." She chuckled, her mood lightening.

"What about your walls?"

"They are the color of the ocean. I guess you could call it French blue."

I pictured it in my mind and, in a flash, knew just what she needed. "You know what would look amazing in your decor? Blue-and-white Chinese porcelain—you know, garden stools, temple jars, that sort of thing."

He eyes lit up with excitement. "You're right. Why didn't I think of that?" She looked around. "But I don't see anything like that here."

"I have an idea," Marnie said. "Why don't I weave you a couple of samples in those colors—no charge—and if you like the way it looks, I could make you place mats, decorator cushions, rugs, even afghans?"

Her eyes brightened with excitement. "How soon will it be ready?"

"How about a couple of days?"

Once we'd reached an agreement, she wandered around

the shop. I had the feeling she wanted to talk about something with me, but was hesitant to bring it up. I had a pretty good idea what that something might be. After flitting from display to display for a few minutes, she started talking.

"I heard something upsetting," she said. "It seems that Judy has been spreading rumors about me. Did she say anything to you?"

"Nothing bad. The only thing she mentioned was that Swanson made your life miserable when you did your renovations."

"That's all? I'm surprised. She told others that I recently did more remodeling without a city permit."

Judy's comments had made me suspect Susan for a few days, but I'd since dismissed her as a possibility. "Now that you mention it, she did say you did more renovations recently. But I didn't pay it much attention."

"I had all the construction done months ago, and *with* a permit. And then recently, I finally got around to the details—things like new tiles in the bathrooms, new kitchen cabinets, counter and backsplash. Those jobs don't require a permit. Renovating is expensive. By the time we finished the big jobs, we couldn't afford to continue. So we waited until just recently to do the rest."

"It sure does cost a fortune. Even for a small job," I said, gesturing toward my new wall. "I found that out too."

The tenseness left her mouth and she smiled. "But it's all worth it in the end. I love my new floor plan. And your place looks great too." She smiled, suddenly embarrassed. "Anyhow, what with Inspector Swanson being murdered, I wanted to clarify the situation. I did not do anything illegal, whatever Judy may have told you, and I most certainly did not have any arguments with him." With those words, she headed for the door. "Give me a call the moment the sample is ready," she said, and walked out.

Marnie, who had been quiet during most of this exchange, said, "It's interesting that she thought it important to tell you there was no bad blood between her and Swanson."

"Perhaps, but I really don't think she had anything to do with it, if that's what you're implying," I said.

Marnie gave me a teasing smile. "Just checking. I know how your suspect list keeps changing."

She counted on her fingers. "Mona, Syd and Dempsey. And for a while you were considering Susan, and even Swanson's ex-wife, Sondra. Am I forgetting anyone?"

Chapter 24

One o'clock came and went, and there was no sign of Mercedes. If I didn't leave soon, I'd miss my appointment with Sondra Andrews.

"I don't know what could have happened to her," Marnie said. "She's usually so reliable."

I was beginning to worry also. "If she shows up now, I might not make it back before closing. And I'm not sure what time Matthew will be back either. Can you keep Winston if neither one of us is back by then?"

"No problem." She scratched Winnie's head. "You and I get along great, don't we, big fella?" He licked her hand—probably looking for a snack.

I was trying to convince myself it was all for the best anyhow—why should I drive to Charlotte just to talk to some woman who used to be married to Swanson?— when the door flew open and Mercedes came rushing in. "I'm so sorry I'm late. I was at the library, studying, and I completely forgot about the time."

"Don't worry about it," I said. "We're just glad you're all right." I turned to Marnie, already heading for the exit. "Give her a hand with sales. You'll be fine."

"Don't worry. It's not as if this is my first time." It wasn't, but it also wasn't as if she had lots of experience. But I had no time to worry about any of that at the moment. I made a dash for my Jeep and I was off.

My appointment was for two o'clock and by the time I got on the highway it was already one forty. I put the Jeep into cruise control and drove at the speed limit all the way, hoping the ex-Mrs. Swanson would be home to see me when I got there.

It always felt strange, leaving Briar Hollow and driving to Charlotte—like going back in time. Charlotte was where I'd grown up, made friends, started dating—all the activities that make up the fabric of a person's early life. I'd gone to college there, and studied to be a business analyst.

It was also where I was falsely charged with embezzling money just a few years ago. That had been a defining event in my life. It was when I'd seen my life with crystal clarity. I recognized that I had a financially rewarding job that brought me no enjoyment. That I had continued to do it because it was expected of me, to please others.

I decided that when I was exonerated—because if there was any justice in the world, there was no question that I would be—I'd change my life. I'd quit my job. I'd sell my condo and open a weaving shop. And, the day my boss was caught and confessed, I had done exactly that. Except for a few financially hairy moments, I had not regretted it for a minute. My mother, on the other hand, had nearly had a heart attack. The one bright star she saw in my leaving the city and moving to Briar Hollow, was that Matthew also lived here.

The image of the engagement ring in Matthew's kitchen drawer popped into my mind again, and I considered telling my mother about it. I dismissed the thought as quickly as it had come to me. Knowing her, I wouldn't put it past her to call Matthew and strongly suggest—if not order—that he propose.

As I approached Charlotte, I followed the directions Sondra Andrews had given me, got off the highway and pulled to a stop in front of a quaint bungalow on an oak-

lined street in Dilworth. The house was so pretty—
yellow painted clapboard with white trim and a black
door. I liked the owner already.

I knocked. After a few minutes, I knocked again. I was
listening for the sound of footsteps, anything to indicate
someone was home, when I heard a faint voice. I couldn't
be certain, but I thought it was calling for help. A cold
dread came over me. I turned the handle—thankfully
unlocked—and rushed in.

"Mrs. Andrews? It's Della. Are you there?" I heard a
moan and followed it. I pushed open a door and found
myself in a dining room, where on the floor, not three
feet away, was a woman bleeding from her chest. She
tried to raise her head.

"H-help," she gasped, breathing short, shallow breaths.

"Don't move. I'll call an ambulance." I grabbed my
cell and punched in 9-1-1.

"What is your emergency?"

"I need an ambulance at—" I consulted the scrap of
paper on which I'd written the address and read it aloud.
"She's been shot or stabbed. I'm not sure which."

"I've got an ambulance on the way. In the meantime,
can you see a knife in the wound?" the dispatcher asked.

The woman's pink blouse was soaked with blood, but
there was no weapon in sight. "No. But she's having difficulty breathing."

"Is her injury in her chest?"

"Yes. What should I do?"

"Find a towel, a bedsheet—anything that looks clean—
and press it firmly against the wound. You want to stanch
the bleeding." I dropped the phone, running in the direction I imagined the kitchen would be and snatched a
dishcloth, returning to the dining room and pressing it
hard against the woman's chest.

"How do I know if I'm pressing too hard?" I asked,
picking up the phone again.

"Listen to her breathing. Does it sound any better?" The woman's eyes fluttered and focused on me.

"I think she's breathing better."

"Good. Just keep the pressure the way you're doing and the ambulance will be there soon."

"You're going to be all right," I said to the woman. "An ambulance is on its way. You're Sondra, right?" She gave a slight nod and closed her eyes again. "Stay with me, Sondra," I said. "Can you tell me who did this to you?" I had to lean down and put my ear near her mouth.

"It was h-her," she whispered. "Sh-she killed him . . . tried to k-kill me." The corner of her mouth twitched as if she was trying to smile. "I p-played dead." And then she closed her eyes.

In the distance came the wail of an ambulance siren. It got closer and closer until it came to a stop in front of the house. Not a moment too soon. Sondra's already pale complexion was turning gray. In the next minute, the sound of footsteps came storming through the front door.

"She's over here," I yelled, and they rushed down the hall, bursting into the room. Two young EMTs, carrying a dizzying amount of equipment appeared.

Suddenly I realized the operator was still on the phone. "I'll let you go now. You're in good hands," she said.

"I've got a pulse," one of the men called out, and I almost cried in relief. I had never met Sondra Andrews before, but I couldn't bear for her to die. "But she's got a pneumothorax." He looked at me. "You did good. Keeping the towel on her chest is the only reason she's still alive."

"Is she going to be all right?"

"We'll do everything we can." His answer didn't reassure me, but soon they had hooked her to an IV and her grayish complexion improved slightly. They lifted her onto a gurney and were wheeling her out when a squad car pulled up and two officers climbed out—not Harrison and Lombard, thank God. One of the cops, a blond man, spoke briefly to the attendants before they sped off, sirens blaring.

"You the one who called this in?" the dark-haired one asked. Not trusting my voice at that moment, I nodded. "Can you tell us what happened?"

"I'm not sure. I had an appointment with her at two o'clock, but I showed up late—more like a quarter to three. Nobody came to the door when I knocked. But I thought I heard someone calling for help inside." I gestured toward the dining room. "That's where I found her." I went down the hall, and pointed at the bloody spot on the hardwood floor. "Right there."

"Was she alert when you found her?"

I nodded. "But she was very weak. I tried to keep her awake, but she passed out just before the ambulance got here."

"Did she say anything?" the blond officer asked.

"I asked her if she could tell me who did this to her and she answered, '*She* did it.' And that she had killed her husband and tried to kill her."

"You mean there's another victim in the house?" the other officer asked, already prepared to dart down the hall.

"No. Not here. Her ex-husband was murdered in Belmont about a week ago." I explained about Swanson's murder followed by Syd's.

"Is it just my imagination or are you closely involved in those two murders?" the first officer said, studying me.

"If by connected, you mean interested then, yes, I suppose I am."

He nodded slowly, his eyes not leaving mine. "If you don't mind, I'd like you to come to the station with us to make a witness statement," he said.

In the meantime, his partner was on his cell phone. I

overheard him saying something about an assault with a deadly weapon. "I'd say it's an attempted murder," he continued. "But it could turn into murder, if the victim doesn't make it." He was quiet, listening for a few minutes. "It's hard to tell. I spoke with one of the attendants and he couldn't tell with all the blood. Send the forensic team, STAT."

I turned back to the dark-haired officer. "Of course," I said. "Anything I can do to help." I went outside with them. "I'll follow you in my Jeep."

"Sorry, but it'll be better if you come with us. Don't worry about your vehicle. There's no time limit on street parking in this area."

He opened the back door, and from the way he put his hand on my head and sort of guided me onto the backseat, I suddenly knew I was not being brought in to give a witness statement. They considered me a suspect.

As soon as we took off, I snatched my phone from my purse and hit the speed dial button for Matthew.

"Della," he answered. "Where are you? I just stopped by the shop, but Marnie wouldn't tell me where you went. She was being very mysterious about it. Are you snooping again?"

"I'm in Charlotte," I said. "At the moment I'm in the backseat of a police car, being driven to the station."

"What!" He said this so loudly that the officer who was driving, threw me a glance in the rearview mirror. "What the hell kind of trouble did you get yourself into this time?"

"I just found another victim." I heard him gasp, and continued. "Swanson's ex-wife. She's alive, but in bad shape. I called an ambulance and she's now on her way to the hospital. And the cops who answered the call want me to make a statement."

There was a long silence, until I thought the connection had been broken. "Hello? Matthew?"

"I'm here. Ask them which station they're taking you to, and I'll drive there right away."

I knocked on the glass partition until the blond cop turned around. "What station are we going to?" I asked.

"Mecklenburg," he answered, and I repeated it to Matthew.

"I'm leaving right this second," he said, and hung up.

The station was swarming with uniforms. I walked up the sidewalk, flanked by the two officers, and everywhere I looked, were cops. They were going in, coming out. They huddled around desks gathered in conversations. I should have felt safe. Instead, being here brought back memories of my arrest for embezzlement three years ago. And just as had been my experience that time, they fingerprinted me—"to differentiate yours from any others we find," they said. Then, also like the last time, they put me in a small room with a camera mounted in one corner and a metal table facing a wall with a one-way mirror from which, I just knew, somebody was studying my every move. Then they left the room and closed the door.

One thing, however, had been different. This time, after taking my prints, they had also wiped my hands with some sort of plastic film. And when I asked what that was, I was told it was a gun residue test.

After half an hour of waiting, the dark-haired officer came back in. "Am I being arrested?" I immediately asked.

"No, of course not," he said, closing the door behind him. "Where did you get that idea?"

"Then why the gun residue test?" He walked over to the corner and turned on the camera.

"We don't even know whether the victim was shot or

stabbed yet, but if she was shot, we have to get all our ducks in a row for when we go to trial against the perpetrator," he said "A good defense lawyer could argue that you might have been the shooter. This way, we'll have proof that you didn't."

I digested this. "Then why did you just turn on the camera?"

"Normal police procedure," he said, joining me at the table. "Why don't you tell me again, how you happened to find the victim?"

I went over the story again, explaining that Sondra Andrews was the ex-wife of Howard Swanson, who had been murdered in Belmont, and that there had subsequently been a second murder.

"So, I started poking around," I said, as if this was the most natural thing in the world.

"Poking around?" he repeated. "In what way?"

"Oh, you know, asking questions, getting people to talk. That sort of thing. And I must have been getting close because last night somebody called to threaten that what happened to the others could happen to me."

"Really," he said, with only slightly less skepticism.

"I couldn't tell if it was a man or a woman. And the number was blocked. But if Sondra's attacker also killed those men, I'd be willing to bet the killer is Swanson's new wife." I went on to repeat what I'd been told—that she was young and beautiful and nobody could understand why she'd married him, unless it was for his money.

"Didn't you tell me he was a building inspector? Did he win the lottery or have family money?"

"No, but he had a lucrative sideline," I said. "Extortion." His eyebrows jumped up. "Turns out he wasn't inspecting, so much as selling occupancy permits."

"And what you're telling me can all be verified?"

"It sure can."

"Why are you so sure his wife killed him and the second victim?" I explained my theories, that either Syd had killed Swanson for her, and she got rid of him afterward, or he confronted her and she got nervous and killed him to stop him from going to the police.

"Any other suspects?"

"Well . . . There is one other, a local developer by the name of Ronald Dempsey." I told him how Ronald had lied and told the police he'd seen me wiping blood from my clothes, and how he'd sold Swanson a house for half its price, and how I'd gotten the threatening phone call only minutes after getting home from confronting him.

"Sounds to me like you've been busy. Why do you think Sondra Andrews was attacked?"

"I think Sondra must have known something about Mona," I said. "Mona's sister is the only person who knew I was coming to Charlotte to meet with Sondra. And she must have told Mona." I explained about the car I'd seen leaving city hall the morning of Swanson's death, and how Mona's car was identical to it, right down to the bumper sticker.

He nodded. "Interesting. Can you think of anybody else who might have known you were going to interview Sondra Andrews?"

"No. Not a soul—unless you count my shop assistant, and my friend who owns a coffee shop next door. But they both spent the morning at work."

There was a knock at the door and the officer went to answer. There was a muffled conversation, of which I couldn't make out a word. He came back.

"There's somebody here—says he's your boyfriend. He's making a ruckus, insisting on seeing you."

"Matthew's here?" I said, brightening up. "He's ex-FBI, you know. He'll vouch for me."

"Actually, my superior just looked you up. Seems you were arrested for embezzlement a couple of years ago—"

"Falsely accused," I said.

"—and that you were instrumental in catching the real culprit. So you were snooping even back then?" His attitude had changed. I now detected amusement in his voice.

"I was a business analyst. That was my job, checking the company's financials. That's how I found the discrepancies in the accounting."

"You want to see your boyfriend?"

"Yes. Of course," I said, hoping Matthew wouldn't be *too* angry at me.

Chapter 25

"How do you do it?" Matthew asked, trying to sound amused, and not very successfully. "I leave town for less than twenty-four hours, and somehow you manage to get yourself into another fix." We were alone in the interview room, the officer having left.

"First of all, I am not in a fix. All I did was call 9-1-1 and save a woman's life—if she survived the trip to the hospital," I added grimly. "By the way, did anybody mention how she's doing?"

"I didn't ask about her. I was worried about you."

"I'm perfectly fine, as you can see."

He sighed. "And that's why you sounded so scared when you called me?"

"I guess I was a bit worried."

"A bit?"

"I thought the police saw me as a suspect again. Honestly, who would be so stupid as to call an ambulance after trying to kill someone?" I gave him a tentative smile and was rewarded with a hand squeeze.

"I happen to know you're smart, but they might not have noticed that yet."

I gave him a quick kiss. "Can you make sure the Charlotte police let the local department know about the attack on Sondra Andrews?"

"I'm sure they will if they believe the crimes are connected."

"But of course they're connected," I replied, more than a little incensed at the thought that the cops could be so dense. "Who in their right mind would ever doubt that?"

"The cops don't always take well to civilians telling them how to do their jobs."

He made a good point.

"I'm sure the Charlotte police know what they're doing," he continued. "So you can keep out of it."

I saw the teasing glint in his eyes and my outrage at the Belmont police descended a notch. "So, do you know how much longer I have to stay here?"

"They finished interviewing you. You're free to leave."

"I am? Well, then. What are we waiting for?"

On my way out, I stopped by the dark-haired officer's desk to ask about Sondra's condition.

"Last I heard, she was still in surgery."

"Will you let me know when she comes out?" I gave him my contact information, which he already had. "I just want to make sure you remember."

"I will, I promise."

"Er, if you happen to call the Briar Hollow police, you might not want to mention that I found this latest victim."

He narrowed his eyes. "And why wouldn't I want to do that?"

"Let's just say that I'm not exactly popular with one of the officers. She seems to think I'm a busybody."

He chuckled. "Where did she get that crazy idea?"

Matthew drove me back to my Jeep, which was surrounded by squad cars.

"How do you want to do this?" Matthew said. "I follow you? Or you follow me?"

I grinned. "I'll let you take the lead this time." I hopped out of his car, but when I got closer to my Jeep, I saw it was blocked, one car was parked tightly in front and another in back. There wasn't more than six inches of space all together.

"How am I supposed to get out of here?" I looked over at Sondra's house. Two officials were standing at the door. A second later an officer wearing navy forensic overalls walked out with a cardboard box, which he carried to the trunk of a police car. I hesitated, hating to bother a cop as he worked. Then, the two officers at the door split up and one of them headed to his car. I marched off in his direction.

"Hey," I called as he climbed into his car. "That's my Jeep over there. Could you please ask one of the drivers to move theirs?"

He got back out. "You're the owner?"

I snatched my wallet and shuffled through credit cards until I found my registration and driver's license. "Yes, I am. See?"

He came closer. "Sorry, ma'am, but this vehicle has to go through forensics."

"What?" I was shocked. "What do you mean, forensics?"

"You know, evidentiary procedure. You'll have to call the station and make arrangements to pick it up once they're through with it."

By this time, Matthew had climbed out of his car and was coming over to see what the fuss was about. "What's going on, Officer?"

"I was just telling this lady that she can't have her car until we check it for evidence."

"But I need my car," I said, looking at Matthew for help. "I don't understand why it has to go through the lab. It's not as if it's part of the crime scene."

He put a hand around my shoulder, steering me back toward his car. "No problem. I understand, Officer."

"Before you go, let me get you a receipt." He went back into Sondra's house, returning with a signed form and a card. "This is the phone number you can call to get more information."

"Let's go. We'll drive back together. And when you make arrangements to pick it up, I'll be happy to take you."

I followed him to his car. "I don't understand why they would keep my Jeep. What's it got to do with Sondra's attack?"

He opened the passenger door for me. "They'll run it for traces of blood. If they find any, they'll then test it to make sure it isn't the victim's."

"I don't get it," I said as Matthew climbed in.

"You found the victim. If you were the attacker, you might have run back to the Jeep and hidden the weapon, before calling 9-1-1." Seeing the worry on my face, he added, "It's just procedure. Nothing to worry about."

Easy for him to say. He wasn't a suspect. I, on the other hand, was now a suspect for a third crime within the span of one week. And I was getting quite fed up with it.

"It's already almost seven," he continued in a tone meant to cheer me up. "With rush hour traffic, we won't be back home until close to nine. I vote we drive directly over to the Longview and have dinner there."

"I'll call and make reservations," I said, already scrolling in my cell-phone contacts for the number. "And the first thing I want when we get there is a tall glass of wine. Actually, make that two or three."

The traffic was horrendous, of course. Crazy drivers sped by only to brake once they passed us, and then, when we got on the interstate, everything slowed to a crawl.

"I swear this is one more reason I love living in Briar Hollow." There was only one traffic light in town.

He chuckled. "You used to complain that folks there are so laid-back they'll wait through green lights rather than honk if someone falls asleep at the wheel."

"I guess I've gotten used to driving at a more leisurely speed."

By the time we made it to the restaurant it was nearly nine thirty—a drive, which in normal traffic, shouldn't have taken more than an hour.

As we walked in, Bunny, the owner, was behind the counter. "There you are. I was getting worried about you. Come on in." That was another thing I loved about Briar Hollow. People here knew their neighbors and genuinely cared about one another. She proceeded down the hall to the restaurant and opened the door for us. "Enjoy your evening."

A waiter pulled a chair for me at the same table where Matthew and I had sat just a few days ago. He handed us the menus and took our drink orders.

"The lady will have a glass of chardonnay," Matthew said after consulting with me. "And I'll have a glass of pinot noir." As soon as the waiter returned with our wine, Matthew raised his glass. "To you."

"And you," I answered. After a few sips the stress of the day began to dissipate. Only then did I realize just how tense I'd been. "Boy, did I ever need this," I said, taking another sip. "It's been a crazy day. First, I'd gotten off to a late start for my meeting with Sondra. I worried the whole way that she might be gone when I got there. If I hadn't heard her calling for help, she would have died."

"She's lucky you got there when you did. She's got you to thank for saving her life."

"That's if she lives," I said. "We still don't know if she did." I held out my hand. It shook. "No wonder I was stressed."

"Are you all right? Are you sure you want to stay?" Matthew asked.

"I'm fine. It just hit me that she probably got attacked because of me."

"Why would you say that?"

I told him about Lori Stanton walking in just as I was telling Jenny my plans for the afternoon. "I'm convinced either she or her sister did it. She overheard me, and then drove to Charlotte before I got there. It couldn't have been anybody else. Nobody knew I was going to see her."

"Does this Lori spend her days in her store the way Jenny does?"

"I think so. Whenever I walk by she's there."

"In that case it should be easy enough to find out if she was there all day today. If she was, you can eliminate her from your list of suspects."

"Which is down to two after today's events," I told him. "At least for Syd's murder. I think Syd might have killed Swanson. He and Mona used to be an item before she married Swanson, and I suspect he had hopes of getting back together with her."

"And that's why he would have killed him?"

"Whether it was his idea or she put him up to it, I don't know. But I'm convinced she was involved in killing him."

"If she did, wouldn't that imply they were involved?"

"Or he was hoping they'd pick up their romance, and when she refused, he threatened to tell the police that she planned the murder."

He gave me a crooked smile. "You never cease to amaze me, how good you are at this sort of thing. But what about that real estate developer, Dempsey? Have you dropped him as a suspect?"

"I think so. I just can't think of why he'd want to kill Sondra, or for that matter, how he would have known I was going to see her. The only person Sondra has any connection to or might have known something about is

Swanson's new wife. Sondra might have gone out of her way to find out what she could about the woman who broke up her marriage."

Matthew nodded. "A woman scorned."

I thought of something. "You know who could find out whether Lori was in her shop all day is Marnie." I fumbled through my bag for my cell.

"Don't call her from here," Matthew said.

"I was just going to pop out for a moment." I got up. "Be right back." I called her from the hallway. "Marnie. I need you to do something for me."

"It's almost ten o'clock. Can't this wait until morning?"

"Sure. I can't explain now, but I promise I'll tell you everything tomorrow."

"Uh-oh. Does this involve spying on anyone?"

"Not really. Is there anyone you could call to find out if Lori Stanton was in her store all day, or if she was absent for any significant amount of time this afternoon?"

"How significant?"

"At least two hours."

"I think there are a couple of people I can still call at this time. And I'll just casually ask the question during the conversation," she said, and hung up.

When I got back to the table, Matthew said, "I forgot to tell you. Winston is at my place. I picked him up from Marnie before driving back to Charlotte. And I ordered the fresh salmon for you. That's what you wanted, right?"

"Yes." I was about to launch into more theories as to why the two sisters killed Swanson, when from the corner of my eye I noticed somebody walking toward us. It was the saleslady I'd met at Prestige Homes, and she was wearing a big smile.

"Jenny," she said to me. "Fancy meeting you here." Matthew opened his mouth to say something and I gave him a swift kick under the table.

"Ouch."

"And you must be Jenny's fiancé," she said, sounding chirpy. "Have you picked a date for the big day yet?"

"We're still debating," I said, aware of the blood rushing to my face, and Matthew's mounting confusion.

"Now that I've got you both together, how about we make an appointment for you to visit our project?"

"Actually, I don't have our agenda with me, so I'll have to call you back on that."

"All right then," she said, and then she turned to Matthew. "I know this is probably a bit late, but congratulations on your engagement. I hope you will both be very happy." From that moment on, I have no idea what was said. All I was aware of was the growing look of displeasure on Matthew's face.

"What was that all about?" he said when at last she'd left. "Are you telling people that we're engaged?"

"No. Of course not. Let me explain. Marnie and I went to visit Prestige Homes. I just wanted to see what kind of a project it was. I thought that maybe Swanson had discovered something, like subpar materials being used. But it's a really beautiful project." I became aware of speaking too fast. That always made me seem guilty. I forced myself to slow down. "When we met her, I pretended I was shopping for a house for my soon-to-be husband and me."

"I see," he said. "For a moment there, I thought you had a secret agenda."

I laughed, but it came out like a bray. "That's just silly. I'm very happy with the way things are."

"That's good, because marriage is not something I want to think about."

The sip of wine I'd just taken went down the wrong way and I coughed. "Are you saying you never want to get married?"

"I'm not saying never. But certainly not in the foreseeable future. At the moment, my life is perfect just as it is."

I thought of the engagement ring in his drawer, and swallowed hard. Luckily the food arrived at that point and I hid my disappointment by concentrating on my salmon.

"You seemed preoccupied over dinner," he said later, as he drove me home.

"I'm a bit worried about my mother," I said, for lack of a better excuse for my quiet mood. "I haven't heard from her in a few days, not even after I found Syd's body. And that is not like her. I hope nothing's wrong."

"She's fine," he said. "I saw her yesterday."

"You did?" I said, shocked. "Whatever for?"

"I went to visit my mother and yours happened to be there. She looked well."

That was so weird. Everybody seemed to have talked to my mother lately but me. Jenny had. Then Marnie had told me my mother called her when she couldn't get in touch with me. And now Matthew had seen her. I might have been tempted to give her a call as soon as I got home. But if she asked me if Matthew had proposed yet, I might fall apart. I was so upset by Matthew's comment at dinner that it had taken all I had not to burst into tears right then and there.

Chapter 26

The headline of the *Belmont Daily* the next morning read MURDERS STILL UNSOLVED. The article, however, said that the police had found new evidence and that they were looking at a new suspect. It had to be Mona. I scanned the rest of the piece, looking for anything about Sondra's attack, but her name wasn't even mentioned. How odd, I thought. I retrieved the card the police officer in Charlotte had given me yesterday and picked up the phone. When he picked up, I introduced myself.

"Yes," he said. "Of course I remember you. You're the snoop."

I chuckled. "I've been called worse things," I said, and went right to the point. "I was wondering if you have any news about Sondra Andrews' condition."

There was a long pause. "I'm afraid we're not at liberty to divulge any information about that case at the moment."

"Oh," I said, taken aback. "Can you at least tell me which hospital she's in?"

There was another pause, this one briefer. "Sorry, but I can't tell you that either. But here's what I will do. As soon as we get clearance to talk about it, I'll let you know."

There was nothing I could do but thank him and hang up.

If Sondra was still alive, the police might want to keep

her condition and location a secret in order to keep her safe. That thought bolstered my spirits.

I folded the paper and looked up to see Marnie struggling with boxes while trying to unlock the door. I dashed over to help.

"These are for Jenny—except for this one," she said, dropping all of them on the counter. She set the top one aside, and picked up the others. "I'll be right back." I opened the door for her again and she went over to Jenny's. When she returned a few minutes later, it was with muffins and coffees. Winston, who had been snoozing on his cushion behind the counter, sat up.

"Sorry, big boy. These are not for you," she said.

I snatched a liver treat from my catchall drawer and threw it. He hopped up, grabbing it in midair, then went back to his cushion.

"At what time did Matthew come by this morning?" she asked, handing me a cup.

"He dropped Winston off around nine o'clock."

She eyed me critically. "You look like hell. What's wrong? Didn't you sleep last night?"

"Not very well," I said, taking a sip.

"Why not? Did Sondra Andrews refuse to see you?"

"No, that's not it. Sondra was there, but she'd been attacked." Marnie's face fell. "I found her bleeding on the dining room floor and called the ambulance."

"Please, don't tell me she's dead."

"I have no idea how she is at the moment. She was alive when the ambulance got there, and she was in surgery when I was at the police station. But I called the police this morning and they wouldn't give me any updates. They wouldn't even tell me which hospital she was taken to. I hope she's alive and they're keeping her condition a secret for her protection. But I can't help feeling that it's all my fault. If I hadn't made an appointment to meet with her, she'd probably be fine right now."

"Don't be silly. How were you to know somebody would try to kill her?" She furrowed her brows. "Who else knew you had an appointment with her?"

"Except for you, Jenny and me, there was only Lori Stanton. She overheard Jenny and me talking yesterday before I headed over."

"Well, that proves it. It had to be her."

"That's why I asked you if she was gone from her shop for any length of time yesterday."

Marnie's face fell for the second time in as many minutes. "I forgot about that. I called a few people, but they all said she was at work all day."

"Well, then, she must have told her sister. Mona is the only other person who could have done it." At that moment the bell above the door rang, and Officer Lombard walked in.

Uh-oh.

This was not going to be pleasant.

"I hear you found another victim yesterday," she said. I detected an edge to her voice, but rather than get on the defensive, I put on the charm.

"Yes, and I was just about to call you," I said. Her eyes registered surprise, but only for the briefest of instants. I continued. "I could be wrong, but I think I might know who's behind both murders and also the attack on the ex-Mrs. Swanson."

She rolled her eyes.

"I don't blame you for being doubtful," I continued. "But you can be the judge." I was being so nice and polite, she had no choice but to listen. She shifted her weight and planted her hands on her hips.

"All along, I kept going back to the same question. Who had the best motive for killing Swanson? And no matter how I looked at it, I kept coming to the same answer. His new wife. From the very first, all I heard about her was how attractive she is, and how nobody could figure out why she married her husband. Before he died, Swanson bought a house from Ronald Dempsey. That model is listed at one point five million dollars, but Dempsey let Swanson have it at a fifty percent discount. That didn't surprise me too much. Considering Swanson was extorting money in exchange for permits, I figured Swanson gave Dempsey an easy pass for his permits in return for the discount. And for a while, I was sure Dempsey had killed him. It made sense. Dempsey had the opportunity. He was at city hall when I found Swanson's body. And now that he is starting the second phase of his project, I'm sure Swanson must have demanded some form of payment for the new permits Dempsey would need to move forward."

"A minute ago you said you thought Mona killed him."

"I know. I'm just going over all the different theories so you understand how I arrived at that conclusion."

She crossed her arms. "I'm listening."

"Well, supposing the attack on the ex-Mrs. Swanson is related to the two murders, I doubt Dempsey would have done it. For one thing, he had no idea that I was driving to Charlotte to see her. Also, I couldn't imagine what Sondra might know about him that he'd want to kill her for. The only person Sondra might know something about, would be the woman her husband left her for—Mona."

She nodded. "That's a good point."

"There could have been any number of reasons Mona wanted to get rid of her husband—his money, another man. She was probably planning to divorce him from the day she married him. Now, getting back to the house Swanson bought from Dempsey, it turns out that he'd taken out mortgage insurance on the property. And by signing that policy, I suspect he signed his own death warrant. As his wife, Mona stands to inherit, not only his pension plans and life insurance policy, but also a one-point-five-million-dollar house, free and clear."

Officer Lombard's eyes widened.

"I think she planned the murder and, if she didn't do it herself, she got somebody else to do it."

"A hired killer," she said, nodding to herself.

"Syd Shuttleworth."

Lombard's demeanor had slowly changed until she had lost all the stiffness in her bearing.

"If I'm right, then as soon as Swanson was dead Shuttleworth became a liability. That's the only logical reason she would have had to kill Syd."

"Murder for hire," Lombard said, her eyes glazing with determination. "But how do we prove it?" I couldn't help noticing that she'd said "we."

"There are a few possibilities. There might be some evidence that would prove she killed Syd."

Lombard shook her head. "No such luck."

"Or that she attacked Sondra Andrews."

"I didn't get all the information from the Charlotte police yet. What other ideas have you got?"

"There's always Sondra herself. She was conscious when I found her. And when I asked her if she had seen her attacker, she nodded and said, '*She* killed Howard, and *she* tried to kill me.' I figure Mona attacked her."

"Let's hope Sondra can tell us."

"I called the Charlotte police this morning to find out how she is. They wouldn't even tell me if she's still alive, or which hospital she was taken to. The only reason I can imagine they would keep it a secret is if she's survived. They're keeping her condition and whereabouts a secret for her protection."

"Anything else you care to share?" she asked in a friendly tone.

"You know, I saw her just before finding Syd's body," I said. "I happened to drive by her house—"

"Happened to?" Lombard said, the corners of her mouth curling.

"I admit I was curious. I wanted to see what kind of house Swanson had—whether it looked like a mansion. Mona happened to be in the window. Not only that, but when I walked around the car to see if there was a bumper sticker like the one on the car I saw at city hall that day, I happened to put my hand on the hood, and it was hot. It wasn't ten minutes later that I found Syd's body."

"What's this about a bumper sticker?"

"I told your partner," I said, and explained that I'd forgotten about the sticker when they first interviewed me. "It was the same one that I saw on the car the day of the murder."

"So the killer, whether it was Syd or Mona, used her car that day. Why would they do that?"

I shrugged. "Syd's van was highly recognizable. As for her sister, I don't know if she even has a car."

Lombard nodded again. "I hate to admit it, but it all makes sense."

I gave her a tentative smile. "I know you and I got off at a wrong start. I hope we can leave all of that behind and start over again."

She gave me a crooked smile. "Well, you must admit you have a way of butting in where you have no business."

"She does do that," Marnie said, laughing.

"But from now on," Lombard continued, "if you find out anything, do me a favor and give me a call." She pulled a card from her pocket and handed it to me. "Don't go through dispatch," she said, heading for the exit. "And by the way, why don't you call me Roxanne from now on?"

As soon as the door closed behind her, Marnie dashed to the window, staring at the sky.

"What are you looking for?" I asked.

"If anybody had told me you and Lombard would make peace, I would never have believed it," she said. "I'm looking for flying pigs."

*   *   *

A short time later, Marnie got us fresh cups of coffee. "You still look troubled," she said, handing me one. I'd been trying to put Matthew's comments about marriage out of my mind, with little success.

"I need your advice about something."

"Uh-oh. This sounds serious."

"Maybe I'm overreacting. You remember how I gave the saleslady at Prestige Homes Jenny's name and told her I was shopping for my fiancé and me?"

"I remember."

"Well, Matthew and I were at the Longview for dinner last night and she was there. She made a beeline to our table as soon as she saw me, and started congratulating Matthew on our engagement, asking him about the wedding. You should have seen the look on his face. After she left, he gave me a long speech about how he's happy with the status quo and has no intention of getting married."

"Ever?"

"Not in the foreseeable future was how he put it."

"So what's your question?" she asked.

"What am I supposed to do?"

She crossed her arms and thought about it. "I can't see that there's anything you can do," she said at last. "What was his behavior like when he dropped Winston off this morning?"

"Totally normal. As if nothing had changed."

"I guess that's because nothing *did* change—at least for him."

"But I don't want to *date* for the rest of my life. I want to get married, have children and build a family. If he can't give me that, I might as well break it off and make myself available to other men." I squeezed my eyes shut, thinking of my mother. She'd be at least as devastated as me.

"Is that what you want to do?"

"What I want is for him to *want* to marry me. I've been in love with him for years, waiting for him to feel the same about me. At long last, I thought he and I had a future together. But no. We're *dating*. And that's all it will ever be."

Marnie patted my back. "There, there. Don't get yourself all worked up. You know men. A woman mentions the word marriage and they put on their running shoes. But that doesn't mean he doesn't love you. All it means is he's not ready for *now*."

"You think so?"

"Well," she said, sounding hesitant. "Some men have been known to change their minds." That didn't make me feel any better.

Chapter 27

The day went by with me watching customer after customer enter Jenny's shop. If my sales hadn't picked up as much as they had, I might have been a bit envious. Sometime midafternoon, Jenny crossed over to my side, looking exhausted.

"I just heard," she said. "It seems the police have just arrested Mona Swanson."

"You're kidding," I said.

"I thought you'd like hearing the news," Jenny said.

"She's been arrested? When did this happen?" Marnie asked.

"Well, since we just heard, I figure it can't be more than a half hour or so ago. You know how fast news travels around here." She glanced at her watch. "I'd better get back. It's been so busy, I don't even have time to breathe. And it's only going to get busier."

"And to think," I said. "Just a short time ago, you were worried about not being able to get your customers back."

She chuckled. "And now, I have so much work I've been thinking of hiring another employee."

"You have?" Marnie said. "That's wonderful. I'm so happy you're doing well."

Jenny was turning to go when she stopped and looked

at me through narrowed eyes. "Your aura is muddy. Something's wrong. What is it?"

"Trouble in paradise," Marnie said. "Yesterday Matthew announced that he doesn't want to get married, and Della doesn't like the idea of dating him for the rest of her life."

"Give the man some time. You only started dating a few months ago. I'd love to talk about it, but I left Margaret by herself."

Marnie followed her, calling out something about grabbing us something to eat.

As soon as the door closed behind them, I noticed the way they brought their heads together, whispering and giggling. For some reason, I had the strangest feeling they were enjoying a laugh at my expense. But as soon as that thought crossed my mind, I knew I had to be wrong. These were my friends. When I hurt, they did too.

I was finishing the grilled-cheese sandwich Marnie had brought back with her, when the phone rang. It was the Charlotte police officer I'd called earlier.

"I'm sorry I couldn't give you any information before," he said. "But as long as the victim's attacker was free, we couldn't risk anybody knowing she was still alive."

"Thank God she's alive. How is her condition?"

"I wouldn't say she's all right," he said. "The bullet was very close to her heart and she went into cardiac arrest during the surgery."

So she had been shot. The idea conjured an awful image in my mind. "Has Sondra said anything yet?"

"They've got her in an induced coma," he said. "Her condition is critical. That's all I know so far. But that isn't the reason I was calling you. I wanted to tell you that you can pick up your car now." He gave me the address and I wrote it down.

"Can you tell me which hospital she's in? I'd like to visit her."

"She's at the Carolinas Medical Center. But, seeing as she's in a coma, I doubt the doctors will let her see anyone." I thanked him and went online to order a flower arrangement to be delivered to her room.

"That's nice of you," Marnie said, just as Judy Bates walked in.

"What's nice?" she asked.

"Inspector Swanson's ex-wife, Sondra Andrews, was attacked yesterday. She's in critical condition at the hospital. Della just ordered her some flowers."

"Sondra was attacked? But she's alive, right?"

"She is," I said.

"How did it happen?" Marnie told her the story while I concluded my online purchase. "You know," Judy said, "I think I'll send her some flowers too."

"I didn't know you and Sondra were friends," Marnie said.

"I wouldn't say we're friends, more like friendly acquaintances," she said. "We used to be members of the same book club, before she moved away. I liked her. She was nice. In what hospital is she?" I told her. Judy nodded. "I hope having all those flowers around her will make her feel better when she wakes up."

"That's *if* she wakes up," Marnie said. "She was shot. They'll probably find the gun hidden somewhere in Mona Swanson's house. With the weapon as evidence, the case against her will be a slam dunk."

"Thank goodness that woman is off the streets," Judy said. "Word is you had a lot to do with her being arrested. That's why I stopped by—to thank you."

"I didn't really do anything. I'm sure it was all Officer Lombard," I said, earning myself a thumbs-up from Marnie.

"I also wanted to tell you that the article about my

house is appearing in tomorrow's paper," Judy continued. "I hope it brings you lots of new customers." She gave us a little wave and left.

"Do you really think Mona Swanson would have been stupid enough to keep the weapon?" Marnie asked.

I froze, as an idea hit me. "You know, it never occurred to me before, but there were two murders and one attempted murder. And for the three attacks, a different weapon was used each time. Isn't that strange?"

"What's so strange about that?"

"For one thing," I said, thinking out loud. "If Mona was planning to murder her husband, don't you think she would have used a weapon other than a bookend? If a person premeditates a murder wouldn't you think they'd bring a weapon along?"

"You can't say that about her attack on Sondra Andrews. She brought a gun with her."

"Hmm. I wonder if Syd's murder was planned," I said as another thought came to me. "I guess there's one way I could find out. The police probably know whether the knife belonged to him. If it did, then Mona didn't bring a weapon and probably went there to talk. And for some reason, probably during a heated argument, she grabbed the knife and stabbed him."

"What difference does it make, whether she planned the murders or not? If she didn't, the lady sure has some anger management issues."

I was still laughing when the phone rang. "Dream Weaver, Della speaking."

"Della, this is Johanna. I can't believe what I just heard. Mona Swanson got arrested?"

"That's right."

"Anyhow, that's not why I'm calling. I heard something else that really upset me. Sondra was attacked? I hope she's all right?"

"She's alive," I said. "But she suffered a cardiac arrest

on the operating table. They've got her in an induced coma. I hope she recovers, but right now her condition is listed as critical."

"Oh, that poor woman. What a terrible time she's had of it lately, first the divorce, now this. I don't even think she has many friends."

"I know Judy Bates is sending her flowers," I said. "And I just did too."

"Judy Bates? Really? How odd. I had no idea those two even knew each other. You know, I should do something for her, too. I think I'll pick up a get well card and get everyone at the office to sign it."

"That would be a lovely gesture," I said, and gave her the name of the hospital. We said good-bye, and as soon as we'd hung up, I called Roxanne before it slipped my mind.

"I know this is none of my business," I said. "But—"

She laughed, and it hit me that I had never heard her do so before. It made her seem all the more human. "Since when has that ever stopped you?"

I laughed too. "Do you happen to know whether the knife that killed Syd Shuttleworth belonged to him, or whether she brought it with her?"

"We think it was his. It was a hunting knife and there were other hunting tools in his garage. Why do you ask?"

I told her my theory that if the murder was premeditated, she would have brought a weapon. "That's why I'm now thinking that maybe she and Syd argued and she grabbed the knife and stabbed him in a fit of anger. Also, I'm beginning to think that she might not have planned to kill Howard. If she had, I'm sure she would have brought a weapon along. Killing somebody by hitting them over the head can't possibly be premeditated. That would also explain why she was driving out of that parking lot like a bat out of hell. She was probably shocked at what she'd done. If she'd thought about it ahead of time, she would probably have come up with a less noticeable exit."

"Please don't tell me you're having doubts about her guilt," she said, sounding the tiniest bit worried. "Anyhow, that's not my problem. I'll let the DA decide whether the murders were premeditated or not."

Afterward, I told Marnie about the conversation Roxanne and I had. "I might even start liking her," I said.

Marnie rolled her eyes. "Now, I know hell has just frozen over."

At five o'clock, Matthew appeared in the doorway, and my heart skipped a beat. I was still upset with him, but he looked so handsome, dressed casually in jeans and a camel-colored suede jacket, that it took all my willpower to not drape myself all over him. Winston galloped over to greet him, hopping on his hind legs and prancing.

"Hey, big boy. How've you been? Did you miss me?" He pulled out his leash as he spoke and hooked it to Winston's harness.

"Hey, gorgeous," he said turning to me. "How was your day?"

"Good," I said, determined to behave normally. "Did you hear? They arrested Mona Swanson."

"I take it that means no more detecting for you?"

"I guess not. By the way, I got a call from the Charlotte police. My Jeep is ready to be picked up."

"Okay. When would you like to go?"

"How's early tomorrow afternoon? That way you can do your word count in the morning and we can head back before rush hour."

"Sounds great. Pick you up at one, how's that?"

"Perfect."

To my surprise, he opened the door and left without

so much as making plans to get together. Marnie, who had been in the studio, came over.

"What happened? Did you two have a fight?"

"No. He just picked up Winnie and left."

"So why do you look so miserable?"

"Normally he hugs me and gives me a kiss. And he didn't say anything about the next time we'd go out together."

"Didn't I hear him offer to drive you to Charlotte? You'll see him then."

I knew what she was saying was logical, but I had a bad feeling Matthew was pulling away rather than getting closer. What I needed was a shoulder, and much to my surprise, the shoulder I wanted most was my mother's.

Tonight I'd give her a call and ask her advice—something I hadn't done in years.

I was returning from making my nightly deposit when I saw somebody waiting by the door to my building. It was Officer Lombard and for the first time since I'd met her, she was dressed in civilian clothes: casual beige pants, a floral shirt and a sweater.

"I almost didn't recognize you," I said. "You look nice."

"You mean, wearing normal-people clothes?" she said. "I was hoping you might have a few minutes."

"Sure. Come on up." She followed me up the stairs, and I offered her something to drink.

"Thanks—anything but coffee. I must have had half a dozen cups already." That was something we had in common.

"Good idea. I always drink way too much of it. Since you're not in uniform, does that mean you can have a glass of wine?"

"That'd be great. Anything you have already open

will be fine." I hurried to the kitchen and checked the fridge. Sure enough I had a half bottle of chardonnay. I carried it back along with two glasses.

"Sorry for the mess, by the way. I don't always have a loom in the living room."

"And here I thought it was part of the decor." I saw the teasing glint in her eyes. I could hardly believe it, but the woman was growing on me. Could it be that she and I could actually become friends?

"This almost feels festive," I said, handing her a glass.

"Well, we certainly have something to celebrate," she said as we clicked glasses. She leaned back into the sofa. "Considering much of the case we have against Mona Swanson is from information you provided, I thought I at least owed you an update on everything that's happened. After leaving here, I went to Judge King and got a search warrant for Mona's home."

"You found the gun."

"No such luck," she said. "But we did find a pair of jeans and a shirt she'd buried in the backyard. They were covered in blood and the type matches Syd Shuttleworth's. But until we get the DNA, we can't be one hundred percent sure."

"Buried!" I said in disbelief.

She nodded. "She wanted to get rid of the jeans but was afraid of throwing them in the garbage in case we searched. She thought burying them would be the best way to go. The good news is she's admitted to killing him, but claims it was in self-defense. She swears she had nothing to do with her husband's murder, or with the attack on Sondra Andrews."

"I don't get it. Why would she admit to one murder and not to her other crimes?"

"For one thing, it would be near impossible for her to claim innocence in Syd's murder. We may not have the results of the DNA test of the blood on her clothes yet, but she must have known it would be just a question of time."

That made sense. "What does she say about her husband's murder?"

"Oddly enough, she admits to driving over to city hall that morning, to supposedly show him the picture of a sofa she wanted to buy for the new house. But she insists that he was already dead when she got there and she panicked. All she did was walk into his office, and run back out. According to her, that's why she drove out of there like a bat out of hell. And she also insists that she had nothing to do with the attack on Sondra Andrews."

"A likely story," I said, harrumphing. "But if she's already going up for murder, why not admit to both? Everybody already knows she did it. But she probably feels that a jury will be more lenient toward her for one murder than two, plus an attempted murder." I snapped my fingers. "Also, legally a person cannot profit from a crime. So, in order to inherit her husband's estate, she can't be convicted of killing him."

Lombard nodded. "Even if she got convicted of second-degree murder, or maybe even manslaughter, she won't serve more than ten years. She'll still be a young woman when she gets out."

"And a couple of million bucks will go a long way in rebuilding her life," I added.

"That hardly sounds fair," she said.

"I agree with you there," I said. "Sounds like things are lining up nicely." I noticed her glass was empty so I poured her a bit more.

"Hopefully, when Sondra Andrews comes out of her coma, she'll be able to testify against Mona. And that will be the last nail in the lady's coffin."

"Have you heard anything more about how she's doing?" I asked.

"I spoke to her doctors and her condition has improved slightly. She's no longer critical, but she's still listed as serious. They couldn't tell me how long she might remain in that state."

"I'm going to Charlotte tomorrow to pick up my Jeep. The police impounded it for forensic testing. God only knows why."

She gave me the eyebrow. "You *did* find the body," she said. "I spoke to one of the officers. You're getting a bit of a reputation in Charlotte, too. Seems you helped them solve an embezzlement case a few years back."

"They'd caught the wrong guy," I said. "Me."

She laughed. "I guess you had no choice but to get involved that time." She looked at her watch and got to her feet. "Anyhow. I don't want to keep you. Just thought I'd stop by and share the news."

"Thank you. I really appreciate it," I said, walking her to the door.

"By the way," she said, "I just wanted to tell you what a nice-looking couple you and Matthew make." Before I had a chance to respond, she was gone.

I was in the kitchen, tossing myself a salad for dinner— my attempt at a healthy diet—when the telephone rang. I glanced at the call display.

"Mom. You must have read my mind. I was just going to have a bite and then call you."

"It must be telepathy," she replied. "I was thinking about you all day. I had a feeling something was wrong. Are you all right?"

To my surprise, my throat constricted and tears welled in my eyes. As soon as I could speak, I found myself blurting out the whole story about Matthew's declaration of the previous night. "He doesn't want to get married." She was silent for a few long seconds. "Mom? Are you still there?"

"Yes, yes. I'm just thinking, before you do anything

drastic—like breaking up with the man—why don't you have an honest conversation with him? Tell him how you feel."

"You think I should tell him I want to get married and have children? What good is that going to do? He's already made it plenty clear that he doesn't."

She hesitated. "Well, sometimes men can be dense. In my experience—"

"You're drawing from the one relationship you've had in your life again?" I said, hearing the smile in my own voice.

"Yes, I am," she replied seriously. "Joke all you want about my lack of experience, but I have learned a lot about men from your father. He once gave me a speech much like the one Matthew gave you before we were married."

"He did? What made him change his mind?"

"I left him. I was very nice about it, but I was firm. I sat him down not long afterward and told him that as much as I loved him, what he was offering me was not enough. And I said that I respected him too much to make him change his mind, and that in my opinion we had irreconcilable differences. Therefore, the only intelligent thing to do was to stop seeing each other."

"How did he take it?"

"Oh, he put up a big fuss. Starting telling me things like, he couldn't predict the future. That maybe he'd change my mind someday. Or maybe I would. So I gave him a peck on the cheek and walked out."

"Weren't you afraid you'd never hear from him again?"

"Of course I was. But I knew I was doing the right thing, and that if he loved me he'd be back. Of course," she added gently, "that's the kind of measure a woman takes as a last resort."

"Thanks, Mom."

"I love you, sweetheart."

"I love you too."

I returned to the kitchen, poured myself another glass of wine and sat down to a lovely dinner as I reflected on everything my mother had told me.

For the last few years, she'd been so obsessed with my getting married and giving her grandchildren, that our entire relationship had become contentious. We couldn't have a conversation without me wanting to beat my head against the wall. But today's conversation had been lovely. I couldn't remember the last time she had given me such good advice.

Maybe my mother still had lessons to teach me after all.

Chapter 28

The next morning I woke up after a good night's sleep, feeling more positive than I had in days. I hurried through my routine and was in my shop by seven thirty, having coffee with Jenny at my counter as I poured over the paper. Today's headlines were all about Mona Swanson's arrest. But I flipped right by the article and searched until I found the article about Judy Bates' house.

"Here it is." I was looking at a full-page spread with color pictures of an elegant decor with rustic overtones. And smack in the middle of the center shot was the sofa with my cushions and throw. "They look great."

"Let me see," Jenny said, crowding me away. She squealed. "Look. They mention your name and the name of the store."

Halfway down the first column, the writer described the details that pulled the decor together. And, sure enough, there were the credits—Della Wright of Dream Weaver, complete with address and phone number. "That kind of advertising is priceless."

"It might not be the best timing," I said. "Matthew is driving me to Charlotte this afternoon so I can pick up my Jeep. I got Mercedes to come in and help."

"She and Marnie will handle everything like pros. I have no doubt the article will bring in more business, but I imagine it will come in a gradual trickle rather than a boom." She chuckled. "Did you happen to notice that I predicted everything that's happened? Remember? I told you a friend would do you a favor. And Judy Bates just did. I also told you that your business would become profitable. And see? The article, on top of your new merchandise will keep customers coming. Now do you believe?"

"Weren't there more predictions?"

"Why, yes. There was the friend who would recover. And your mother would surprise you."

"I wonder," I said, "if the friend could be Sondra. I'd imagined a recovery from an illness, but the prediction could just as well be regarding an injured person." It came to me that the last prophecy had also come true. My mother had surprised me last night. She had given me excellent advice. I shared with Jenny the conversation I'd had with my mother. "Now all I have to do is put it into action. Easier said than done."

"Don't forget," she said, her forehead scrunched worriedly, "that she also told you to only do this as a last resort."

"True. But I wonder if waiting might be a mistake. I don't know how good I'd be at keeping calm and waiting patiently. When I'm stressed I tend to get snappy. If we're arguing all the time, there's no way Matthew will ever want to marry me. And I wouldn't blame him. Who'd want to tie themselves down to a woman who's an emotional mess all the time?"

"You're not giving yourself enough credit. You're the last person I'd describe as an emotional mess."

"I've been known to have a crying jag once in a while." I brushed the subject away and submersed myself in the article. We both read it in full—the section pertaining to my shop aloud—until Jenny had to return to her own shop. Soon, Marnie showed up.

"Didn't you say that with both shops having their own private entrances you would be able to come in later?

When are you planning to start doing that?" It was only a few minutes past eight and I was already at my Navajo loom, working away.

"Look at who's talking. You're here early every day."

"It's different for me. I have to drop off Jenny's pastry order. Once I'm already here, why would I want to go back home?"

"Well, I have a very good reason for coming in early today." I pointed her toward the paper on the counter. "The article about Judy's house is out."

"I totally forgot about that," she said, making a bee-line over. She studied it quietly for a few minutes. "I think this deserves a celebration. How about a coffee?"

"A refill sounds good."

Soon, she was back carrying a tray with mugs and brioches. "Any news from the man?" she asked.

"If by 'the man' you mean Matthew, no. Not a word."

"Have you decided what you're going to do?"

"I had a long talk with my mother about it last night." Her eyes registered surprise. "It seems my father pulled the same stunt on her before they got married."

"You're kidding. And what did she do?"

"She told him she had too much respect for him to try to change his mind. So she broke it off with him."

"Are you serious? Well, it seems to have worked. They got married, and they had you."

"And stayed married for over four decades," I said.

"So you're going to give Matthew his walking papers?"

"I think we should have a talk first." I glanced at my watch. "And that will be in about six hours."

"That could turn out to be a tense drive," she said, voicing my fears aloud.

The morning went by swiftly with customers coming in to congratulate me on my new collection, which they'd seen in the newspaper article. By the time Mercedes came in, we had sold twice as much as we would have on a normal day. But soon after, the sunny day changed to a light drizzle and now the shop was empty.

"There's no question that Marnie and I can handle the store on our own now," Mercedes said, looking out the window at the empty sidewalk.

A few minutes after one, Matthew showed up with Winston in tow. "I thought I'd spend the morning with him and drop him off now since I was coming by anyhow. And since we're only driving to Charlotte and back, I can pick him up at five as usual. If that's okay with Marnie."

"Of course it's okay with me. Winnie's never any trouble. He doesn't do much more than sleep behind the counter."

Winston gave her a bleary look, as if to say, "Are you calling me lazy?"

"The place is simply not the same when you're not here," Marnie added, scratching his ear. "Did you hear that, Winnie? We all love you."

He gave her a bark that I interpreted as, "If you love me so much, where's my liver treat?" I riffled through the drawer and found one. Satisfied, he trotted over to his cushion, and Matthew and I took off.

We were on the highway, with the radio playing some romantic song from the eighties, when I turned it off.

"Don't you like that music?"

"It's not the music," I said, a lump already forming in my throat. "It's just that I think we have to talk."

"Uh-oh. Sounds ominous."

I strove for a lighter tone. "Not at all. It's just that all relationships, sooner or later, come to the same questions. 'What have we got here? And where are we going?'"

"And you think we're already there?"

"I do."

"Feels to me like we just started."

"I know we haven't been romantically involved for

very long. We've only been officially a couple for—
what—six months?"

"About that." There was amusement in his voice.

"On the other hand, we've known each other our entire lives. So perhaps this talk isn't about you and me, so
much as about what each one of us wants from our lives,
and if our goals are compatible." This was met with
heavy silence. I gathered my courage and continued.
"The other night over dinner, you mentioned that you
don't see marriage in your future."

"I never said never."

"You said 'in the foreseeable future.' I don't know
about you, but when somebody talks about the foreseeable future, I interpret that as being five or ten years,
maybe more. If I'm wrong, then tell me."

Instead of answering, he came back with, "Aren't you
happy having me as a boyfriend?"

"Yes, very much."

"Don't you agree that we get along?"

I nodded.

"So why don't we take it one day at a time and see
where it goes?"

"Matthew, that's like saying, 'Isn't this a nice boat? It
doesn't have oars or paddles, but let's just get on it all the
same and see where it takes us.' That might be fine for
somebody who has all the time in the world, but not for
me." I stopped. I had almost said the words "my biological clock." I was beginning to sound like my mother.

"Why not? We do have all the time in the world.
What's the big rush?"

My voice took on a defensive tone. "Here's the thing.
You might not know or care where you want to go. But
I do. I want what my parents had—a happy marriage and
children."

"Ah," he said. "So that's what it is. The famous biological clock." I could have clobbered him.

"It has nothing to do with my biological clock. I know where I want to go and I don't want to go on a long ride to nowhere," I said, noticing that the discussion was suddenly going very differently from what my mother suggested. It was quiet in the car for a long time after this. The silence grew until we got to the outskirts of Charlotte.

At last, Matthew said, "How long have we known each other?"

I look at him, puzzled. "What kind of a question is that?"

"All our lives, like you said. You should know by now that I'm honest and loyal. Why don't we keep seeing each other? Who knows? Maybe you'll change your mind." He was giving me the same argument my father had given my mother.

I had prayed I would not have to use them, but all at once, I heard myself speak my mother's words.

"I'm glad we had this discussion." He glanced at me, and I continued onward. "I think it's important for two people who are in a relationship to know each other's goals and objectives. The problem is that you and I don't want the same thing, and I have too much respect for you to try to make you change your mind."

A look of relief washed over his face, but it disappeared as soon as I said, "So, that's why I think it best if we stop seeing each other. This way, we will each have fond memories of each other. If we don't, we risk the relationship deteriorating into one of frustration and resentment. And that way, we can each look for a partner whose goals will be more compatible to ours."

When I finished, I noticed that we had arrived at our destination. I couldn't have planned it better if I'd tried.

Matthew pulled to a stop and turned to me. "So that's it? You're breaking it off with me?"

"We're just traveling different roads," I said. I leaned over, gave him a kiss on the cheek and hopped out of the car. I walked over to the police building, without turning around. If I had, I would probably have had a meltdown.

Inside the building, I made my way to a counter where I presented my claim ticket. The clerk pointed me to a bank of elevators.

"Take the first on the left down to P and hand in your ticket there."

Fifteen minutes later I'd initialed and signed half a dozen forms, inspected my Jeep and was already driving out of the garage. As I wove my way through the city, I spotted a hospital sign and remembered that I was only blocks away from the hospital where Sondra was being treated.

On a spur of the moment decision, I turned at the next light and made my way there.

The drizzle had grown to a light rain. I was lucky and found a parking spot near the hospital. I dashed inside and stopped at the information counter.

"Can I help you?" the clerk asked.

"I'm looking for Sondra Andrews' room."

She consulted her computer. "She's in room five oh six. Take a right at the corner and take the elevator to the fifth floor." I followed her directions, amazed at the number of people in the building. I had to keep an eye on where I was going or risk bumping into someone. I stepped into the elevator, sharing the space with a gurney and a couple of men dressed in surgical greens. On the fifth floor a nurse pointed me in the right direction and soon I found myself facing Sondra's room. I had no more than touched the door when somebody called out to me.

"Excuse me, but you can't go in there."

"This is Sondra Andrews' room, right? I'm a friend of hers."

She marched over. "That patient is allowed only one visitor at a time. Those are the rules."

"She's got a visitor?" I grabbed the door handle to take a quick peek inside.

Sondra was on her back with her eyes closed. Machines were all around her, beeping at different intervals. I had an immediate impression of countless tubes connecting her to machines and vice versa.

Next to her bed were flower arrangements. And then a person moved into my view. It was Susan Price. As she noticed me, a look of guilt washed over her face.

"Della," she said. "Come on in. I was just about to leave."

I looked at the nurse and she nodded reluctantly.

Susan snatched her bag and hurried out, whispering a quick, "See you." I stepped in, waiting for the door to shut and then grabbed my cell, punching in Roxanne's number.

"Lombard," she replied immediately.

"It's Della."

"Hey, how are you?"

"I'm at the Carolinas Medical Center, in Sondra Andrews' room. Maybe I'm overreacting, but something strange just happened. Susan Price was here when I came in. And I had the strangest impression that she wasn't happy being discovered here."

"Susan Price? What's she got to do with anything?"

I remembered that I had never even mentioned her name in relation to Swanson's murder. "It's a long story," I said. I gave her the *Reader's Digest* version.

"We already have the killer," she replied, sounding none too pleased.

"I hate to ask you this, but is there any possibility that Mona might be telling the truth, that she killed Shuttleworth, but had nothing to do with her husband's death or with the attack on Swanson's ex-wife?"

"Are you telling me you think you got it wrong?" she asked. I couldn't help noticing that all of a sudden it was

"I" got it wrong. Not the "we" she'd used earlier. "Because if that's what you're telling me, I'll be one very unhappy cop."

I hesitated. "Maybe I am just being paranoid."

I didn't know the first thing about any of the machines plugged into the patient, but there were no red flashing lights, no alarms screaming for medical personnel. Everything looked like it was working fine. If Susan had done something, surely I'd see evidence of it somewhere. I glanced into the wastebasket by her bedside table. No syringe, no ampoule. I gave myself a shake.

"Sorry, Roxanne. I think I let my imagination run away with me."

"I guess after all the evidence you've uncovered, it's natural to be a bit overly suspicious." I could hear the relief in her voice. We said good-bye and hung up. But I had a little niggling feeling that something was not right. I was overlooking something.

Since there wasn't much I could do but sit and stare at Sondra, after a few minutes I decided to leave. I was walking down the hall, toward the elevators when I happened to glance up and noticed a man among a group of patients walking in my direction. His appearance caught my attention. He looked frail; over a pale face, his hair was gray and perfectly coiffed. He looked around nervously. Must be a cancer patient, I thought, realizing that his strange appearance had a lot to do with his painted on eyebrows. As I climbed into the elevator I watched as he made his way down the hall, and something about the way he moved also struck me as familiar. I'd met this man before, I thought. I had lived in Charlotte my whole life until a couple of years ago when I'd moved to Briar Hollow, but I couldn't place him for the life of me. I chased the thought away and was on my way to the parking lot when my cell phone rang.

"Hello?" a male voice said. "Is this Della Wright?"

"It is," I said, balancing the cell between my ear and my shoulder as I riffled through my purse for the keys.

"This is Ronald Dempsey," he said. "I've been meaning to call you ever since that day you stormed into my house. I thought I should clarify a few things with you." I was stunned, not certain how I should react.

My phone started to slip and I dropped my purse catching it. "Where did you get my number?"

"I called your shop and a nice lady—much nicer than you, I should add—was kind enough to give it to me. All I want is two minutes of your time. After the way you treated me, I think you owe me that much."

He had a point. I'd accused him of murder. And now that Mona had been arrested, I felt somewhat embarrassed by that little episode. "I'm listening," I said.

Even before he spoke, my heart was already pounding in my chest, as if I knew that what he was about to tell me would change everything all over again.

"One of the things you said was that I'd tried to deflect suspicion from myself by putting it on to you. I want you to know that I never did that. I wasn't the one who told the police that I'd seen you wipe blood off your clothes."

"It wasn't you?" Half a dozen thoughts flashed through my mind. Was he lying? If he was, I couldn't see the point. If he was telling the truth that could only mean— Suddenly all the pieces of the puzzle fell into place. "Oh, my God. I have to go," I said, already running as fast as I could.

I must have looked like a lunatic racing down the sidewalk, then up the hospital corridor. Inside the elevator I kept pressing the fifth-floor button, praying that I wasn't already too late. The doors opened and I sprinted to Sondra's room and burst through the door.

"Stop!" I screamed. The strange-looking man I'd noticed earlier was holding a pillow over Sondra's face. He dropped it, and made a dash for the door. But, just as he was passing me, I stuck my foot out and he went flying.

I poked my head out the door and called for help. A moment later the nurse who'd tried to stop me from going in earlier came rushing in.

"What's going on here?" she asked.

"I just caught this person trying to smother her." I pulled out my cell phone again and punched in 9-1-1. "I'm calling to report an attempted murder," I said, keeping my eyes fixed on the man on the floor.

"I'll get security," the nurse said. She ran down the hall, coming back a minute later, followed by a burly man in uniform. "That's him," she said, pointing to the man now cowering in the corner.

The guard grabbed him by the arm, lifting him up to his feet. I walked over and snatched his gray wig. Thin, wispy blond hair came cascading out. "You sure had everybody fooled," I said. "And you almost got away with it. Almost, but not quite."

I was looking at none other than Johanna Renay.

"Howard deserved it," she said, her face a deep shade of crimson. "He strung me along for years, promising to leave his wife and marry me. And all that time I covered for him at the city, and he never once shared any of the money he made with me. And then, he meets that little piece of trash—"

"You're talking about Mona?" I said.

She nodded. "Of course I'm talking about Mona. That bitch wrapped him around her little finger, and within weeks he up and left his wife and married her."

"But he married Mona almost a year ago. What else happened to make you so angry?" I asked.

"He suggested we pick up where we left off, adding that he promised he was going to leave Mona and marry me, just as soon as he figured the timing was right." Just talking about it was making her so angry her voice was coming out raspy. "The bitch almost caught me that morning."

"You saw her at city hall, the day you killed Howard?"

"I was just walking out of his office when I spotted her turning the corner down the hall. I slipped out the back entrance before she saw me."

I had a few more questions I wanted to ask, but there was a commotion down the hall, and when the nurse opened the door to check, two policemen walked in. Soon, Johanna was cuffed and escorted away.

"You'll have to come to the station with us to make your witness statement," one of the officers said.

"Gladly." I said good-bye to Sondra, who was being attended to by a nurse, and promised to come back. I followed the police out of the building.

Chapter 29

The news of Johanna's arrest flew like wildfire—as it always does in Briar Hollow. By the time I got home, it was already seven o'clock. Matthew had picked up Winnie hours earlier, yet to my surprise, Marnie and Jenny were both sitting in the staircase to my apartment waiting.

"You didn't really imagine we'd wait until tomorrow to get all the details, did you?" Marnie said.

"But I'm famished. I haven't had anything to eat since lunch," I said.

"So are we," Jenny said. "So I brought the wine and Marnie said she'd get the pizza."

"Sounds like a plan," I said, unlocking my door and letting them in. "But you know who we really should invite is Roxanne."

"Roxanne?" Jenny said. "Who's she?"

"Also known as Officer Lombard," Marnie said. "Didn't you know? She and Della are BFFs now."

"Don't be silly," I said. "We had a talk and patched things up. That's all. At least I won't be worried about being arrested every time some crime is committed. Besides, I owe her. I fed her all this information and half of it turned out to be wrong."

Without waiting for another teasing comment from Marnie, I went to the kitchen and gave her a call, followed by a call to The Bottoms Up for pizza. "She's on her way," I said, carrying a tray of wineglasses and a bottle opener to the living room.

Marnie filled glasses all around, leaving an empty one for Roxanne. "You haven't said a word about Matthew. So, I take it the talk didn't go the way you expected?"

I sat and took a deep breath. "Actually, it went exactly as I expected. He'd made it pretty clear that he doesn't want to be married. But, I suppose a small part of me was still hoping."

"You broke it off?" Jenny sounded shocked. "But—" She looked at Marnie who shook her head slightly. "That's just not right," Jenny continued. "You two belong together. You should—"

Marnie cut in. "Della knows what she's doing. If they're meant to be together they will be." She turned to me. "I bet he's going to call. And when he does, don't be a fool."

"Okay. Define fool. If he asks, am I supposed to see him or not see him?"

"See him, of course."

That was the answer I'd hoped for. But regardless of what she might have said, there was no way I would have turned him down. "Fine. If you think that would be the right thing to do."

Marnie gave me an amused smile—as if knowing exactly what I'd been thinking.

The buzzer from downstairs rang and I let Roxanne up. She was wearing a skirt and jacket—civilian clothes. I couldn't get used to it.

"Nice outfit," I said.

"Thanks." She handed me a bottle of red. "Hope I'm not too late. Is there any pizza left?"

"I just ordered it," I said. "Come on in. Roxanne, you know everybody, don't you?"

"Yes, I think I've questioned just about all of you at one time or another."

"Must be hard to make friends," Marnie said with a touch of sarcasm in her tone.

But instead of bristling, Roxanne laughed. "I don't know. Look at Della. I didn't just question her. I arrested her, and now here we are, sharing pizza and drinking wine together."

The buzzer rang again and I answered. This time it was the delivery guy. Marnie paid him while I carried the boxes to the kitchen, where I'd already stacked plates and wrapped the cutlery in napkins.

"Come and get it," I called. Soon we were all back in the living room and everyone was looking at me expectantly.

"How in the world did you figure it out?" Marnie said. "We were all convinced Mona had killed Howard and Syd and that she had also attacked Sondra."

"So was I. She was the most logical suspect," I said. "But I still had a nagging feeling that I was missing something. Judging from the look of fear in Mona's eyes when I saw Syd arguing with her, I think that Mona might be telling the truth about killing him in self-defense."

"I agree with Della," Roxanne said, turning to me. "I have to say you almost gave me a heart attack when you called and questioned whether we'd gotten it right. But it started me thinking, so I went back and questioned Mona again. She told me that when Syd found out that her husband had been murdered, he jumped to the conclusion that she'd killed him. He took for granted that they would get back together. She went to his house the morning he died, to make it clear to him that she would never get involved with him. That's when he attacked her."

I remembered the mess I'd noticed in the garage. It had looked like a fight had broken out, but I'd believed that Mona had attacked Syd.

"In the end," I said, "it was just luck that helped me

figure it out. If Ronald Dempsey hadn't called me when he did, Johanna Renay may well have gotten away with murder."

"By the way," Roxanne said, "you'll be happy to hear that Sondra is awake. And she's confirmed that her attacker was, indeed, Johanna Renay."

"That is really good news," I said. Maybe it was because I had held her hand and tried to keep her from dying until the ambulance got there, but her death would have devastated me.

"Get back to Ronald Dempsey," Marnie said. "What did he say that made you solve the case?"

"He told me that he never said a word to the police about seeing me wiping blood from my clothes."

"That's it?" Jenny said. "You figured everything out from that?"

"It was simple. You see, Johanna was the one who told me he'd said that. And she'd very cleverly made me think he was pointing the police in my direction in order to prevent them from suspecting him. So once he told me that he hadn't, I had to question why Johanna would have lied. The only reason that made sense was if she was doing exactly what she had accused Dempsey of doing. Then I remembered a number of things that didn't make sense and I put everything together."

"Give me an example," Jenny said, while I hurriedly had a sip of wine.

"For one thing, I'd noticed the way Johanna spoke about Swanson. One minute he was wonderful and she had been close to him. Then the next, he was a philanderer who had broken his first wife's heart. It may not seem like much, but to me it showed she had mixed feelings about the man. And she was doing the same thing when talking about Sondra. One minute Sondra was a nice woman, and then the next she was a neurotic person who wouldn't even talk to anyone on the phone. Yet, I remembered Judy saying Sondra had been a member of her book club. So she couldn't be as antisocial as Johanna was painting her out to be."

"The Charlotte police questioned Johanna at the station," Roxanne said. "And she admitted everything. It turns out that she and Swanson had been having an affair for years. All along he'd been promising her that he'd leave his wife—someday. But when the someday came, he fell for a girl less than half her age and married her within weeks of meeting her."

"That was another thing I'd noticed. She'd once told me that he had married her only a short time after meeting her, and then during another conversation she implied that they had been having an affair while he was still married. But what was really the clincher was when I remembered that I had told Johanna that I was trying to reach Sondra. She was the person I first went to see when I was trying to locate her."

"How did she find out you'd located her?" Jenny asked.

"She didn't," Roxanne answered, taking over from there. "She decided to kill her just in case. With Sondra dead, nobody would ever find out that she and Swanson had been carrying on this long-term affair."

Marnie nodded. "I get all that, but what I don't get is how Sondra knew that Johanna had killed her ex-husband."

"She didn't," Roxanne said. "The ironic part of this is that Sondra was convinced Mona had killed him. But Johanna was afraid that if the police ever found out about her relationship with Swanson, they might figure it out."

"Wow," Marnie said.

Roxanne looked at me. "I've been meaning to ask you. How did you recognize Johanna in the hospital? From my understanding, she was disguised as a man."

"It was her eyebrows. She draws them in such a peculiar shape, and when I saw that man in the hospital, I noticed his odd appearance, but it wasn't until Dempsey phoned me that everything fell into place. And by the way, I'd noticed she wore wigs, and imagined she was suffering from cancer, but the reason she wears them is because her hair is so thin."

"All I can say," Roxanne said, "is I'm very much relieved we didn't have to release Mona after charging her. I would have hated to have made a false arrest."

The evening wore down, until everybody went home. I climbed into bed, thinking about Matthew again. I wondered if Jenny was right and that he would call.

The next few days went by in a blur of activity. Still, my heart thudded every time the telephone rang. But still no call.

On the fourth day, Jenny came rushing into my shop.

"Did you hear the news? There's a sign in the window of Good Morning Sunshine. The place is closed for business. Much as I feel sorry for them, I admit I'm thrilled to officially be the only game in town again." She squealed. "Isn't that great?"

"Wasn't it just a few days ago that you were complaining about being too busy? Have you found a new employee yet?"

"No, but I've got some feelers out. I'll find someone soon." She left, walking on a cloud.

As for me, my shop sold more in the following few days than it usually did in a month.

"Jenny predicted your business would do well," Marnie said. "I hate to tell you she told you so, but she told you so. You've got to be a believer now."

"Like I always said, Jenny has an above average ability to read people. That, combined with a little common sense, and anybody could predict the future."

She harrumphed and busied herself for a while, then, almost timidly, she asked, "Any word from Matthew?"

I shook my head. "Nothing."

He had even stopped dropping off Winston at the shop every morning. I went back to weaving and forced myself to think of something else.

It was the evening of the fifth day. I was home, sipping a glass of wine and feeling lonely, when the phone rang. When I saw Matthew's number on the call display, my heart went into a gallop. I took a deep breath and picked up.

"Matthew," I said. "This is a surprise."

"I've been mulling over the talk we had, and I think you and I should sit down and discuss a few things. Are you free tomorrow night for dinner?"

"I am," I said, already dying of curiosity. But I kept my cool. We agreed that he would pick me up at six, and hung up. Then I spent half the night worrying about what I would wear to look absolutely irresistible.

Chapter 30

"You look beautiful," Matthew said, holding the door open for me. I was wearing my blue dress—the one I knew was his favorite—and my highest heels. I'd done my hair and it now fell onto my shoulders in soft curls. And I'd paid particular attention to my makeup. As a result, I looked as good as I could, without looking like an entirely different person.

"Thank you," I said. He went around the car, slipped into the driver's seat and we took off. Minutes later we walked into the Longview. Again, he went around and held the door open for me.

"Mademoiselle."

"I always did have a weak spot for Frenchmen," I said, sliding out. "You're being so formal tonight," I said. "What's the occasion?"

"The occasion is you solving not one, but *two* cases. So your snooping—"

"Investigating," I corrected him, keeping my tone light, even though my heart had just dropped like a brick. If the whole point of the evening was to celebrate my solving the case, I might as well go home.

"Fine. Investigating," he repeated after me. "The point is you're alive and I don't have to worry about you getting into trouble. I don't know about you, but that, to me, is worth celebrating."

"Hi, Della. Hi, Matthew," Bunny, the owner, said from behind the registration desk. "Everything is ready for you," she added with a wide smile. She waved us toward the restaurant entrance with a grand gesture, worthy of a *The Price is Right* model.

"Wow. What was that all about?" I asked as soon as we had walked out of earshot. "It's not like we've never been here before."

"Who knows?" Matthew said, opening the restaurant door.

"What the heck?" The inside of the restaurant was pitch-black. Suddenly the lights went on and people were jumping out from all over the room. I spotted Jenny and her boyfriend, Ed. A few feet away were Marnie and my mother. "What the heck?" I said again, dumbfounded.

"Surprise!" they all yelled at once, almost sending me into cardiac arrest.

"What—" I looked at Matthew, confused.

"This was your mother's idea," Matthew said, grinning wickedly. "And I decided it was an excellent idea."

People were now standing around, waiting for God knows what. I looked among the crowd seeing more people I knew. There was Margaret, and Mercedes with her mother. Even Roxanne was here, and at least a dozen other people. And then my mother was coming forward with her arms open. She wrapped me in a bear of a hug.

"Surprise, sweetheart."

"But . . . It's not even my birthday," I said when she released me. "I don't understand." Rather than answer, she just smiled and pointed to Matthew. I turned toward him, and to my surprise, found him on one knee.

All at once, tears gathered in my eyes.

"Della," he said, retrieving a small silver box from his pocket, and opening it. "Will you do me the honor of becoming my wife?"

This was the moment I had dreamed of for so long.

But when I opened my mouth to say yes, it came out like a croak, and in the next moment I had rivers running down my cheeks.

Everybody I knew was watching as my makeup was quickly becoming ruined. My nose was running. And I just knew I was doing the ugly cry. But I had never been so happy in my life.

"Was that a yes?" Matthew asked.

I nodded. As he slipped his grandmother's ring on my finger, the whole room broke into applause.

Weaving Tips

Navajo weaving is easily recognized for its bright geo-metrical patterns in reds, blues, yellows and greens, often on tan or gray backgrounds. Although originally it was used to create blankets and little else, today we find it in everything from rugs, and upholstery fabrics, and home linens such as place mats and decorator cushions, and yes, even in fashion. A few of my favorite projects were sleeveless vests (worn over a shirt and jeans) and a shoulder bag.

What most people don't know is that the original Na-vajo designs were simple stripes of white, gray and brown. In the early seventeenth century, few Native cloths con-tained blue. The blue pigment, indigo, could be obtained only through trade with Mexico and was difficult to come by. It wasn't until the mid-nineteenth century that many of the colors we now associate with Native weaving actu-ally came into popularity.

One important characteristic of Navajo weaving is that it is constructed wide rather than long. This is be-cause traditional Navajo weaving used upright looms with no moving parts. Often they were simply two trees six to eight feet apart, and the weft was prepared by sim-ply wrapping the yarn around from one tree to the other, again and again, until the desired length was reached. And then the weaver would work on the project until it was finished. The artisan sat on the ground during weaving and wrapped the finished portion of fabric underneath the loom as it grew. The average weaver took anywhere from two months to many years to finish a single rug, depending on the size of the project.

Another characteristic of Navajo weaving is in the threads used. Historically, the Navajos raised their own sheep, and produced their own wool, which was coarser than most seen today. For a more traditional look, use natural 8/4 wool yarn.

Before starting on your project, I recommend always making a sample. Simply use an empty frame and wrap your weft around and around until you have the desired width. Aim for five threads per inch. This should be perfect for the recommended thickness of yarn. Remember that the more yarns per inch, the finer your thread will need to be and the more challenging your project. For the first time, I also recommend a simple stripe pattern, working with three colors, off-white, gray and red, for example. It will result in a pleasing yet easy project. A first-timer's biggest challenge is usually in beating the weft evenly so that the rows and stripes are straight.

Although there are Navajo looms available on the market, you can always start with a small project, such as the decorator cushions I mentioned earlier, and use the proverbial frame loom with the wraparound technique I described above. Once you've mastered that, you can move on to bigger projects.

Happy weaving, everyone!

About the Author

Carol Ann Martin is an author and former television personality who divides her time between San Diego and the Canadian coast. She lives with her husband and their ever-expanding collection of dogs. When she is not writing, Carol Ann enjoys baking and beekeeping.

ALSO AVAILABLE FROM

Carol Ann Martin

LOOMING MURDER
A Weaving Mystery

Della Wright left her career as a business analyst
in Charlotte to open a weaving studio in the
picturesque Blue Ridge Mountains. At her weaving
workshop, she meets many of the town's colorful
characters as they come together to weave
baby blankets for the local hospital.

But Della soon discovers the beautiful town hides a
killer. When suspicion falls on two of her clients,
Della—distrusting of police authority after being
falsely accused of a crime in her past—decides to
use her natural curiosity. Can she weave together the
clues in time to stop the killer from striking again?

"Carol Ann Martin has created a new series
featuring engaging characters, a puzzling mystery,
and the promise of romance."
—Amanda Lee, author of the Embroidery Mysteries

**Available wherever books are sold or
at penguin.com**

ALSO AVAILABLE FROM

CAROL ANN MARTIN

TAPESTRY OF LIES
A Weaving Mystery

Della Wright can't believe her luck when celebrity designer Bunny Boyd walks into her weaving studio in small-town Briar's Hollow, North Carolina, with a large custom fabric order. Bunny needs materials for her latest design project: Bernard Whitby's mansion. Bernard is Briar Hollow's resident millionaire, and Della soon discovers that Bunny has designs on the man as well as his house. And he's happy to have a celebrity at his side when he announces his candidacy for governor.

But the buzz surrounding Bernard's announcement is quickly overshadowed by the murder of a local coffee shop owner. When her good friend Jenny becomes one of the suspects, Della decides to unravel the mystery. But she'll have to work fast—before she gets tangled in a killer's clutches.

"Fabulously entertaining."
—*Suspense Magazine*

Available wherever books are sold or at penguin.com

ALSO AVAILABLE FROM

Carol Ann Martin

WEAVE OF ABSENCE
A Weaving Mystery

It's a joyous time at Dream Weaver—Della Wright's studio in small-town Briar Hollow, North Carolina—as part-time employee and full-time friend Marnie Potter is preparing for her upcoming marriage. Della has enlisted a tight-knit group of close friends to handweave a beautiful collection of fine household linens as a wedding gift for the happy couple.

But when Della notices Marnie's suave fiancé engaged in a heated argument with one of her students at the engagement party, she starts to worry that there may be something wrong with Marnie's Mr. Right. After the student turns up dead the next day, Della must weave together the clues to find the killer—before Marnie agrees to "Till death do us part."

"I really love it when I find a new series and can't put down the book until I finish it."
—*MyShelf.com*

Available wherever books are sold or at penguin.com